ALLY

OCEAN
HEART

THE SOUL HEART SERIES: BOOK ONE

OCEAN HEART copyright © 2020 Alison Aldridge

All Rights Reserved

This is a work of fiction. Names, characters, places and incidents are products of the author's imagination or are used fictitiously and are not to be construed as real. Any resemblance to actual events, locales, organisations, or persons, living or dead, is entirely coincidental.

Published by Redfae Press

Conditions of Sale

This book is sold subject to the conditions that it shall not, by way of trade or otherwise, be lent, re-sold, hired out or otherwise circulated without the publisher's prior consent in any form, binding or cover other than that in which it is published and without a similar condition including this condition being imposed on the subsequent purchaser.

No part of this book may be used or reproduced in any manner whatsoever without written permission of the author except in the case of brief quotations embedded in critical articles, and reviews. Fans are welcome to share their images of the book and quotes on social media and review sites. In addition, copies of the book may be purchased for educational, business or sales promotional use. For more information please contact via author's website: www.allyaldridge.com

OCEAN HEART - FIRST EDITION

Formatter and interior art by Julia Scott of Evenstar Books Ltd
Cover designed by Natalie Narbonne of Original Book Cover Designs

Paperback ISBN: 978-1-8382084-0-0

To my nieces,

There will be times you feel like you don't fit in, but don't change. You belong, one hundred percent as you. You're mermazing.

Love, aunty Ally.

CHAPTER 1

WRIGGLING MY WAY UNDER THE FENCE on my elbows, I breathed in the rich scent of soil. It warmed my heart and reminded me of a lifetime of sneaking through this gap, into the garden of my best friend and neighbour.

I barely made it to my feet before I was soaked in an icy, cold shower. I shrieked in surprise and turned to find Jace laughing, holding the garden hose in his hand.

I narrowed my eyes. "Jace!"

With a mischievous glint in his eye, he lifted the hose and soaked me again.

"Cut that out!" I ran at him to pull the hose out of his hand.

He dodged out of my way and ran past me. As I chased after him around the garden, he kept spraying me over his shoulder. I welcomed the cool relief in the heat of the summer sun.

Finally, trapping him by the shed, I grabbed the hose. He still wouldn't let go and, as we wrestled over it, he kept managing to spray my face. Using my fingers, I changed the direction of the water and sprayed him back. He made a funny gurgling noise and shook the water from his blond mop of hair.

"That doesn't sound like my plants getting watered!" Denny yelled from the kitchen window.

"Sorry, Mum," Jace yelled back. His lip curled on one side as he tried in earnest to appear sincere. "You need to let go so I can continue with my chores."

"No way," I giggled, knowing as soon as I let go, he'd spray me. "We'll just have to do it together."

We started watering the plants together, both refusing to let go of the hose.

"This is stupid, Mariah. Let go. I promise I won't squirt you." His blue eyes twinkled.

I grinned and shook my head. "I know you too well, Jace. Why don't you let *me* do it?"

"I couldn't shirk my responsibilities like that," Jace countered.

"I don't mind."

I felt him attempt to tip the hose towards me but I managed to stop him and the water ran up the fence instead.

"Cut it out, Jace!"

"Oops!" he mocked.

We finally finished the watering and stretched out

on the grass, eating ice cream whilst our cold drinks sweated in the heat.

"Summer's almost over," Jace said, sounding oddly sad. He'd taken his t-shirt off and I could see he'd become less boy and more physically grown up.

"Then back to school," I groaned. "I hope we're in the same classes."

"You'd miss me if I wasn't."

"Careful, big head! You'd miss me, too."

"Maybe I would, maybe I wouldn't," he teased.

I shook my head. "You can't fool me, Jace Walker."

"I fooled you into watering the garden, didn't I? And what about when I told you that if you eat enough lettuce it starts to taste like chocolate? Or the time I tricked you into swapping your little pound coins for my big fifty pences?"

"Wow, you are a shitty friend. Maybe I won't miss you at all."

"Fine, we'll miss each other. And summer. Summer is great," Jace sighed, leaning back on the grass.

"It really is," I agreed.

"Be even better if I didn't have a little, whiney voice chittering in my ear."

I gave him a playful shove. He squinted one eye as he tried to look at me but caught the sun. My stomach flipped in a new way as I realised, for the first time, that Jace had changed over the summer holidays. He had got hot! I shook the stupid thought away. He was Jace Walker, my best friend forever.

Denny came over to see Mum. It was odd Jace hadn't come over with her, as we always found excuses to hang out together.

Jace's mum had delicate features and high cheekbones framed by her dark, pixie cut. She was quite young and followed current trends. Whereas my mum was that strange woman with dark, flowing hair who tells fortunes at spiritual fairs. She wore hippy-looking, loose, flowing clothes and was a tad overweight. You wouldn't expect them to be best friends, but they were.

I hovered around the kitchen. Denny's eyes stared down into a mug of tea, slowly stirring her sugar spoon, her gaze lost in a deep spin of thought.

"Are you going to drink that or spit out what's on your mind?" Mum asked.

Denny sighed, "I was hoping you already knew."

I stood on my tiptoes to reach the cake tin, helping myself to one of the buttercream cupcakes; a product of Mum and Denny's 'Sparkle Cake' bakery business. Even though they had the use of a proper kitchen and cafe now, Mum still liked experimenting at home.

"Don't make me dig out my crystal ball…," Mum threatened Denny. Her tone made me think I was caught with my sugary delight. For a moment I paused, wincing as I waited for 'don't spoil your dinner' or 'stop eating our profits', but she was too focused on Denny to notice me.

Denny took a deep breath like she was conjuring up the courage to speak. With an awkward smile on her face, she said, "Dave and I found somewhere to live together, a home of our own." Her blue eyes shone, brimming with tears.

"That's great news." Mum cheered.

"But…," her face crumpled.

"What is it, Denny?"

"It's been a tough decision. It's perfect, except we'll no longer be neighbours and it's all the way over on the other side of town. I'm gonna miss you guys."

Her words were like the icy blast from the hose but without the warm relief of the sun or uplifting sound of Jace's laughter.

"You can't!" I snapped. Jace was my life! I needed him close! I needed him next door! I no longer wanted the cake; it was too sweet and I cast it aside on the counter.

"The cakes!" Denny gasped.

Mum frowned. "Mariah, go get the washing off the line!"

I stormed out of the kitchen through the back door of our small terrace house, slamming it shut behind me. Without bothering to unpeg the clothes from the line, I yanked them free and dumped them into the laundry basket. The haphazard approach completed the task too fast and I wasn't ready to go back inside.

I tugged at the loose panel of the fence, but it wouldn't move. I spotted the evil glint of a new nail, hammered in to keep the plank in place, keeping me out. I kicked at it, succeeding only in injuring my foot. Holding it, I collapsed onto the grass and pressed my back against the fence. As I gazed up towards Jace's bedroom window, my heart felt like a rock; unpleasant and heavy in my chest. A sinking feeling consumed me as I realised, he was really going and there was nothing I could do about it.

The beautiful, blue sky darkened. Heavy, rapid rain soaked through my t-shirt as I raced inside. I didn't stop in the kitchen with Mum and Denny but ran straight up to my room. Dropping onto my bed, I stared out the window at the raging storm. It spoke to my soul, mirroring my anger.

The August sun blazed down on us, making me hot and sticky. Jace and I sat side by side on my front doorstep looking at the gravel. Neither of us wished to face what was going on next-door at his house. We were both wearing shorts, my freckled left knee pressed against his tanned right knee. My head hung heavy, red curls falling around my face.

The short picket fence acted like a protective shield from all that was happening. For weeks, I hadn't dared to think about the move, as if by not thinking about it I could prevent it from happening. But, now, the removal men were carrying cardboard boxes marked 'Jace's Room' to load onto the lorry. I scrunched up my eyes to push back the image of him being taken from me.

"Are you okay?" I asked, seeing his jaw twitch.

"Fine," he huffed.

"Are you going to cry?"

"Only pansies cry," Jace said. He fiddled with the bracelet on his wrist and lowered his voice. "You know, I could live anywhere in the world as long as you lived next door."

With Mum's help, I'd made him the bracelet he was wearing as a goodbye gift. I'd used fifteen silver and blue beads to represent each year of our friendship. I'd intended to tell him that I'd chosen blue, not because of his favourite colour but because the colour represents friendship; Mum and I had soaked it in white wine and crushed basil leaves. She said it would encourage him to visit more. Now, those facts seemed pointless and the words remained unspoken.

I wore a bracelet, but mine wasn't one of friendship. I'd begun wearing it shortly after our holiday in Spain when my skin had a bad reaction to the salt water. It makes people aware of my unusual allergy. Mum had done a good job of finding one that was pretty. It had a metal plate with the typical medic alert symbol, a six-point cross and snakes down the middle. The symbol was engraved onto a background of waves, and the band was made with small aquamarine beads.

My thoughts were interrupted by the loud clang of the lorry door slamming shut. The sound rang with injustice, like a gavel on a silent courtroom when the wrong sentence was served.

I flung my arms around Jace, desperate to hold onto him a little longer. I breathed in his smell: a mix of boy and the great outdoors. It brought back memories of splashing in puddles wearing bright, yellow wellies, climbing trees, and scraping our knees, racing along the seafront, and camping in the backyard sharing spooky tales by torchlight. All those memories that had once made me blissfully happy began crashing into my mind and caused an aching hollowness in my heart. It felt so final. A solitary tear ran down my cheek.

"Don't cry, Freckles," he whispered as his thumb wiped my tear away.

I took a deep breath and exhaled to try and calm myself down. A frown creased Jace's forehead and his eyes were heavy with sadness.

"I'm sorry," I croaked.

"Chin up," he smiled. "We'll make it work."

Denny lent over the fence. "Come on, you two, it's not like you'll never see each other again." In her hands were the basil plant and new broom that Mum had given her as a housewarming present.

"Are you all packed up?" Mum asked.

Dave stood next to his car, keys in hand and a smug grin plastered on his face. "Yep."

My blood began to boil... except the bubbling felt more like a tingling. Didn't he have any compassion for what he was doing to Jace and I? The angry current coursed through my veins. So charged, I felt a need to defuse. I threw my hands in the air and screamed.

"Mariah-," Mum began but stopped.

Dramatically, the sky lit up like a stormy backdrop to my anger. Lightning pitched down from the sky and hit the lorry, cutting the engine out. The black cloud moved in to darken the before clear sky. The first plop of rain sent a chill through my cotton t-shirt. In no time, the sky was emptying buckets of rain.

"Temper, temper," Jace teased.

"Quick!" Mum yelled over the rumbling sky as it began to chuck it down, "Everyone inside."

We ran in. Denny invited the removal men to take shelter in our home with the promise of sampling their famous Sparkle Cakes and a brew.

As Jace and I were about to run up the stairs, Mum pulled me to one side.

"Are you okay, Mariah?"

"What do you think?" I snapped at her stupid question.

She tugged on my sleeve. "You must stay in control of your emotions."

I shrugged her off me and hurried up the stairs with Jace. In my room, we revelled in the storm's blessing of extra time together. I grinned, as pleased with myself as if I had caused the storm.

CHAPTER 2

*H*ere, under the ocean, I could forget my loneliness. My troubles were a distant memory. Instead of legs, I had a beautiful, shimmering tail that reflected a kaleidoscope of blues and greens. It fluttered up and down as I propelled myself forward through the crystal blue waters.

My hands hung by my side as I flew through the water, free as a bird in the sky. Rays of light shone down from above, illuminating my underwater hideaway. My red hair swirled around me. I was miles away from anyone or anything. I'd stay here, blissfully unaware of reality, safe in my dream world.

But, my mermaid dream was always brought to an abrupt end by my alarm.

So much for what Denny said!

Three weeks later, Jace and I still hadn't seen each other. We messaged each other, but as we ran out of things to say, our messages became less and less frequent.

I had dreaded the holidays coming to an end, but now I welcomed it. Mum had bought my new uniform and new, shiny black shoes. They were flat shoes with a small, crystal apple embellishment by the toe. It was only a short walk to school but I was quickly falling out of love with them as they were rubbing the backs of my heels.

Dark clouds threatening rain circled above as I tried to walk flat-footed and avoid the pain, making me appear awkward and clumsy. Everyone seemed to have grown over the summer, except me. I headed into the school hall for my new schedule.

The room was filled with the rowdiness of hundreds of voices all talking at once. A mass of kids, all my age, stood in groups or queued to speak to someone behind the tables. I searched the room for Jace. As his familiar face appeared, my morning troubles melted away. The vision of him soothed the ache in my heart like aloe-vera on sunburned skin.

Racing across the room, I gave him a huge hug. He looked older in his new uniform, wearing the smart blazer jacket. He was taller, too, and smelled different. I frowned, disappointed the boyish smell I craved was gone. In its place was a rich, spicy smell, mixed with something fruity and sweet cinnamon. As I adjusted to his new smell, I appreciated that it was delicious and comforting, like an apple crumble on a winter's day, but it wasn't Jace. I didn't like him smelling like a stranger.

"Freckles!" he squeezed me back with a crushing bear hug. "I missed you so much!"

"I missed you, too."

The room suddenly filled with sunlight.

"I think we have to join one of these queues." He indicated to the nearest line of people with his head.

We both made our way over and instantly fell into a ramble of excited chat about everything and anything. I wanted to know all about the new house and living with Dave. He wanted to know how Mum was getting on and what I'd been up to. We talked about the music we had been listening to and the shows we had watched. I felt so alive to have him back. I felt whole again. He filled the space in my heart of everything I was missing. Chatting without pause, we soon found ourselves at the front of the queue.

"Name?" asked Mr Griffen, a young, male PE teacher with short, dark hair. He addressed me but I didn't answer. I always let Jace do the talking.

"She's Mariah Turner, I'm Jace Walker."

"I can only do one name at a time," the teacher said, irritated as he tapped on his keyboard. There was a whirring noise and I realised the box next to him was a printer. "Walker!" He announced pulling out the piece of paper. "You're one of mine. Welcome to form six."

Jace took the piece of paper handed to him. I peered

over his shoulder. It was his timetable. The printer made another whirring noise.

"Turner!" Mr Griffen announced and handed me my timetable.

Jace pulled me out of the way of the people waiting for their turn and we compared our sheets. We were in different forms.

"I wanted us to be in the same form!" I complained as I compared our timetables. I felt sick as I realized we were starting to have less and less in common. I searched hopefully for any lessons that matched but we weren't even taking the same subjects on the same days. My eyes widened in horror. We would never see each other!

"Just 'cause we have no classes together, doesn't mean we can't be friends," Jace reassured me, registering my panic.

"I'm going to hate it. This sucks!"

I wanted to go home. I kept staring at my schedule, willing it to change; for there to have been some mistake. We looked glumly at our sheets as the bell loudly interrupted us from overhead.

"I guess that's the signal that we have to go find our rooms," Jace said, fidgeting with a stray thread on his bag strap and screwing up his face.

I nodded. There was nothing more to say. He hugged me, but it was so rushed that I got no joy from it. He headed towards the double doors as if he already knew where he was going. As the students swarmed in the same direction, he disappeared and became one of many. I followed, pulled along into a dimly lit corridor, dragged by the tide of people. I felt I was drowning, slipping under, helpless and unable to stop what was happening.

The school had suddenly become a dark place, I didn't want to be.

It had been a long week and the last thing I needed was for Mum to be poking her nose into my business the moment I walked through the door.

"How's school? Mum asked.

"Fine," I sighed. Lying to Mum felt pointless as I knew she could use her witchy powers to check on me but I didn't have the energy to discuss it.

"What's wrong?" she probed.

Standing at the foot of the stairs, I groaned. I might as well tell her.

"I'm bored. I never see Jace. And, he isn't bothered, he has all these new friends."

"Don't be so dramatic. You'll see him -"

"He doesn't want to see me. He doesn't have time to see me."

The more I unleashed the more I could feel myself heating up as my emotions rose to the surface.

"I'll speak to Denny and work something out."

"Don't bother! It's her fault they moved!" I ran up the stairs and slammed my bedroom door shut, and threw myself on the bed. I could feel tears peppering my eyes. I rolled over and unlocked my mobile phone.

I searched Jace's social feeds and could see all these posts of him taking selfies with people I didn't really know. There were tags and comments and inside jokes that I didn't understand.

I went to send him a private message but when the app opened, I could see my last message to him two days ago.

Mariah: How are you doing? We need to catch up. Feels like forever since we chat.

The icon showed he'd seen it but hadn't replied. I could see he was currently online. Maybe he was busy and would reply later this weekend...

Except, he didn't.

Over the next few weeks, I saw him a few times but always from a distance. He made friends quickly and I often sighted him with a group of lads, laughing, having a good time. He danced in the sunlight whilst I lurked in the shadows. Like a magnolia wall, I disappeared into the background. I sat in class as an observer, not a participant. I brooded over the loss of my friend and my miserable disposition. It didn't make me very approachable.

Soon, the opportunity to make friends had passed. Everyone was in their groups and had their place. The popular kids had been identified and Jace was one of them.

For the first time ever, he wasn't associated with me.

I woke to the sound of laughter. Groggily, I put on my dressing gown and slippers and made my way downstairs. As I passed the mirror I ran my fingers through my hair and tried to pat it down curly, red strands so they didn't stick out all over the place. My slippers had little cat heads on the tips, and as I made my way down the narrow staircase they bobbed up and down as if giving me an enthusiastic, positive 'yes'. I paused at the bottom to see if I could figure out who Mum's visitors were.

I heard Denny's laugh: "I don't know, is it your magical basil plant or just plain luck?"

"My basil plant," Mum said proudly. "Never doubt the power of a basil plant."

"I followed your instructions exactly and still can't believe it"

"I can't believe you're still a sceptic after all this time."

Denny chuckled again. "I just wanted to say thank you."

"You're practically family. No need to thank me."

I'd heard this sort of conversation before.

Just like me, Denny would not have believed in magic if it wasn't for Mum. She'd tried a few spells under

Mum's direction but they'd never worked. Mum said the caster has to see and believe in what they are doing, otherwise they are just going through the motions. My attempts at casting had never been successful, either, but Mum's magic always worked.

The step creaked under my foot.

"Someone is awake!"

I heard the voice I longed to hear and bounced down the last step to greet him.

"Jace!" I cheered as I threw myself into the kitchen for a big hug. The feeling was like magic bubbling up inside me, bringing me awake and alive.

"Morning, sleepy head."

"It's such a shame they split you two up," sighed Denny.

I frowned in response. She could blame the school all she wanted, but I had never felt as divided as the day that removal van took off with Jace and his belongings.

"... Guess you two have a lot of catching up to do?" Denny wriggled under my glare.

I couldn't help but admit to myself that Denny was glowing. She was happier than I'd ever seen her.

Jace was the opposite of his mum in appearance, with sandy blond hair and piercing blue eyes. I had to assume his colouring came from his dad, whom we'd never met. I'd never met my dad either. It was something our mums had bonded over and forged a lifelong friendship.

It was difficult to stay mad at Denny. She was so happy it was impossible to stop a little rubbing off on you. Giving in, I allowed myself to share a smile with her.

I grabbed Jace by the hand and led him up to my room, leaving our mums to gossip. Somehow, we managed to race up the thin stairwell gap, side by side. We crashed into my room and fell onto the bed.

Jace rolled over and grinned at me. "Still miss you."

"Miss you more," I said and stuck my tongue out. It was so true that the statement weighed heavy on my chest. I had to laugh otherwise I might cry.

"You need to get dressed so we can go out," Jace said.

I quickly grabbed my denim shorts, a vest top, and underwear. "Two seconds."

I headed off to the bathroom. I didn't want to waste any time I could be spending with Jace. I washed my face and threw on my clothes, and quickly yanked a wide-toothed comb through my rebellious locks. My hair was not behaving today, it stuck out sporadically where it shouldn't, giving the effect that I'd been electrocuted. The only way to tame it was to pull it back into a hairband. Even tied back, wild strands escaped and curled down my face. I didn't like my hair, there was nothing pleasing about it.

"Ready," I announced as I opened my bedroom door. It served more like an invitation to race. There was no need for an 'on your marks, get set', with just a grin at Jace, we charged like loose bulls down the stairs.

"Careful!" Mum yelled.

She had told us countless times not to race on the

stairs but we never listened. We headed out the front door and I found myself skipping next to him down the road.

"Are you alright?" he asked.

"I'm just so happy to see you," I answered.

"I'm happy to see you, too," he skipped next to me in mockery, but he was the one looking stupid. With his long legs it was more like a gallop. Realising he was making me laugh, he carried on until I punched him in the arm.

"Cut it out!"

He started running and we were racing again, bounding carelessly down the street, dodging into the road to avoid pedestrians, acting like a pair of goons. By the time we reached the park, we were both out of breath.

"Who would have thought that'd be so exhausting?" he gasped, bent over, and leaned on his knees.

Hunching over and trying to get my breath back, too, I said, "Perhaps we're really unfit?"

"You maybe, but not me!" he jabbed me in the waist. He headed for the tree we usually hung out by and sat down at its base.

"What's new with you?" he inquired, giving me his full attention.

I shrugged my shoulders and slumped down beside him. I really didn't have anything to tell, so I didn't answer his question.

"You seem to be making lots of new friends."

"Yeah," he grinned. "I joined the footie team. We

practice most breaks and after school."

"That's cool..."

I concentrated on how happy I was for him but deep down I was jealous. Jealous of his new friends, who now got to spend so much more time with him than I did, and jealous that he found making friends so damn easy.

"How about you?"

"What about me?"

"Are you making friends?"

I felt my cheeks turning red. I was annoyed at my inability to speak to anyone.

"It's different for girls. We don't have a football team!"

"You could start one," Jace suggested.

I shook my head. "Not really my thing."

Jace traced patterns in the soil with a twig. In a low voice, he said, "Sorry you're struggling, I'm sure you'll make friends soon."

He sounded sincere but we both knew it was too late for me. I was doomed to be a friendless loner. Even the outcasts and weirdos were in groups.

I glanced down at the pattern he'd drawn and saw the outline of a love heart. He was drawing something in the middle. I glared at it. He had definitely drawn a K. Then, he drew another line. He dragged the stick through the dirt, cutting a rough O shape. Finally, he stabbed a dot between the two letters. His actions had a physical effect on me, like that stick was stabbing me in the chest and making my heart bleed.

"Who is K. O.?" I demanded, reading his doodle.

He quickly scratched out his sketch with his stick. "K.O.?" he acted dumb. "'Knock Out' like when I beat you on Combat?"

"I'm still reigning champion, don't you forget!" I playfully reminded him. "Don't change the subject. I saw you draw a heart and her initials - assuming it is a 'her'?"

"Of course, it's a girl!"

I felt a strange heaviness as the truth was confessed. There was officially another girl in Jace's life. A girl I knew nothing about.

"Who is she, then?"

"Kiely O'Neil. Just a girl I like," he said nonchalantly.

"Does she like you, too?"

"Everyone thinks so. She watches me play but could be watching anybody."

His smug smile told me his coy attitude was just for show. He knew she liked him back. Would Jace have noticed me if I'd watched him play? Maybe if I had he'd be carving my name in the soil.

What a crazy thought. Jace and I are just friends!

Hearing him talk about another girl hurt. It hadn't ever bothered me before. The difference was, usually, I was the one pointing it out to him, encouraging him to go for it. Usually, he couldn't be bothered to go there and laughed it off. This was an unknown threat; I didn't know who Kiely was and I didn't like her influence over him. I didn't like *not* being involved.

"Are you going to ask her out?"

Jace nodded.

I dropped my head to hide my eyes, prickling with tears. Awkwardly, I laughed to throw him off the strange sensation I was feeling. Inside, I was slowly dying.

I didn't want him to be with anyone else.

The thought was new and scary and I didn't know what to make of it. It was supposed to be us, forever. My mouth fell open at the revelation of my own feelings for Jace.

"Are you alright?" he asked.

I gulped. "Yeah, I'm just so happy to spend time with you again. I've missed you so much."

"Come here, you silly girl."

He pulled me into his arms and I didn't want him to ever let me go. Suddenly, the afternoon felt too short.

Jace was not yet aware of what had changed between us, but the gentlest touch from him felt like electricity. Even his voice could cause my body to stir with excitement. I found myself giggling more than usual and just wanted to touch him all the time. I didn't recognise the person I was turning into and if I could just get a grip of myself for five seconds, I'd slap myself really hard.

As we walked back to my house to get lunch, I clung to his arm and leaned against his chest.

"Mmm, cheese sandwiches," I grinned up at him.

"With cherry tomatoes."

It wasn't even funny but I giggled. "And pickles."

"And salad cream?"

I giggled some more and my hand ran its way across his chest.

Jace shook his head. "I don't know what's gotten into you. Maybe I should stay away more often?"

"No," I gasped in horror and pouted.

We passed his old house, pushed open my little, white gate, and entered the house. Sure enough, laid out on the dining table were the jars of different pickles, butter, salad, and a cheese board. We both loved 'Saturday Sarnies' and it seemed like forever since we had shared one together.

As I sat at the table, I didn't feel that hungry. My stomach felt all over the place, yet I had this stupid, goofy grin on my face. I tried to force a sandwich down but I wasn't interested in eating. I found myself picking at little chunks of cheese and popping cherry tomatoes in my mouth to feel them explode.

The time came, too quickly, for Jace to go.

"Can't you stay?" I begged.

"I can't. Brian's invited the team over for a game," Jace said apologetically.

"You were never that into football before," I complained.

"Things change," he said with a shrug and gave me a hug goodbye.

He had no idea how true that statement was.

As we hugged, I had an urge to kiss his cheek. It was such a simple act but the rush it gave me was scary. My lips briefly touched his skin but the warm tingle was undeniable. I was terrified of how he might react. It made my head spin. His lips gently brushed my cheek, reciprocating my kiss. A delicious warmth coursed through my body. My heart raced in response to that simple act. Had it affected him the same way?

"I'll see you soon," Jace promised as he went out the door.

CHAPTER 3

"**H**E WAS DEFINITELY WHAT YOU NEEDED," chirped Mum behind me. "I haven't seen you that happy in ages."

I watched the front door close behind them, then threw myself into Mum's cosy cuddliness. One thing Mum was better than anyone at was cuddles – except maybe Jace. Hot tears ran down my face.

"Whatever is the matter?" Mum cooed in my ear.

"I don't feel well," I grumbled between sobs.

She put a hand to my head. "You don't have a temperature. What sort of not well do you feel?"

"I have a funny tummy and I feel dizzy."

Mum was instantly concerned as she guided me up the stairs to bed. She pulled back the covers and tucked me in. The curtains lifted and waved angrily into the room with the wind. Mum leant over the bed to pull the window shut.

She frowned. "The weather has turned suddenly."

She looked at me with the look she gave me when I'm in trouble and, for a moment, I thought she was accusing me of something, but I had no idea what.

Her expression softened and she wrapped the top sheet around me, kissed my forehead, and gave me a cuddle as she whispered:

"Wrap her in cotton and surround her with love,

Send peace for her body on wings of a dove,"

I smiled, comforted by the familiar words she always says when I'm poorly.

She drew the curtains.

"Give her your blessing on this shadowy night,

The brightest of light, reap her pain and take flight."

She walked towards the door and winked.

"I'll make you a lemon peel tea. That's always good to stop dizziness."

I rolled over and stared at the wall as I gripped my tummy. It felt empty but I wasn't hungry. Shutting my eyes, all I could see was Jace grinning at me, his eyes sparkling, as he spoke about Kiely. I pictured us kissing. Not on the cheek, but on the lips, gentle and warm. My lips would tingle, just as they had when they'd brushed his skin, but it would mean something more, a connection deeper than friendship.

During the week, I saw Jace but he didn't notice me. I stood in the stairwell, on the top floor, watching out the window as he played football with his new friends.

I'd a good idea who Kiely was. A group of pretty girls sat at the benches watching the boys play. Kiely had long, blonde hair and as soon as the bell rang, she'd jump up and run to Jace so they could walk in together.

They weren't ordinary girls. Even though they wore the same uniform as everyone else, they stood out. Kiely's hair was usually pulled back from her face by a colourful band. It caused the layers of her hair cut to flick out and frame her cheekbones. Her heeled shoes made her legs appear longer, and she had a rich, golden tan, the sort earned from a tropical holiday.

Her beauty made me feel plain. I knew I would have to make an extra effort on Sunday if I wanted Jace to see me in the same light as her. To make matters worse, the ache in my belly had not gone; it had been heavy with sadness since saying goodbye to Jace at the weekend. It hung like a weight just above my left hip.

I got my mobile from my knitted satchel and decided to check how his date had gone. He was on the sidelines, squirting juice into his mouth. He put the juice down and began chatting to the girls at the benches. I stabbed the send button - it was better to know than torture myself with soul-destroying scenarios of 'what if'.

Mariah: Hey Jace, how's it going with Kiely?

Seconds later, I saw him reach into his pocket and check his mobile. I waited for him to text back but he just glanced at the screen, shrugged nonchalantly, and shoved it back in his pocket.

He just ignored my text!

I felt as if he had punched me in the stomach. This was ridiculous. I shouldn't be so worked up about something so silly, but as his best friend, I thought responding to me would be high on his to-do list.

What if I'm no longer his best friend?

I thought about how he'd ignored my messages on social media, but then he'd come over and we'd had a great day together. My head spun trying to make sense of his hot and cold behaviour. He was now running back on the field to play with my replacements.

My phone chirped with the familiar sound of a text message. My heart fluttered with joy that I was wrong. I pressed to read it.

Mum: Meet me at the bakery after school. Doing a food shop and will need help carrying it home. X

My smile fell when I saw it wasn't from Jace. I let out a heavy sigh. All I wanted to do was curl up and sulk in bed. But, after school, I took the detour, as requested, to meet Mum. The town centre was full of busy, noisy people that didn't appeal to my cranky mood, and to make matters worse, I could feel a headache brewing from the exhaustion of just getting through the day. Not only did I not feel right, but my shoes were making my feet hot and itchy. Thankfully, they had now moulded to the shape of my foot and weren't rubbing anymore.

I was definitely coming down with something. Maybe Mum could whip up one of her magic concoctions. I saw her on the other side of the road. She'd already locked up the shop and now stood in the centre of her makeshift island of reusable cotton bags waiting for me to join her.

"Are you alright?" Mum asked as I approached. Her warm hand pressed against my forehead as she gauged how worried she should be.

I just grunted. I was feeling progressively worse and my bed couldn't come soon enough.

She carefully selected the lighter bags for me to carry and took the remaining ones. I struggled to keep up as we walked home. I felt defeated and heavy. The fifteen-minute walk felt like forever as I replayed Jace's shrug over and over in my mind.

Arriving home didn't give me the pleasure my pitiful mood had desired. I just wanted the ache in my belly to stop. I dumped the bags in the kitchen and unpacked the items. The task was robbing me of my final reserve of energy.

"What's that?" Mum gasped.

"What's what?" I turned to identify what she was pointing at. Following her finger down towards my leg, I saw a dark red line that ran down my inner thigh like paint. It was bright and vivid and I felt faint just looking at it.

"I don't know," I mumbled weakly.

"Quick!" Mum gasped. "Go to the toilet. I'll fetch you some sanitary pads."

The burning heat that had plagued me all day suddenly rushed to my face. I ran to the toilet and locked the door. Sinking down onto the seat I inspected the damage. Sure enough, my knickers were soaked. *'Just a teaspoon of blood!'* That's what my Sexual Education teacher had taught me, but this was more. Way more!

I felt sick and wriggled my knickers off and over my ankles, trying my best not to touch them. Pulling a piece of tissue from the roll, I rubbed at the stripe on my leg but it was dried on. *How long had it been there? Had anyone else seen it?*

The humiliation eventually got to me and a stray tear found its way down my cheek. I sat there helplessly on the toilet waiting for Mum to return with clean knickers and a sanitary pad. I hadn't pictured my first period being like this, I thought I'd have some warning and be more prepared. For the first time since the move, I was glad that Jace wasn't here.

There was a knock at the door and I wondered if I could leave the toilet to let her in. I didn't want to make more mess and I worried if I got up I could bleed all over the floor. I leaned forward trying to reach the door but it was too far away.

Mum knocked again. "Come on, Mariah, it's only me."

Well, I couldn't sit on the toilet for god knows how many days... I quickly made a dash for the door. As soon as it was unlocked, Mum barged her way in, forcing me backwards. She handed me what I had been waiting for. I quickly put on the clean knickers and stuck the sanitary pad on.

Mum's eyes sparkled proudly: "My little girl is growing up."

"Get out!"

"It's a good thing," Mum nodded enthusiastically. "Now, you go and get changed and I'll cook you something nice for dinner. Then we'll have a proper chat about this and celebrate."

Was she deaf? Celebrate? If looks could kill...

"Get out! Get out! Get out!"

"Alright..." Mum hurriedly exited the small room as if I'd wounded her. She grabbed my discarded knickers without even flinching at how unpleasant that must have been. She closed the door behind her.

Safely alone with my privacy, I was able to cry properly. I felt bad for yelling at Mum but I just wanted to be alone. Too many things were changing and it was all happening so fast. It made me feel unstable and I didn't think I could handle any more.

Finally, my phone beeped.

Jace: Not great. Best I explain in person.

I wiped the tears from my cheek and smiled. But the smile soon left. I felt awful for feeling pleased things hadn't worked out for Jace. I dropped my head in shame.

CHAPTER 4

OVER THE NEXT FEW DAYS, Mum's homemade ylang ylang shampoo helped to lift my spirits and alleviate the cramps. She referred to menstruation as 'the blob', which sounded as unglamorous as I felt. I'd downloaded an app to help determine my cycle, and today was the first day I'd not marked the date in red. A fact I was truly grateful for as today I was getting ready to visit Jace.

Wrapping a towel around myself, I headed for my wardrobe to choose what to wear. I wanted something feminine to remind Jace I'm not one of the lads. Unfortunately, I didn't have much in the way of 'girlie'. I lived in jeans or shorts. But, at the back of the wardrobe, was a yellow, crinkle summer dress that I'd forgotten about.

I threw the dress on and checked my appearance

in the mirror. I scrunched up my hair and studied my face. I still was plain, old Mariah. Freckles speckled my face and my eyes were small and almost invisible, framed by my blonde lashes and eyebrows. They were so pale, they may as well have not been there.

I headed back to the bathroom for Mum's makeup bag and got out the mascara. Very carefully, I applied it to my lashes. I like how it opened up my eyes.

I searched through the makeup bag to see what else I could use and discovered a red lipstick. I applied it but it was a bit daring for me. I blotted on some tissue paper but it wasn't coming off.

Was I confident enough to carry this off? I bet Kiely wouldn't be scared of red lipstick.

I blinked.

Now, a row of little black dots appeared around my eye. I tried to rub them away with my finger but ended up with dark smudges. I tried using soap and water. No matter how hard I rubbed, they wouldn't come off.

"Mariah, are you ready?"

No! No! No!

I couldn't go to Jace's like this. I rubbed harder. My skin stung and was turning pink, but I had to get this off. I heard Mum coming up the stairs.

"Mariah? Are you alright in there?" she asked as she knocked on the bathroom door.

"No!" I wailed.

I kept splashing water at my face. I wanted it all off! But, it wasn't budging! Plus, it was getting worse. With red and black smeared across my face, I feared I was going to be stuck with the Joker's face forever. I felt so stupid. My eyes prickled with tears.

"Open this door!"

My face crumpled as I reached for the lock in defeat.

"What have you done?" Mum's face began to crack into a smile and then she was laughing.

"Mum, it's not funny!"

She bit her lip, and then reached into the bathroom cabinet and pulled out a bottle. "Sorry, let me help you get it off."

I sat on the toilet with the seat down while she applied some olive oil to a cotton pad and wiped it across my face. It was soothing against my flushed cheeks.

"Some of this stuff can last 24 hours, you know?"

My eyes bulged in horror. "Can you get it off?"

"Hold these against your eyes." Mum passed me two pads.

I did as I was told whilst she took care of the lipstick. She began to rub harder, to get the more resistant smudges off my cheek. It started to hurt but I didn't complain. I sat with my eyes shut whilst she said soothing words throughout the process. *"Almost done,"* she would say, or *"I'll just get this bit, here."* She took the pads from my eyes and swept them across my face.

Finally, she said: "That's it!"

I opened my eyes and glanced in the mirror. My face was a little pinker than before but I was me again.

"Thanks."

"Why were you putting on makeup?" Mum asked.

"You're pretty just the way you are."

I wasn't sure how to explain, so I just kept quiet. I rubbed my damp, cotton socks together, like Dorothy in Oz, I wished myself somewhere else, somewhere where I wasn't the next disaster waiting to happen. Although, what I truly wished was to be someone different, someone who fits in and doesn't need to try. Someone like Kiely. I slumped. I was no match for her.

"Is it a boy?" Mum probed. Her finger raised my chin so she could search my face. "Are other girls saying you should wear makeup?"

"No!" I snapped. "I just wanted to try it but I won't do it again."

Mum sighed. "You don't need to be like that. We can get you your own makeup with colours more suited for you. These shades suit people with dark skin like me."

It was true. I looked nothing like Mum and had always wondered who my dad was and whether I looked like him. Mum never spoke about him, and if I ever asked she'd dodge my questions or respond with silence. But today, I couldn't help but ask: "Where do I get my looks from?"

"Tidy up this mess and hurry up. We're already running late."

Mum gave the taxi driver the address. I watched the neighbourhoods change as we headed over to the other side of town. The houses got wider, taller, and had real front gardens, driveways, and garages. Jace had certainly moved up in the world. His new house was modern and big. It had that new, yellow, brick look and all the windows and doors were double glazed. Dave's car sat on the driveway.

I was already knocking on the door before Mum had even paid the driver.

Denny opened the door and Mum demanded a tour. Denny proudly showed us around, room by room. Every room was immaculate, as if straight out a catalogue. We ended in the conservatory. My heart skipped a beat as I saw Jace playing on his console.

"Hi Freckles," he gave a brief wave and quickly returned to clicking buttons on the controller. "One minute."

I went to sit next to him on the floor but Denny called me over.

"Mariah, come sit with me." She tapped the seat next to her on a small, wicker sofa.

Politely, I joined her and Mum, but willed Jace to hurry up so we could hang out.

Denny continued happily, "I have some news..." Her eyes went wide and she drew up her hands to her mouth as if trying to conceal a secret or an excited scream.

Mum grinned as if she already knew, which she probably did. "Ah, so you're telling people now."

Denny gasped. "I should have known! Nothing is a secret from you."

Mum grinned and nodded at me. "I haven't told anyone."

Denny twisted around and grabbed my hands. "Dave and I are having a baby."

"Congratulations," I said happily and hugged her. I checked to see what Jace's reaction was but he was engrossed in his game.

"I hear you have some exciting news, too?" She smiled whilst holding me at arm's length.

"What?" I said, confused.

Denny squeezed my hand. "Becoming a lady!"

"You told her?" I glared at Mum.

Mum frowned. "It's nothing to be ashamed of."

"Finished," Jace announced and got up. He chewed his cheek like he was trying to contain a laugh. "Yeah, congratulations, Freckles."

Oh no, he'd heard everything.

"She wants to wear makeup now, too," Mum chuckled. "Her disaster is why we're running late."

"Mum!" I felt hot and prickly and wriggled uncomfortably.

"Come on," Jace beckoned. "I want to show you this place I found, you're gonna love it!"

I welcomed escaping my humiliation where the mothers' meeting's hot topic was my puberty.

The bus to Ipswich was full of non-stop chatter about Jace's football team, his new bike, and morning paper round. He promised he'd visit me more often and I hoped it was true this time. Once off the bus, we made our way to the 'bigger, better' park that Jace wanted to show me. With a heavy heart, I realised that everything seemed bigger and better in Jace's new life.

With nothing to offer, I felt deflated. No-one even noticed I was wearing a dress. I didn't feel like skipping this time. Always up for some self-torture, I asked: "What happened with Kiely?"

Jace rolled his eyes. "She got grounded. Her parents are insisting our dates be chaperoned and her brother is constantly cock blocking me. She tried to sneak out but got caught. Her brother is fucking everywhere."

It was odd hearing Jace talking about another girl like that but I was pleased the date hadn't happened. He was my Jace for a little longer.

"If you're meant to be, there'll be another date."

He nodded. "Yeah, tonight."

I swallowed a lump in my throat. I knew I should be happy for him, but it hurt. Selfishly, I didn't want things to work out. How was he supposed to miss me if he had her? I wanted him to want me, in the same way I wanted him.

"Where are you taking her?"

"Nowhere fancy, just the cinema."

We entered the park, and he was right, it was much bigger. There were even signposts to tell you which way to go. He took me down the left path and we followed it around a wooded area.

When we reached the play area, Jace hopped over the fence.

I paused.

"Are you coming, Freckles?" he asked.

I rolled my eyes. "I can't climb over that in this. Where's the gate?"

Jace chuckled and pointed, "Over there, princess."

He jogged over and held the gate open for me. There was something very gentlemanly about the gesture that made my stomach squirm with feelings I was trying to ignore.

On the swing, I concentrated on my arms and legs swinging back and forth, taking me higher, to keep my mind off him and his new romance. It was a relief to face forward and not look at him.

Swinging my legs, caused my dress to slide up my thighs, revealing my pale legs. So white, I was sure they illuminated the play area. In fact, they were so bright, they should have come with a health warning: '*Do not look directly at Mariah's legs! Sunglasses recommended!*'

To my horror, I caught Jace looking.

"You don't normally wear a dress."

"No, I don't," I felt humiliated, and planned to avoid making this mistake again. The dress had not had the effect I intended. I thought of Kiely with her gorgeous, tanned body. My heart weighed heavily as I asked, "Are you nervous?"

"About the date?" he asked.

I nodded.

"I don't know if you would understand," he sighed and tried to change the subject. "How are you getting on with making friends?"

I glared back with a sulky expression. "No progress."

He leaped off his swing at the highest point, flying into the air and then landing on his feet a few yards in front. I followed suit. My dress floated up around my waist, before falling back to my knees.

"I saw your knickers," Jace smirked.

I blushed. "How old are you?"

"Thought you were a lady now?" he teased. "Flashing ain't very lady-like."

"At least I act my age and not my shoe size!"

Childishly, Jace stuck out his tongue. Laughing, he grabbed my hand and all the anger washed away in a second, replaced by a fast running bubbling brook that was turning a whirlpool inside me.

"I want to show you the duck pond," he said.

Once out the gate, he dropped my hand and I was instantly disappointed. The idea of us running through the trees, hand in hand, had conjured up beautiful images in my mind.

We wandered through themed landscaped gardens. One was a herb garden, in which everything was edible. Another had plants to attract butterflies and other wildlife. Finally, we came to a nature reserve and pond. It had two benches, but a family was already there enjoying their lunch.

"We can sit down here," Jace said as he led me

towards a willow tree and parted the long branches. We disappeared under its hood. The branches seemed to separate just in front of us, giving a private view across the pond.

"This is beautiful," I said, impressed. "It's our own secret hideaway."

"I knew you'd love it." Jace was already sitting down, leaning back against the slope of the bank.

I sat next to him and leant back in the same manner. Some ducks swam over to see if we might have some bread. Once they discovered we had nothing they quacked their complaints, and with bowed heads, dejectedly waddled back into the pond. The pond was large, more like a lake. The water sparkled and the long willow branches trailed down to meet the grass, like a leafy green waterfall. I turned to capture a glance of Jace, so I could picture this later and discovered he was watching me.

"What?" My cheeks flushed.

He reached out and held my hand. "I wish we did this more often."

My heart raced. "Me too..."

"Promise, you'll come again?"

"Of course."

He seemed relieved. Why'd he think I wouldn't? I loved his company, more than he'd ever know. Surely, on some level, he must sense how much I love him, even if he thought it was only as a friend.

He stared at the grass, twisting the green blades between his fingers and biting his lip.

"What's wrong?"

"Nothing."

I wanted to know what was going on in his head, more than ever. I wondered what he wasn't telling me. Then, I remembered what he'd told me at the swings.

"You said I wouldn't understand why you're nervous, but I do."

He shook his head again. "It's not that simple."

"Everyone gets nervous on dates. It's natural."

He sat up and leaned forward as if he was about to tell me a secret. His blue eyes searched mine. "We haven't seen each other much since the move, but I need to know… can I still trust you?"

"Always." I leaned forward.

"No matter what, we'll be friends? Right?"

I didn't really want to promise that. I frowned. "What is this about?"

"Promise?"

"Friends forever," I promised reluctantly. I regretted the words as soon as they were out. Was it possible to keep that promise and still have more? Perhaps, he knew how I felt and that was the reason for the strange questions, to stop me from making a mistake.

"I need your help with something?"

"What?" I was curious.

He stared intently into my eyes, then shook his head and got to his feet. "It's stupid. Forget I said anything."

For a moment, I thought he was about to run off and leave me. I got up and grabbed his arm.

"Don't go!"

He stopped and faced me. I noticed again how tall he had become.

"Whatever it is, you can tell me. I'm sure it's not as stupid as you think."

"What if she..."

He seemed to be having trouble getting the words out. I didn't like how he wouldn't look at me. His eyes roamed around our leafy dome as if seeking a way out. He opened and closed his mouth several times as if he were about to say something but changed his mind.

Finally, his eyes rested on me and he blurted out: "I've never kissed a girl! Not properly!"

"Oh," I gasped and let him go.

"I know it's wrong but... I shouldn't have brought it up. Please don't hate me," he said, gripping my hands as if he was worried that now I'd be the one to run. "I thought, perhaps, we could practice? There's no-one in the world I trust like you."

My face dropped in surprise. "Are you saying you want to kiss me?"

"Sorry, Freckles," his head dropped, and he stared at the grass. "I know your first kiss should be special but I'm begging you."

My heart began to race and I could feel my palms sweating. We were going to kiss. He was begging me to kiss him!

"It's okay," I said softly, sounding way more calm than I felt.

He scrunched up his face. "Do you mean okay... as in... you know... are you saying I can kiss you?"

I nodded. My whole body tingled in anticipation.

We both awkwardly stared at each other.

"How do we do this?" he asked, staring at my lips and slowly closing the gap between us.

"You know I've never been kissed either," I whispered nervously and shrugged. "I think we just do it."

The urge to kiss him gripped me. I wasn't sure how long this burst of confidence would last, so I closed my eyes, leant forward, and kissed him on the lips. It was brief, but it felt amazing. I opened my eyes.

His eyes widened, as if I'd caught him off guard, before he grinned at me mischievously.

"I think we need more than that."

He wrapped an arm around my waist and pulled me up against his body. I felt his hot lips press against mine. The heat raced through my body to greet his kiss. I didn't know what to do with myself and my arms dangled by my side. He held me to him, our lips locked in a heated bond.

Suddenly the air was cold between us. I opened my eyes, and felt a bit dazed.

Jace raised an eyebrow. "Good?"

"Mmm," was all I could muster.

"Let's try with tongues," he said eagerly, and before I could say another word I felt his hot lips against my mouth gently teasing them open and then his tongue was in my mouth. It felt more intimate and a little invasive. My arms reached up around his neck and I hung onto him for support. I felt unsteady on my legs.

Too soon, he let me go. "Any good?

Breathlessly, I nodded. I looked up at him through my eyelashes and slid my arms away. My legs felt wobbly and my head was spinning.

"Thanks, Freckles." He wrapped an arm around my shoulder as he led me out of the green canopy, back into the real world.

I slid an arm around his waist. That kiss had brought to life feelings inside me that I wasn't prepared to handle. The journey home was painful as he continued to treat me as he always had, as his best friend, and I needed more.

CHAPTER 5

I COULD BARELY SLEEP. When I closed my eyes, I saw his smiling face beaming at me like a burst of unrelenting sunshine.

You're just friends! I kept reminding myself but my heart didn't listen and responded with a flutter at the mere thought of his name.

He is going out with Kiely! I argued with myself but my mind didn't care and skimmed over the fact like an overused meme that's no longer relevant.

He found you attractive. After all, the idea to practice had been his; not that I would say no to any further sessions. In fact, I hoped the next time I saw him he might be ready to practice again.

He's using you! The vicious, inner voice brought me back to reality and I finally listened.

You're just friends… But, did friends use each other

like that? The idea that Jace would use me felt like the ultimate betrayal. Was keeping my true feelings from him deceitful? If he had known, would he still have wanted to kiss me? Perhaps, if he had known he'd forget Kiely. The idea made me smile. A world where Kiely wasn't the apple of Jace's eye. Picturing Jace and I under the willow tree was how I finally fell asleep with a silly grin upon my face.

My fantasy wasn't the only positive thing that came from the weekend. I now had my own makeup.

My positive attitude seemed to rub off on the other students. They started making small talk with me. It's amazing the difference a smile makes. I still had no-one to lunch with, but I quite enjoyed my routine of eating lunch whilst spying on Jace from the top window.

Despite Jace's sweet words, he reverted back to barely texting me. When he did reply, they were short, sometimes only one word. But, I could see he was busy. He was posting pics of him out playing football and there was this one picture of him out with Kiely. They were walking a black Labrador. He'd tagged her in it but her account was private so I couldn't view it without sending a friend request.

I watched a few makeup tutorials online and practiced with my new make-up. By the weekend, I had perfected my new look and was ready for Jace to visit. I'd spent the morning watching out the window for his arrival, and repeatedly checking the mirror for any flaws.

It felt like forever until they arrived, Jace glanced up at my window, knowingly. I ducked as if I'd been caught spying and had to remind myself that I'm allowed to look out my own window.

Mum let them in. My breath caught in my throat as I heard familiar footsteps bounding up the stairs. With each step, my heart beat harder, rapidly getting quicker, until it was beating faster than the sound of his steps. As he pushed open the door, I thought my heart might explode at the revelation of that smile I was now so fond of.

"The weather sucks," Jace stated as he flung his arms around me by way of greeting.

I shut my eyes and breathed him in and let out an odd humming noise.

"How are things with you?" He bounced onto the bed next to me, reached over me for the remote and selected Top Hits from the Prime playlist.

"Fine."

The room filled with an upbeat tune as I pressed my feet against his. Somehow, his feet were always warm.

"Wow, you're cold!" He leapt off the bed as if electrocuted. Grabbing my arm, he pulled me off the bed and lifted the duvet. "Get in."

I got in bed and he tucked the duvet around my feet and then got in with me. He propped a pillow behind our backs. Once settled, my bed was cosier than ever, especially with Jace in it!

"How was kissing Kiely?" I'd been torturing myself wondering and now needed to know. I clenched my teeth, bracing myself for the truth.

"I chickened out."

"You haven't kissed her?" I was almost mad. All that worrying for nothing. But, somehow knowing it hadn't happened gave me a strange sense of hope. "So, what happened?"

Jace shrugged. "Her brother won't leave us alone, but I held her hand and we're officially going out now."

"Don't move too fast," I teased.

"Don't you start! I get enough of that from the lads!"

I felt a mixture of jealousy that the 'lads' knew more than me. I felt threatened and alarmed that their banter could encourage him like a dare.

"There's no rush," I said and meant it on so many levels. I dreaded the day that he got closer to some girl, any girl that would take him away from me. "If you ever need to practice again, I'm your girl." I cringed as soon as the words were out.

"Sorry, about that, I never should have asked that of you." He ran a hand through his hair.

"What are friends for?" I giggled to hide my disappointment. "Just say the word."

"What word?" he raised an eyebrow, in a flirty way.

"Umm....," I said thinking. "I guess it's two words, kiss me."

"Kiss me?" he laughed.

I hesitated for a moment. Was he asking me or

testing the words? I decided it best not to question it; if I didn't kiss him now, I might lose my chance. I leaned over and quickly pressed my lips against his.

Almost as quickly, I felt his hand on my breast. Alarm bells rang, as I realised what was happening.

He was pushing me away!

His lips left mine and he jumped away from the bed. The duvet fell to the floor and the cool, November air gripped me. I wanted to undo what I'd done; I wanted to wrap up in quilted goodness with Jace by my side, like nothing had happened. Instead, he was frowning, casting a dark shadow across his facial features.

"What're you doing?"

"You wanted me to," I whispered.

"I'm with Kiely," he said. "I told you! Officially."

I took a big breath, bit my lip and swallowed the lump in my throat. How had everything gone so horribly wrong, so quick.

"Mariah, I do need your help, but not like that." He rested his hand on my shoulder. "I'm sorry if you got confused and thought…"

"I'm not confused!"

"Sorry." Jace walked towards the door. "Maybe I should go."

"No!" I'd waited so long to spend some time with him. "Stay."

His hand rested on the handle. "I never should've kissed you."

How could he say that?!

I hated him moving away, us being split up at

school, and regretted not pushing harder for more visits. It's painful enough to listen to him talk about wanting to kiss Kiely but to hear him wish he'd never kissed me was cutting me up inside in a way I could never tell my best friend.

It hit me. Jace was my everything. But to him, I was one friend out of many. I needed somebody, somebody who wasn't Jace.

Jace continued, "I don't want it to ruin our friendship."

I put on a brave face and nodded. "I agree. Friends forever?"

"Forever and ever," Jace smiled.

He returned to my bed and sat down. He casually rested his hand on my leg and it sent a current up my body.

"I do need your help, though?"

Jace's words made my whole body burn up and my eyes creeped to his lips, reminiscing over their capabilities. I tingled with willingness to please him. My eagerness made me feel dizzy, like I was in an out of control car heading for a wall, without brakes.

"What do you need?" This would end badly unless I accepted our friendship and stopped trying to make it into something more.

"A plan to get rid of Kiely's brother."

I joked to cover up my reluctance. "Shall I search for pig farms or incinerators?"

One of his mum's creepy boyfriends had told us once that pigs will eat anything and are the best way to dispose of a dead body. He also told us some other random facts about murders. We weren't sad to see the back of him.

Jace lightly punched me on the arm. "I was thinking more you could date him."

"What?!" I choked.

"Loads of girls are into him. I hate to admit it but he is a catch."

"Well, he's hardly going to be interested in me."

"Of course he would. You're his type - female."

"Thanks, Jace," I said sarcastically. "I'm really not liking this plan."

"What's not to like?" Jace grinned. "You and him, while me and Kiely…"

"No!" I did not want him and Kiely to do whatever he was thinking. "You're on your own. Promise me you won't set us up!"

"But, I can hear wedding bells," Jace smirked.

I grabbed his little finger with my own. "It's a pinky promise. You can't break it."

"Fine." Jace snatched his hand away. "I'll come up with something else."

Being 'just friends' was incredibly painful. I couldn't switch off my feelings and I found myself writing lists, comparing myself to Kiely. After using the lists for weeks to torture myself, I had a revelation. I needed to do something to impress Jace to get him to see me differently. I had to stop being such a loser. But how?

I wanted to make friends, as Jace had with the football team, but I wasn't good at sports, or magic, despite my efforts. I checked the noticeboard in the school library for something that might appeal to me. It was covered in bits of paper and card, secured by pins. There were several different groups that didn't interest me: chess, drama, art, and netball. I grimaced.

Then, I saw 'swimming' and was filled with a wave of excitement. The club met after school on a Wednesday at the pool. My hand reached for one of the paper tags with the details, and my allergy bracelet jangled, reminding me why I can't join.

When we were in Spain, Denny got me a swimming costume from the gift shop and let me swim in the pool. My body took to the water, in no time I was swimming like a pro. I thought Mum would be pleased when she saw me, but she hauled me out in front of everyone and dragged me to our room. She dried me off and confessed her concern about my fair skin burning in the sun. She made me promise never to swim again and, even once I promised, she wouldn't let me out of our room.

The next morning, my legs were coated in a strange rash that gave my skin a silvery sheen. I'd never seen anything like it but Mum recognised it. She called it meralloitis, and said it was a rare skin condition that runs on my father's side, caused by sea water. I asked more about my dad but she got angry. She threw my swimming costume in the bin and notified the school that I'm not allowed in the pool. I argued that I'd be fine, the school's pool is full of chlorine, not sea water. But, she refused to discuss it. It broke my heart. I'd never felt more myself than when I was in the water.

I sulked. How could I join a swimming club without a swimming costume? I let go of the piece of paper.

"The swimming club is awesome," a girl with dark hair chimed next to me. She pulled a piece of paper off and handed it to me. "There, you dropped yours."

I recognised the girl. She was in my year group and called Ana. I shrugged.

"I haven't got a costume."

She pulled a face. "Really? Well, you're welcome to borrow one of mine. I love swimming and always have spares in my locker. I keep them just in case I forget to bring one in."

"I dunno…"

As awkward as I felt accepting a swimming costume off another student, it also felt like fate wanted me to go.

"Come with me," she said and hooked her arm through mine and smiled brightly as if we had always been friends. Once we reached her locker, she rummaged through her swimsuits. I tried to think of an excuse to thank her for her kindness and back away. But, my heart raced at the thought of swimming almost as if Jace was near. Ana passed me a black costume.

"You can keep it. As you can see, I have plenty." She handed me some goggles. "You need to wear these because the chlorine is harsh."

"Thank you."

"You're welcome. See you there."

I slipped into my one piece swimming costume, black with a rainbow travelling from my hip to just under my bust - if you could call those two nipple-shaped lumps a bust.

A mix of girls and boys bobbed in the water near the edge and I was relieved to see they wore goggles, too. The swim team was easy to identify as they all wore matching silver goggles and wore swimwear in the school's emerald green colours.

A teacher stood on the side in red shorts.

"A new girl," he beamed at me.

I nodded and blushed.

He had a clipboard in his hand. "Name, year group, and form number?"

"Mariah Turner, form three of year eleven."

"You can train with us but the team's already been selected."

I felt relieved. If I'd thought I had to compete I wouldn't have come. I nodded and smiled.

"That's okay."

"In you get."

I couldn't see Ana and everyone was staring at me, 'the new girl', so I went to the edge and slid in. The water wasn't like the pool in Spain. It was cool, and I felt like it was rejecting me. I lowered myself down. Soon, I was bobbing away with the other enthusiastic swimmers.

"For the benefit of our new swimmer, Mariah, I am Mr Griffen." He nodded at me. "Team A, I want you to race against Group One. Team B, I want you to race against the sub-team." He began walking along the side, passing a stopwatch to different students near the edge.

"First, try and beat your best time, which should be recorded in your log book." He glanced down at me. "Mariah, group one is down the shallow end. I'll bring you a logbook in a minute."

I nodded and began making my way towards the group I'd be part of. As I made my way through, I noticed most girls wore bikinis. I felt childish in my one-piece swimming costume. Then, I saw Ana. I was thankful she was also wearing a full swimming costume and was in group one with me. She sat on the poolside with the stopwatch in her hand, whilst her legs dangled in the water.

"Hi," I smiled.

"You came," she beamed.

"Do you know each other?" Mr Griffen asked and I realised he must have followed me along the poolside.

"Sort of," I said with a smile. Ana nodded and blushed as she grinned at Mr Griffen.

Mr Griffen passed Ana my logbook. "Can you record Mariah's times so I can get an idea of what she can do?"

Ana nodded and bowed her head as her whole body flushed with colour.

She recorded my times for different strokes and commented that I was the fastest in our group. I asked her if she wanted me to time her but she preferred sitting out on the edge. She came to the swimming club but rarely swam.

Afterwards, Mr Griffen introduced a game to finish the session. We were told to swim out to the middle of the pool and hold our breath underwater. Mr Griffen wanted to see who could stay under for the longest. I moved out into the middle of the water and began cycling my legs to keep myself afloat. I dipped my face into the water and held my breath. I could see legs all around me peddling away. Slowly, one by one the legs disappeared. I guessed those leaving must have come up for air, lost, and left the pool.Until it was just me and one other pair of legs - hairy, male legs.

My chest didn't even feel tight, despite the length of time I had been under. Finally, I was good at something. I saw the other person's legs suddenly kick out and twist around. He had given up; I could see he was swimming towards the step. I searched underwater and, once I was sure I had won, I raised my head to the expectant faces waiting at the edge.

"Impressive," Mr Griffen commended me. "So good, I began to worry you'd never come up for air."

I saw who I'd beaten. Pulling himself out of the water was a guy in dark green trunks. He eyed me over his shoulder. His body was toned but his cool, silver eyes cut me like a knife. He obviously didn't like being beaten. His eyes ran up and down my body with disgust. His glare caused the hairs on my arm to stand up on end.

I swam to get out. Ana was waiting for me by the steps.

"I can't believe that!" she said enthusiastically as her bony body shivered. "Nobody has ever beaten Murray."

I glanced over to where Murray was wrapping a towel around his waist and found he was still watching me. Ana held my towel out towards me. I took it and we headed to the showers to get washed and dressed.

As I combed my wet hair at the mirrors, Ana joined me.

"I come most evenings after school for practice. Next year, hopefully, I'll make the swim team." She smiled. "It's a great way to stay slim."

I laughed; like she needed to worry about her weight. I shoved my brush into my bag. "See you here tomorrow?"

"Looking forward to it."

I was proud of myself. I'd made a friend, without Jace's help.

CHAPTER 6

ANA WAS VIGILANT ABOUT HER TRAINING - and mine. She insisted we came after school every evening. With each session I was getting faster. I began to recognise others from the group who came regularly and they began to know me. Everyone was friendly, except Murray.

He was in the final year of sixth form and the swim team star. He didn't welcome me at training and regarded me with the same cold, steel expression he had when I beat him in the underwater challenge. I pointed out his dislike towards me as I chatted to Ana.

"Yeah. I noticed. I guess he's a sore loser," she agreed and shrugged.

I discovered she was in Jace's form and knew Kiely. I was disappointed when I learned she lived out of town, in the countryside, so we probably wouldn't be able to hang out much outside of school. Her village didn't even have a reliable bus service.

In the pool, she was focused and didn't talk much but once out she turned into a real chatterbox. I was delighted when she said, "You should come over mine for a sleepover!"

I didn't know what to say. I'd never been invited for a sleepover before. Unless, you include staying over at Jace's house, but his home had always felt like an extension of my own.

"Okay..."

Ana picked up on my hesitation and tried to sweeten the deal: "We can do face masks and paint each other's toes..."

"Sounds great." It sounded exhausting.

"...and watch chick flicks, talk about men, and stay up all night!"

"Men? It's just Jace for me," I corrected her with a laugh. "Who are you into?"

Her whole body turned pink, from her cheeks to the tips of her toes. "Promise you won't laugh?"

"Who?" I asked. Her expression was so animated, I wanted to laugh.

"Mr Griffen." She swooned and began fanning herself with her hand, suddenly aware of how hot she'd become.

I laughed, "For real?"

"You said you wouldn't laugh."

"Sorry," I bit my lip, a twinkle in my eye. I tried my best to sober up for her. But, seriously? A teacher? Mr

Griffen?

The next morning, as I exchanged books in my locker, I didn't notice Ana approaching until she bounced next to me making me jump.

"Morning, Mariah!" She said too brightly for 8:40 am. "Are you going to the pool after school?"

"Of course," I smiled back.

"Still okay to come to mine on Friday?"

"Yeah."

"Bring your sleepover stuff to school and we can go straight after swimming," Ana grinned.

"You're obsessed with swimming," I rolled my eyes.

"Not swimming, duh! Mr Griffen," she smirked.

"Pervert."

"Ooo, those little red shorts," she giggled.

It had been a good session in the pool, except Ana's goggles had broken. I offered to return the ones she'd given me but she told me she had more at home. I suggested we could finish up early but she insisted we keep racing, even though I beat her every time.

It was time to get out, I made my way towards the

changing room.

"Best of seven?" Ana chirped from the pool. I stood at the brick-built island where most of us dumped our towels before diving in. Ana sure had stamina – you had to admire how she didn't give up.

I wrapped my blue towel around my shoulders like a cape. "Come on. I want to see your house."

Ana sighed and followed me out. I slid my goggles off and Ana stood pale faced before me. She leaned in close, getting right up in my face.

"What's up with your eyes?"

I blinked and flushed red. "What is it?"

Ana blushed. "Nothing. Just, for a moment your pupils were stretched into a long thin slit like a snake's eye." She shook her head. "Sorry, it's my crazy imagination. They're perfectly normal."

"Of course, they're normal," I giggled uncomfortably under her gaze.

Ana blushed and allowed her hair to fall forward and hide her face.

"Perhaps you should wear goggles, too," I recommended.

Ana nodded in agreement.

"Mariah," Mr Griffen said as he came up beside me. "You continue to impress me. I've noticed your dedication to attend every evening and your log is always up-to-date. It's a catalogue of excellent times."

"Thanks." I blushed. I hadn't done it to improve, just to hang out with Ana. It was her who kept my log up-to-date. I hadn't even tried that hard.

"The team was selected earlier this term during tryouts. It would be unfair to cut anyone, but I need you on the team. You must be our reserve. If anyone can't make the competition in July, I'll be counting on you as my backup," Mr Griffen rested a hand on my back. "To make the school team is an honour, Mariah. You'll be representing us all."

"Thanks," I said and became conscious of how close Ana was standing next to me.

"You'll need to get a swimming costume in the school colours and a parent or guardian to sign this form. I know you'll make me proud." Mr Griffen winked and handed me a piece of paper.

Ana and I stood in silence, side by side, watching him stride away. Once he was out of earshot, my towel was snatched from my shoulders.

"Oi!"

"Have my towel," Ana offered and turned so I couldn't get my towel back. "You're so lucky. Mr Griffen had his hands all over you." She clutched it to her chest and inhaled the scent deeply.

"Barely," I took her towel from the brick island, which was pale pink in colour and softer than mine. "Is this yours?"

Ana nodded at the towel in my hand and I quickly wrapped it tightly around me before she decided she wanted it back.

"He wants you. He notices you. It's so unfair. What do I have to do to get on his team?"

"I'm just a reserve."

"You don't even know how lucky you are," Ana sulked as we headed towards the changing rooms.

She was right of course. Mr Griffen believing in me was the first time I wanted to be good, to make him proud and the team. I also promised myself I'd do my best to help Ana get on the team, too.

"You can keep the towel if you like," I winked.

Ana rolled her eyes. "I forgot about that - he winked at you!" She made a low groan. "I'm so jealous!"

We waited at the end of the road to be picked up. A large, silver car pulled up beside us. I had no idea the car was for us until Ana stepped forward and held the door open for me.

The car had a long bonnet with wings imprinted in the centre of it. Inside, the seats were white leather and the dashboard a polished wood. A large armrest was between our seats.

"What type of car is this?" I asked in awe.

"A Bentley," Ana said, blushing. "My dad's into cars."

"Good day at school?" a suited man asked from the front.

"Yes, Geoff," Ana said before she whispered to me, "He's our driver."

"You have a driver?"

Ana nodded as the car filled with the sound of the

radio.

We left the coastal town I called home and entered the countryside. Many of the fields were ploughed and empty but every so often there would be a field of grass with a scattering of sheep. Finally, we turned onto a muddy track that led us to a gravel driveway. The pebbles crunched under the wheels as the car pulled to a stop in front of the house. I saw a separate building and a double door garage. The garage was newer than the house which still had old, deep red bricks and dark slate tiles.

A woman strutted out to greet us and held out her manicured hand to shake.

"Lovely to meet you, Mariah." She was an Asian lady with glossy, black hair and wore a silk blouse and pencil skirt. She turned to address my friend, "Ana, order a pizza, entertain yourselves; I'm out with the girls tonight." She waved and jumped into the car with Geoff.

"Who's that?"

"Connie. She's alright for a step-mum," Ana shrugged as she held the door open for me. We entered the house decorated with old fashioned, antique furniture. Ana shut the heavy, wooden door behind me. "Want to see my room?"

I nodded, lost for words. Ana was rich and I hadn't realised. I followed her up the stairs and across a galleried landing. Ana took me to the nearest door and pushed it open to reveal a large bedroom, with a very pink theme, and a princess canopy bed scattered with decorative pillows.

"This is my room," she said proudly.

As I followed her in, I could feel the softness of the luxury carpet underfoot.

"Over there is my bathroom," she pointed to a door on the far wall and then her finger moved to point at another door. "And, that's my walk-in closet."

Jealousy was an understatement; I barely had enough clothes to fill a wardrobe let alone a closet big enough to walk around in.

"Well, let's get you unpacked!"

I put my bag down next to the sofa that had been folded out as a guest bed.

"Ana, why do you attend our school?"

"What do you mean?" Ana laughed nervously.

"Your family could take their pick of the best private schools in the country."

Ana blushed. "I got expelled... from them all."

"How?" I gasped, shocked.

Ana was so sweet natured and hardworking; I couldn't imagine her in trouble.

"It's a boring story," she dismissed me and strolled over to a desk. She clicked a button and the mirror folded out to reveal her make-up. "First, I thought we could have a makeover and then take some pictures as supermodels. It'll be so much fun."

"Okay," I agreed, letting her change the subject. "But, I ought to warn you that I'm a disaster at make-up and have very little fashion sense."

"I'll make you over, then," Ana patted the stool at

her dressing table for me to sit. "I love doing it."

"Thanks."

Ana made up my face then braided and backcombed sections of my hair. It stuck out in a crazy, wild way, but Ana called it 'supermodel fierce'. She pulled out a selection of clothes from her wardrobe for me to wear. At first I wasn't sure, but then Ana put on some outfits and started strutting around. We posed together in these big brimmed hats and chunky beaded necklaces. We wore matching flapper girl style dresses and an assortment of feather boas. Ana tried to show me how the girls used to dance in the 1920s, but she just reminded me of a penguin and it made me laugh.

Once she was satisfied I was ready, she insisted we go around the house. She instructed me on how to pose in different outfits as she photographed me. We took pictures in a wooded area by her house and she got me to sit on the fence of a neighbouring field.

Finally finished, we sat on garden chairs by the backdoor and Ana showed me the pictures. She kept complimenting me. It felt weird to be told I was beautiful, but it also felt nice.

"Wow, Ana, these photos are great."

"It helps to have such a stunning model."

"I can't believe that's me."

"Well, it is," Ana beamed. "You should wear purple more often."

"They wouldn't look out of place in a glossy magazine."

"Really? I'm going to study it at university."

"Fashion or photography?"

"All of it. I love shapes, colour, and lights," Ana said proudly, admiring the pictures. "Thanks for playing along with me."

"It was fun. Thanks for teaching me how to use makeup and pick the right outfits and colours"

"Actually, I have some clothes taking up space in my closet that don't fit me anymore. You can have them."

I shook my head. "That's generous of you Ana, but I think I'm bigger than you."

She got up and headed inside. "You might not feel so grateful after you've helped me sort through my closet. I'm sure some will fit you."

I followed her upstairs and we began building mountains of clothes: keep, donate, toss, and a rapidly growing pile for me. Ana wasn't kidding. It was a huge task, but it made the pizza taste even better when we were done. We managed to talk all the way through a film - luckily we'd both seen it before.

I'd never had a friend like this before and the time just flew by. I felt a pang of guilt, like I was cheating on Jace, but I quickly pushed the feeling away. Besides, if anyone had cheated on our friendship first, it was him.

I was shattered and ready for bed but Ana wouldn't let me sleep. She put music on and dealt a pack of playing cards.

"Ana, I'm ready for bed," I yawned.

"You can't sleep! That's not what sleepovers are for. Promise you'll stay awake?" The joy was robbed from

Ana's usual cheerful face and she appeared desperate, almost begging.

"I promise."

Ana relaxed and gave a weary smile.

"If I'm not sleeping, I think you should share why you got expelled."

Ana shook her head and laughed. "If I tell you, I'd have to kill you."

"Come on," I begged.

Ana's smile faded from her face and she became serious. She took a deep breath and frowned. "Maybe one day. I just don't want to talk about it right now. Okay?"

"Okay."

I felt a bit awkward for pushing it and worried that perhaps I'd put off my new friend. Maybe once we knew each other better she'd be able to tell me. She certainly had me intrigued.

"So, you and Mr Griffen?" she changed the subject, teasing.

I shook my head and pulled a face. I didn't get the appeal. "There's nothing going on between us. He's all yours, my friend."

"He has made a special exception for you to be on the team," she gushed.

I blushed, "Yeah, about that…"

"What?"

"It's my mum. She'll never sign the consent form."

"Why not?"

"She doesn't even know I attend swimming."

Ana's face screwed up and she shrugged. "Just tell her."

"I can't." I swallowed a lump in my throat as I realised how upset I was about this. "My mum's against me swimming. She'd kill me. I'm dreading her finding out and banning me."

"What's wrong with swimming?"

I held up my wrist to show Ana my bracelet. "I have an allergy to sea water."

"Sea water?"

I nodded.

"I've never heard of that before."

"I'm fine in the pool but she's worried I might have a reaction and doesn't want to risk it. She doesn't want me swimming at all."

"But you're so good! It's like you were born to swim!"

"I know." I sighed. My body suddenly felt incredibly heavy. The one thing I was truly good at and I was hiding it from my mum.

"Don't worry," Ana got up and walked over to her desk and pulled out a credit card. "I'll get your cossie. You do your mum's signature."

My face lit up. "Really, Ana? You'd do that for me?"

"It would be a crime not to."

CHAPTER 7

A NA'S INTERPRETATION OF A 'SLEEPOVER' didn't actually involve any sleeping.

"Best not to talk about it," was all she'd say when I asked. As a result, I lost my weekend to catch up on shut-eye. By Wednesday, I was only just starting to feel like myself again. I missed the water more than I'd expected. Once the final bell rang, Ana came to find me.

She grinned excitedly as she held up a new, emerald swimming costume by the straps, making it dance like a puppet in front of her.

"Look what came!"

"Thank you. I'll pay you back."

She shook her head. "Don't worry about that. Just tell me you've got your signed consent form." She leaned in close and added with a whisper, "On behalf of your mum."

"Do you think I'll get caught?"

Carrying the form around gave me a prickly sensation. Ever since I'd signed it, I had this fear I'd be caught and expelled from school. I wanted to be rid of it.

"Duh!" Ana laughed. "You said your mum is a psychic, she probably already knows, but guess what? She hasn't stopped you and that's consent in my book."

I giggled nervously. "You're a bad influence."

"You didn't need much encouragement."

She took my hand and we were off to the pool. Once changed we tapped on the 'Staff' door.

"Ah, Mariah," Mr Griffen greeted us warmly.

I guiltily passed him the forged document.

My heart beat and my hand quickly swiped a bead of sweat from my forehead. He glanced down at the piece of paper, checking it over. I waited for alarms to sound. My hands tingled as I contemplated snatching it back and running.

"Excellent." He dropped it into a filing tray. "In you get. Got to train my number one reserve."

I breathed a sigh of relief.

He misinterpreted my discomfort. "Don't worry, Mariah. I wouldn't have recruited you if I didn't think you were up to it."

"Thanks, sir," I mumbled and quickly hurried to get in the pool before I said or did something that would give away what I'd done.

Mr Griffen strolled along the side of the pool with his clipboard already marking attendance.

"Thanks for coming, I value your dedication." He sought me out of the row of bobbing heads. "Mariah," he said with a big smile and I felt everyone's eyes follow his gaze. "I'd like to introduce everyone to the swim team's newest reserve."

"But, I thought the team was only for sixth formers!" an older girl complained.

"She's only a reserve - emergency cover. The rules state it can be any student from the school, and Mariah has demonstrated excellent times and commitment."

I could hear some grumbling and complaints echo around. This wasn't going to make me popular. It seemed despite a number of people saying I was really good, there was an equal number that felt it was unfair.

Ana picked up on my concerns and whispered, "Haters gonna hate."

With Ana by my side, I was able to shrug it off.

"If you ignore them, they'll get bored and leave you alone," she added.

I couldn't blame them for thinking I might not deserve this - I'd only just joined swimming. But, I continued to swim every night after school - not just to prove them wrong and show that I did deserve this, but also because I loved it and I enjoyed being good at something.

Swimming after school didn't just make my times better. I slowly got to know more of the other swimmers, and they stopped feeling like I'd taken something from them that they deserved more. The better I got to know them, the more I belonged.

After Mr Griffen got me to race against the strongest female swimmers in the club, and I won, the complaints died down. Some people even congratulated me! Sure, the actual swim team was still suspicious of me, but I could deal with that now I had people on my side.

Best of all, as my confidence grew, my attitude towards myself improved. I couldn't wait to see Jace and tell him about my achievements.

It was Saturday and two weeks since I had become the swim team's reserve. Jace grinned at me.

"You're bouncy today? Swimming must agree with you."

"How did you know?" I was gutted he'd already heard my news.

"Kiely's brother was fuming about 'Goldie the Goldfish'. He kept going on about it. It took me a while to figure it out, but you're Goldie!" he laughed. "I didn't click until Ana tried to persuade me to come to the pool and watch you swim."

I felt my cheeks burning as I worried what else Ana might have said. She was the only one that knew my secret.

"What did she say?"

"She bragged about how good you are, beating the team's times and being Mr Griffen's favourite."

"Who called me a fish?" I fumed, but already had

an idea.

"Murray." He shook his head. "You should have seen him last weekend. He claims you've been stalking him."

I was furious. How dare he? What else had he said? Jace continued to laugh as if it was the funniest thing ever and it just made me madder.

I punched him on the arm. "Cut it out! Why is he saying that? I've not been stalking him. I've been training!"

"Do you like him? It'd be cool if you did. Then we could double date."

My jaw dropped in disbelief. He had to be kidding. Could he not hear me? Had we grown so far apart that he didn't even know me?

"It's still the best plan. You keep him busy while I get Kiely alone."

My stomach turned at the thought. I was being dragged into a perpetual nightmare. Under no circumstances would I want to spend more time than I had to with Steely Eyes. Especially, if he was calling me a fish and telling people I'm his stalker.

"No way! I've never even spoken to him and all he does is glare. I already told you, no!"

In addition to all that, I didn't want to help Jace get with Kiely.

"Shame, we're meeting them at the beach," he cringed.

"Tell me you're joking," I begged, the colour draining from my face.

"Freckles, I only get to see her at the weekend and I thought it'd be nice for you to meet her."

Nice? He really didn't have a clue! Being stoned to death sounded nicer than watching Jace drool over Kiely. The only thing that could be worse was making small talk with Murray.

"You'll like her," he said getting off the bed and heading past me, out of his bedroom. I followed him downstairs and he passed me my coat. I felt unwell. I knew already, I wasn't going to like her, not at all!

I didn't want to go, but the moment he took my hand, his invisible control over me caused my unwilling body to follow. With a silly smile on my face, he could lead me to slaughter - which was a little how this felt.

He wasn't joking about his planned ambush. Waiting for us at the cliff tops were Kiely and Murray. Kiely was dressed in a cute, little, woollen dress, patterned tights, and knee-high boots. Standing beside each other, I could see the resemblance between the siblings. Their features matched; the shape of their nose, eyes, and lips, but their colourings were different. Kiely was more like Jace with her blonde hair and warm blue eyes, whereas Murray's hair was dark, almost black, and his eyes were an empty shade of grey, almost void of colour.

Kiely's cheeks flushed upon seeing Jace and I was annoyed when Jace responded the same.

"Hi!" I yelled, to ruin the moment.

Murray grunted, being rude as usual.

"This is Mariah," Jace squeezed my hand.

I saw Kiely's eyes flare at our intertwined hands. Jace suddenly dropped it as if I'd burnt him. It was too late. Coupled with Murray's tales and her first impression of me, we were never going to get on, not one little bit. Even if I wanted to, which I didn't.

Jace quickly took Kiely's hand in an attempt to fix any damage caused. They headed down the steps to the beach, leaving Murray and I behind. We followed silently. It was a secluded beach that only the locals really knew about.

Jace and Kiely found a sandy spot amongst the shingle to sit down on and watch the waves. I felt like a chaperone. Jace put his arm around her shoulder, and my world began to run in slow motion. I knew he was plucking up the courage to kiss her.

A stone bounced off Jace's forehead. His gormless expression made me laugh. He was as surprised as I was.

Jace glared at Murray. "Oi!"

Murray chuckled. "Any good at skimming?"

He had another stone in his hand leaning back on his leg and twisting round he turned and spun the stone out across the waves. I saw it bounce two or three times a fair distance off before disappearing under the waves.

"I'm the best at skimming," Kiely said as she got to her feet. She searched the sand for a moment before selecting a stone and tossed it across the sea. It skimmed and bounced on the waves, travelling further than Murray's.

Of course, she was the best! I thought bitterly of her success and rolled my eyes.

"I was just getting warmed up," Murray laughed.

He seemed different out of the pool. When he laughed, he came alive and warm... inviting. Eager for the challenge, Jace joined in. His stone didn't go far at all. He crossed his arms.

"I'm no good at this."

"I'll help you find a good stone. You need a flat one," Kiely told him as she rummaged through the pebbles.

"Are you taking a turn?" Murray asked me. His eyes shone at me like a spotlight, giving me his full attention.

I could see why girls were into him. There was something very captivating about him out here that made my temperature rise. I shook my head and allowed my hair to fall and hide my face.

"Come on, Goldie, I bet you're a first-time champion. Like a duck to water."

"My name is Mariah!" I snapped. My shyness was gone, as irritation got the better of me.

He chuckled at my reaction and offered me a smooth brown pebble he had found. "Try it?"

I snatched the stone from him and threw it at the rough waves. It plopped straight into the ocean. As usual, I was rubbish.

Then, I felt Murray standing behind me. His arms reached around me and placed another stone in my hand.

"You know I don't like losing, but do you know

what I hate more? Winning against someone who didn't even try."

He was so close I could feel his hot breath against my ear.

"I don't know how to do it," I croaked nervously. There was something about Murray's closeness that scared me.

"Here," he handed me another pebble and placed his hands on my hips. He twisted my body so I was facing the sea, side on. He pulled my arm with the stone up and held it straight out. "See where you want the stone to go. See it bouncing. Skim it. Don't throw it. Now twist your wrist. Remember: see where you want it to go."

He let go of me and I took that as the signal to put his instructions into action. I skimmed my stone across the sea and it bounced once before going under.

"Now, I beat you trying," he smiled smugly as I turned to face him. He was crouched down, rummaging in the shingle for his next pebble. He checked on his sister. "Let's all skim on the count of three."

We all found our stones and lined up.

"Girls against boys!" Kiely grinned at me as Murray counted us in. Kiely clearly won again.

"What's my prize?" she cheered between her victory hoots whilst glancing at Jace.

"A dip in the sea!"

Murray charged at his sister and effortlessly tossed her over his shoulder. He raced towards the sea while she let out a high-pitched squeal of a scream and kicked her legs about. From over her brother's shoulder, she pleaded for Jace to save her.

Jace just laughed. I grinned, smugly.

"Jace!" She was insulted that Jace wasn't attempting to rescue her. "Charming!"

Unfortunately, Murray didn't want to get his trainers wet. He gave up and put her down with an excuse: "Can't be dealing with Mum's wrath!"

Murray gave me a knowing glance as if I knew what he meant.

"Oh no!" gasped Jace, his mobile in his hands. "I'm late for Brian's."

"Just go straight there?" Kiely suggested.

Jace turned to me. "Do you know the way back from here?"

"I'll figure it out." I didn't want to be a burden.

"I'll walk her," Murray offered.

Jace hesitated. He looked between Murray and I.

"Nah, Murray, if Mariah needs me, I'll just text Brian I'll be late."

"It's fine. You go." I tried to reassure him.

He stood frozen to the spot unsure what to do.

"See ya," Murray said.

"See ya, Kiely," Jace said with a wave. Then, he grabbed me in one of his famous hugs. He whispered in my ear, "Are you alright with him?"

I nodded.

"Love you," he added and placed a light kiss on my cheek.

My skin tingled where his lips had touched me. My

heart was skipping all over the place as he turned and jogged off in the opposite direction. All Kiely got was a wave. He hugged, kissed me, and told me that he loved me.

As we walked back, Kiely babbled on about all the things she had been told about me by Jace, like how long we'd been friends and memories we'd made. I realised that Jace must have talked a lot about me and I felt flattered. Every so often, Kiely would ask "*Is that true?*" She didn't wait for an answer. In a lot of ways, she mirrored my thoughts on how dreamy Jace was and how much she really liked him.

Murray made me laugh by pretending to stick two fingers down his throat and be sick.

Kiely ran up a driveway of a large house with views of the ocean. "I'll let Mum know where you are."

I was alone with Murray, and the air seemed to thicken. We walked like two individuals that were not associated with each other, just heading in the same direction. Earlier, the walkout with Jace had felt breezy and quick. The awkward silence made the short walk drag on. Murray must have felt it too; he coughed as if uncomfortable.

"So, you're the team's new reserve? I guess we'll be spending more time together."

Talk about good news turned bad! I rolled my eyes and carried on walking. The less I had to do with him the better. I instantly regretted not answering him as the silence hung in the air.

"You don't like me, do you?" he said as an

accusation.

I felt wrongly accused. Who did he think he was, asking me that? It was him with the attitude problem, not me!

"What?" I choked. "I hate to break it to you, Murray, but I really haven't given you much thought."

"And glaring at me is to communicate your desire for friendship?"

"You think I'm glaring at you?"

"How about showing me some gratitude?"

"Gratitude? You didn't have to walk me home - you offered. And for the record, it's not me with the problem!"

"Mum's a redhead," he grinned. "Same fiery temper."

"I don't have a temper!" I gritted my teeth in annoyance.

"There it is."

I clenched my fists. I wanted to scream at him but he'd just blame it on my hair so I kept my mouth shut.

"Besides, that's not why you should be thanking me."

"Thanks for what?" My eyes narrowed.

He didn't seem bothered that he had pissed me off. In fact, his cocky grin showed he was amused.

"Deny it all you want but I saw the way you look at Jace and I'm exhausted. All day, I made sure they never kissed, for you."

He caught me off guard and I didn't feel able to lie. I cringed at my feelings being so obvious. Had Kiely noticed too? Once again, I wondered how Jace couldn't know.

"Thank you," I mumbled.

"Shall we kiss and make-up?"

"Murray!" I felt my blood boil again. I ground on my teeth but the words swimming up inside me boiled over and out my lips. "You're so rude! Ever since I beat you at a stupid swim game. You're a sore loser, going around telling people I'm stalking you, calling me a fish. You're right, I don't like you!"

"Jeez! It's just banter. Jace's house is at the end of the road," Murray said with a nod. His face darkened. Good, I had upset him. "Take care." He frowned as he turned around.

We separated; both moving away in opposite directions.

Suddenly, he called out, "So, that kiss, Goldie, I shan't hold my breath!"

The air filled with his laughter and I realised I couldn't have hurt his feelings too badly. Once again, I was his joke. I clenched my jaw as I carried on along the street, screaming on the inside. He was the most annoying person I had ever met. I picked up my pace to get away from him just as a thunderstorm rolled over.

I reached the driveway, and saw that Murray was watching me from the end of the road. He held an arm up to shield his face from the sudden heavy rain. Wickedly, I gloried in him being soaked.

CHAPTER 8

I REPLAYED MY CONVERSATION WITH MURRAY and it tied me up in knots with all the things I should have said. My only salvation was how Jace said goodbye, and even that was now a tiny teardrop in my massive puddle of misery.

During my lunch breaks, I went to my spot on the staircase where I could sit on the window ledge and watch Jace play football. I longed for him to notice me, almost as hard as I wished the day to pass so I could get in the pool. Swimming after school was what got me through the day.

Everyday, I hoped Murray wouldn't turn up. He had that smug look on his face as if bragging that he knew my secret. Thankfully, he never said anything. Not that I gave him a chance. I made sure I was busy

talking to Ana or swimming underwater.

But today, as I reached the pool, I noticed Ana wasn't around. It wasn't like her to miss practice. Her absence made me feel uneasy.

Setting myself up against the wall, I checked the clock to see the time. I wanted to improve my front crawl speed. I wanted to improve and beat Murray. It was the one stroke he bested me at. I hung forward by my hands, with my feet pressed against the wall waiting for the minute hand to point at the twelve.

"Hi, Goldie," Murray said as he positioned himself next to me.

"Stop calling me that!" I snapped, refusing to take my eyes off the clock. One, two, three, the seconds ticked by.

"You don't know what it means."

I don't care!

The hand hit twelve. I pushed myself off, and free of his taunts. The water rippled past me as I flew through and slowly I rose for my first breath. I reached my arm up and over my head, gently brushing past my ears. My head lifted for a breath and to my horror, Murray was there.

"You remind me of -" he said.

I cut him off before he finished, my head disappearing back under the water.

I kicked my legs furiously, willing my body to go faster. I had to beat him. Swimming was my thing, the thing I was good at. He wasn't taking that away from me. My head rose from the water to take a quick gulp of oxygen.

"I've got beautiful..."

He was still talking.

Couldn't he tell I couldn't hear him under the water? He's such an idiot. I flipped at the end of the pool and got a good kick off. I sailed along under the surface, gathering speed. I began my front crawl again. As I came up for air, Murray swimming alongside me, effortlessly.

"You should come over."

Grrr!

He was so annoying. Finally, I saw the end in sight. I focused my anger on my kicks. And, as I reached out a hand to touch the side, I glided to a stop.

To check my time, I sought out the clock. My shoulders slumped as I saw it took me over six minutes. Murray had broken my stroke with his distractions.

"What are you doing?" I pulled my goggles down around my neck.

"Swimming."

"Why don't you leave me alone?"

"I want to make a deal."

"A deal?"

"Mum insists I chaperone Kiely on her hot date tonight. They're watching a soppy rom-com at the cinema. Sounds as dull as dishwater to me." He shrugged.

"So?"

"I could pretend to go but leave them alone and... well, you know..."

A sharp pain struck my heart at the thought of Jace and Kiely being left to '*you know*'. I felt his wet hand on my chin, turning my face toward him, ripples light reflected in his cool eyes.

"Or, come with me, for a kiss?"

"What? Now?" I shot back from his hand. I was sure everyone must be staring but they weren't. They were doing what we were meant to be doing - swimming.

"Pay me now or later, no difference."

My jaw dropped. *Was he for real?*

"We best hurry if we're going to make it in time." He made his way towards the steps, confident I'd agree. "It's just a kiss!"

Just a kiss! If Jace kissed Kiely would it be 'just a kiss'? Wasn't a first kiss the most important one? So, no matter how good Kiely is, she can't ever beat me. I was first!

Still, something in my heart knew if Jace kissed Kiely it would destroy me. Mum said the most powerful thing is true love's kiss. I found myself, making my way out of the pool to get changed. It appeared as if I were accepting Murray's offer.

After all... it was just a kiss. Right?

I followed Murray over to the bike sheds. He unlocked his bike, while I waited by the back wheel. He glanced up from where he was fiddling with a combination lock that wove between his spokes. It gave me enough time to wonder what the hell I was doing here.

"Most girls who've accompanied me to the bike sheds got more than just a kiss."

His face lit up with a cheeky grin that caused my stomach to flip.

"Don't hold your breath." I shook my head and laughed with satisfaction at using his own joke right back at him. To my surprise, he laughed with me. It kind of annoyed me that he found it funny, too.

"Are you really so desperate for a kiss?" I was scared to hear his answer and quickly added. "That smile of yours won't work on me."

Murray rolled his bike out of the shed. "Works on every other girl."

I was glad for the bike frame between us, keeping him at a distance.

"Whatever. I'm not coming along for you."

"Is that right, Goldie?" he chuckled as he held his bike out. "Hop on, I'll give you a seaty to your house."

"My house?" I eyed him suspiciously.

"You're not going in your uniform."

He tipped his bike closer for me to get on. I felt dangerously high perched on his saddle. My feet dangled off to the side, so I tucked them under to avoid catching on his pedals. The crossbar pushed my skirt up and I blushed at the sight of my ghost legs.

"Hold on," he said, swinging his legs over the crossbar.

Before I could change my mind, we were off.

I gripped hold of the narrow part of the seat. The momentum pulled the unruly strands of hair off my face. He bobbed up and down in front of me as he glided with the spin of each pedal.

"Which way?" he called over his shoulder.

"Right at the gate, then straight over at the lights," I answered, finding myself leaning forward to his ear.

He tipped the bike as he paused one foot on the pavement, checking it was safe before pulling out into the main street. Then we were racing along towards my house.

My heart raced. Every time he dipped the bike to take a corner, my whole stomach dropped with it - I held my breath and closed my eyes. He had control, bringing us upright and speeding forward.

We were at my house in no time and I was surprised by my disappointment.

"That's my house, the one with the white picket fence."

He got off his bike. Compared to his house, mine was tiny. The whole terrace block of four houses was smaller than his home.

"Wait here," I told him.

"This is the second time I've taken you home - most guys get a kiss for that," he said wistfully, eyes lingering on my lips.

I turned away and ignored him. I fumbled with the lock and then tripped as I stepped into the house. I cursed myself for making a fool of myself in front of Murray as I hurried up the stairs to get changed.

Technically, this was the first time he'd brought me to *my* house. I thought about correcting Murray but suspected such details wouldn't matter to him.

"Is that you? I thought you were at art club and not home 'til later," Mum called.

"I was," I said, throwing the contents of my drawers onto my bed as I hunted for anything I could wear.

Mum came to stand in my doorway. "What happened?"

"A group of us are going to the cinema. It's an art club social thing." My skin prickled with the lie.

Mum peeked out my window. "I'm glad you're making friends. Is he one of them?"

"Murray? Yep."

"He doesn't look the arty type." Her eyes narrowed. I could tell she didn't believe me. She'd be checking her crystal ball the moment I'm out the door, seeking answers I won't give freely.

"He is. Very arty. Very good." My chest felt tight.

She made a sceptical 'hmmm' sound and then left me to my fashion dilemma. I considered the clothes Ana had given me but ended up throwing on my favourite blue jeans and an old, black crinkle vest top. I returned to Murray.

Murray wore jeans, a plain white t-shirt and leather jacket. I couldn't help recall the toned body that lay underneath. He waited, poised with one foot on the pavement and the bike tilted towards me.

"Won't you be cold in that?"

"I don't care!" I hoped showing a bit of skin might

garner the attention I craved from Jace.

Murray rode past Jace and Kiely waiting at the cinema entrance.

I waved and yelled, "Hi, Jace – surprise!"

Jace waved back, pleased to see me. Murray rode his bike straight into one of the empty bike spaces across the road with a bump. He got off and left me dangling from his bike seat while he locked up. I could tell Murray found it entertaining so I refused to ask for his help. I made a leap of faith to get down. Once free, I skipped across the road to join Jace. We hugged and I acknowledged Kiely with a nod and she smiled.

Murray wasn't far behind me. As soon as he joined us, we went through the doors, joined the queue, and paired up. Except, I was in the wrong pair. To my dismay, Kiely and Jace were holding hands.

"I didn't realise you two were-," Jace started.

"We're not!" I nipped that rumour in the bud.

"As if! She begged to come with me." Smiling at me, he added, in an over affectionate tone, "My little stalker."

"Tickets?" the little old lady behind the counter said, stealing Jace's attention before I could put him straight.

I threw Murray my best '*you what*?' face. He just smiled back at me and said sarcastically, "Love you, too."

Jace and Kiely took their tickets and moved on.

"Tickets?" She smiled and the skin of her face stretched showing as many lines as her years.

"Two for screen one," Murray said.

I quickly got my purse out. "It's okay, I can pay for my own ticket, thanks."

"No way. I've got this." Murray swiped his card.

The little old lady handed both tickets to Murray.

I took a note from my purse and tried to give it to Murray as we moved along. "Please, take it."

"No. You're my date."

Date! Who said anything about this being a date? A deal! That's what he requested. Perhaps he was just playing for the ruse but I didn't want to owe him anything. Not even a kiss.

"Calm down, Mariah, it's a ticket not a marriage proposal," Kiely laughed.

My eyes narrowed. I wish she'd just butt out of my life, take her grubby hands off my Jace, and shut her mouth.

"If only you were more of a lady, I wouldn't need to be here," Murray said to Kiely causing her cheeks to flush, and I smirked. "Come on, Mariah, let's go find our seats."

I felt a warm hand slip into mine and I was being led towards the stairs by Murray. I saw Jace glance down at my hand as we passed, but I couldn't pull it free. Murray had a strong grip.

"What are you doing?" I whispered through gritted

teeth.

I checked over my shoulder and saw Kiely and Jace were following us up towards screen one. Jace glared at Murray and our interlocked hands with a puzzled expression on his face. He wasn't falling for this. He knew I'd never go out with an arrogant idiot like Murray. I dug my nails into Murray's skin.

"Just being friendly. Boy, you're crabby!" He let go and rubbed the pink crescent indentations printed into the back of his hand.

We found our seats but I didn't enjoy the film one bit. Usually, I love a good rom-com but I couldn't tell you anything about it; I barely watched it. Instead, I spent the whole film fuming. How dare Murray make out that we're together?! How was I ever going to explain this to Jace? I didn't want to be unavailable - I needed Jace to know I was an option.

Every time Murray laughed at the film, I growled. At one point he put his hand on my knee and rubbed my leg. I quickly peeled it off and dropped it back on his side of the armrest which seemed to amuse him more than anything. I was glad when the film was over and I didn't have to sit as close to him anymore. He made me so angry, I felt sick.

Kiely text their mum as the credits rolled. We didn't have to wait long to be picked up. Their mum arrived in her Land Rover, with a bike rack on the back. Mrs. O'Neil insisted I sit in the front as she planned to drop me off first. Murray sat directly behind me and leaned forward in his seat. His head pressed against the back of my headrest.

Mrs O'Neil had red hair, like me, and a warm smile that lit up her face when she greeted us, nothing like the hothead Murray had made her out to be. I instantly liked her. How could she be related to her children I disliked so easily?

"Where was your friend today?" Murray asked.

"I don't know," I shrugged. I needed to text her. She wouldn't believe what had happened since practice today. How would I explain this 'date' to her?

"She was off sick," Kiely Little-Miss-Know-It-All informed us.

"Next week's the Mistletoe Disco. This year's theme is couples so tickets are sold in pairs." Murray said.

"Aww, that's romantic," his mum chimed.

"We should go," Jace said.

I twisted in my seat expectantly but was met by Jace grinning at Kiely who nodded her head, up and down, like one of those bobbing dogs in the back of a car - likely drooling, too. Before, Jace would have gone with me without question. Who'd I go with now?

"I'll get our ticket," I heard Murray say, answering my unspoken question.

I didn't need to turn to know who he was looking at. I slumped in the front seat. I couldn't say no with his mum sitting next to me.

"How sweet," she cooed and I forced a smile for her benefit as we pulled up outside my house.

"Thanks so much," I said to Mrs O'Neil as I exited the car.

"No worries," she smiled back.

"See ya," Jace and Kiely chorused in unison.

I waved from the pavement before turning to my front door.

"Don't forget your promise," Murray cheered, giving the sensation of an opposing team scoring at a football match.

My key froze in the lock as I realised he wasn't going to let that kiss go.

CHAPTER 9

SHOVING MY TOAST IN MY MOUTH, I ran out the door, hoping that eating en route would save me some precious time. As I was about to shut the front door, Mum grabbed my arm. Her morning hair stuck out erratically in all directions. Her eyes were wide and alarmed as she spoke urgently:

"Don't kiss him! Don't kiss that boy with the bike!"

I flushed red as her voice rang alarm bells in my head and I reminded me of the deal I'd made with Murray. She must have had one of her visions. I cringed to think what she might have seen, but it was just a probable future and I was going to change it.

"Don't worry, I won't." I tried to shrug her off but her grip tightened. "Mum, you're hurting me."

It was her turn to flush red as she let go. But her eyes

were wild as she begged, "Don't go near that pool!"

I hurried down the front path like I was escaping a crime scene. She didn't know about the swim club and I couldn't let her find out. The panic quickened my pace and got me to school in record time.

There, I discovered the hallways plastered with poster after poster advertising the Mistletoe Disco. It was as if Murray had hung them everywhere to mock me. I was horrified by the reality. I'd consoled myself that he'd made it up but there was no denying this.

My only hope was that he was joking about buying me a ticket. There was no way I wanted to go to a couples disco, especially if I was expected to spend the whole evening in his company.

I'd avoid Murray. That'd be in line with keeping my promise to Mum. Her odd behaviour troubled me but confirmed my intuition. Murray was not someone I should get involved with.

She didn't have to worry. I'd no intention of giving Murray a chance to kiss me. There was only one guy for me, and that's Jace. I didn't care what promise Murray thought I'd made. I didn't *actually* agree to anything and I wouldn't be bullied into doing anything either. I continued to class feeling strong and confident.

I ran into Ana by the lockers. Her shoulders were slumped, her head bowed over, her hair hiding her face. She didn't even look like herself. The only reason I knew it was she was exchanging books between her bag and locker.

"Hi, Ana."

She attempted a smile that didn't mirror the sadness in her eyes.

"Are you okay?"

"I can't go swimming."

"Why not?"

She shook her head. "People will talk."

I gently rubbed her arm. "What is it?"

She sighed and as she put another book in her locker I saw the sleeve on her blouse rise up and there was a bandage on her wrist.

"What happened?"

"I don't want to talk about it."

"But, Ana, I thought we're friends?"

Her eyes widened with fear. I saw how much I meant to her. In a short time, our friendship had become as important to her as it was to me.

"We are. I just had a rough night."

Her explanation and voice were both feeble, and I didn't know if, as a good friend, I should ask again or let her be.

"It looks like you slit-"

"Shhh!" She pressed a finger against my lips. "It was an accident and that is exactly the sort of thing I don't want people thinking."

"We could hang out instead of swimming?"

"But, you're on the team."

"I know but-" The last bell rang overhead. "Meet me for lunch?"

Ana nodded and this time her smile was more genuine.

Ana and I grabbed sandwiches from the dining hall and found a bench outside. There was a tree opposite that had shed most of its leaves, the last few were brown and crisp, shuffling in the wind by our feet.

"You've got to go on Wednesdays. It's a condition of being on the team that you attend the weekly practice."

I sighed. "I'm trying to avoid Murray."

"Are you really?" Ana said in an over-inquisitive way that told me she knew more than I thought.

"What do you think you know?" I asked as my eyebrows raised.

Ana's face lit up. "I heard Murray's taking you to the dance."

"That's what he thinks, but I'm not going."

"Why not? He's hot."

I rolled my eyes. "And super arrogant."

Ana shrugged. "It's confidence."

"Are you on his side or mine? Plus, Mum warned me to stay away from him and the pool."

I blushed, realising I'd said too much. Now Ana would think I'm crazy when I explain about Mum's visions.

"So? What does it matter what your mum says? She can't stop you."

Ana didn't get why I was taking Mum's warning seriously. She hadn't seen her magic or the way her predictions came true.

"She's a psychic. She wouldn't have warned me unless something bad is going to happen. I mustn't let him kiss me." I blushed deeper as soon as the words came out of my mouth.

Ana squealed. "Your mum had a vision of you making out?"

"Ana, please. And, she could stop me. She's a frigging witch."

"Does she cast spells?" Ana's eyes widened.

"Sometimes." I wish I could shut up.

"Hold up! Do you cast spells? Like a witch -like a wizard - like Harry fucking Potter? Oh my god, that's so cool!"

"Ana, keep your voice down!"

Ana bit her lip to suppress her excitement. "Can you teach me magic?"

I shook my head. "No. I can't do magic."

"Oh, that's a shame." Her smile faded. She'd been eating her sandwich without any trouble but now she wrapped up the other half.

"What would you want magic for anyway?"

"Who wouldn't…" She trailed off as if pondering the possibilities.

"If you could cast one spell, what would it be?"

She shrugged. "To banish demons."

I laughed. "Demons? Are they a real problem for you?"

She gave an empty laugh, the sort used to hide something painful. "I don't know."

I leaned close to her and whispered, "We could look

in Mum's Book of Shadows this weekend, if you want?"

Ana's eyes lit up. "I'd love that."

Not swimming, even for only a few days, dragged me down like a dead weight into the inky depths of misery. By Wednesday, I didn't care about avoiding Murray, I desperately needed to get in the pool.

Despite Mum's vague warning, I found myself at practice. Without Ana here, I was the only one-piece girl, in a sea of trunks and bikinis. I thought I stuck out like a neon light, even though no-one probably noticed.

Mr Griffen stood on the side with his whistle. He made us race to beat our times. After, we got to catch our breaths whilst he split us into two groups. He yelled and pointed where to go.

"Team A and B, the deep end! Group One and Two, shallow end!"

Murray was in team A and made a point of positioning himself opposite me. I looked anywhere but straight ahead.

"When I blow my whistle I want you to start swimming – front crawl! The person opposite you is your competition. Your opposition!"

Yeah, didn't I know it!

"You'll lap until you catch them up. When you catch your opponent, tag their toe. If your toe is tagged, then you're out!" Mr Griffen's gesture was like he was about to break into a *Greased Lightning* tribute dance with one hand on his hip and the other in the air. "If you're out, you'll do a lap of butterfly stroke to redeem yourself."

There was a resounding groan from everyone but me. Butterfly stroke was my favourite so the punishment was trivial.

Mr Griffen went along the edge and checked we all knew who we were racing against.

"Mariah?" he paused to check he had my attention. I nodded to show I was listening. "Race Murray."

I finally looked across to meet my opponent. He grinned, amused, and it dawned on me he knew this game and planted himself there on purpose. He knew I'd have to look at him. I clenched my jaw and focused on beating him.

I'll wipe that grin off your face!

The whistle sounded and we were off. There was a commotion of splashes as the pool came to life. Silently we propelled underwater as far as our push would take us. Then watery windmills of arms whirled around our ears as we raced forward.

Halfway across we came into contact with our opponent. Murray was blissfully swimming straight for me. It reminded me of playing chicken, I was determined not to lose by giving way first.

Murray grinned at me and clearly wasn't going to get out of my way. I dived under the water to avoid contact. I surfaced, and as I got to the end I turned and pushed off again. Murray was already making progress. Forcing me to detour had given him an advantage. He swam at me again.

Once again, I found myself having to give way and dart underwater. I finally reached the other side, turned, and to my dismay he was catching me. He was already halfway back. My anger was slowing me down. This time I refused to go under. I swam straight at him. He gave way to my side and I carried on straight.

He was gaining on me. I felt defeated already. As my body accepted the inevitable, it slowed me down like a heavyweight pulling against my progress. Then, his hand tapped my toe. He'd won.

"I wonder what winners get," he teased as he swam past me.

I'm no sore loser, but right then I could've hit him. I wanted to wipe that smirk off his face so bad. Shame fuelled my butterfly stroke, as I glided past him. If we'd been allowed to freestyle, I'd have beaten him. Slapping the wall a full body length ahead of him, I pulled myself out the pool. A wolf whistle came from behind. I guessed it was him teasing me, but I refused to turn around for his amusement. I was gone.

I got dressed and hurried to get home. As I made my way off school grounds, I was horrified to see Murray standing at the entrance holding his bike, waiting for me.

"Want a lift?"

"No!" I spat angrily and gave it to him in plain English: "Just leave me alone."

"That's no way to speak to your boyfriend." He began wheeling his bike alongside me.

"You're not my boyfriend!"

"Shh!" he whispered loudly. He looked around comically for anyone who might be listening and held his hand to his mouth as if he was letting me in on a secret. "That's our pretence so we can crash the dates together."

"I don't want to pretend."

"We don't have to pretend," he said with a cocksure smile.

My heart betrayed me with a flutter. Ana was right, Murray was attractive and swimming had blessed him with a well-toned physique. He had dark hair and tanned skin, and his eyes sparkled mischievously. For a moment, I wished he wasn't mocking me.

"If you want to spy on your sister, I'm sure loads of other girls would happily help."

He shrugged. "You make a good point."

I'd expected relief that I was rid of him but instead I was insulted he was so easily discouraged. I didn't want him to know he'd offended me, so I took a big breath and gave him an award-winning smile.

"So, who will you ask?"

He was quiet for a moment. "Well, I've bought your ticket. It'd be dishonourable to take someone else."

"You're honourable?" I laughed.

He reached in his pocket and passed me a black piece of card. It had red writing and the picture of some mistletoe in the top right corner.

I pushed his hand back. "I'm sure you'll overcome your moral dilemma. It's someone else's ticket, decide whose."

"Fine, I'll take someone else, but this is your ticket."

"I don't want to go." I shook my head and regarded the ticket with disgust.

"Take it, or I won't give up."

I sighed. There was an offer I couldn't refuse.

My shoulders dropped as I accepted his ticket. I shoved it into my swim bag. I didn't care if it got wet and ruined. After all, I'd only taken the stupid ticket to shut him up; there was no way I was actually going.

Murray seemed pleased with my decision. I allowed myself the pleasure of a Mona Lisa smile. He waved goodbye and turned around in the road, peddling off in the opposite direction, towards his own home.

I returned to school, found Murray's locker and slipped the rejected ticket under the door. Keeping the ticket felt like a trap, I knew he'd somehow manipulate me into going.

Walking home, I expected an elevated sense of freedom. Instead, I felt doomed. I knew my decision meant I couldn't continue swimming, not if I wanted to avoid him.

CHAPTER 10

FRIDAY AFTERNOON CAME AROUND and I reflected that having someone to talk to on the way home made the walk quicker. Once inside, I thought about how much smaller my home was than Ana's and hoped she didn't think less of me. I led her through to the kitchen and put the kettle on.

"Mum won't be back until six. We've got about two hours to find the book."

She shooed me away from the kettle using her hand.

"Are you crazy? We have no time for drinks. Describe it?"

"The book? Black with silver embellishments and silver gilt pages."

"Where should we start?"

"The lounge?" I led Ana back to the lounge where

she promptly sat in front of the cupboard and opened it up and began rummaging through.

"What are you doing?" I asked.

She paused. As she glanced over her shoulder, her eyebrows furrowed, as she asked, "I thought this was the plan?"

I nodded. "It is. I just… It feels wrong to be snooping for her Book of Shadows. Like the ultimate betrayal."

"We don't have to."

Ana's body hung like it was heavy and I heard her sigh with the weight. I could see the dark rings under her eyes. I walked over to the other cupboard and opened the door.

"Let's be quick."

Ana's smile was like a child promised candy. Both of us searched through the cupboards, shelves, and in every nook and cranny. We searched every room downstairs and then headed upstairs.

We'd run out of places to search and slumped on the landing out of ideas. I groaned.

"We've been searching for over an hour."

Ana groaned in reply and tilted her head back and then her expression changed. She squealed, excited, "What's up there?"

Above was the door to the attic. I'd never been up there but had Mum often. I grabbed the stick to open the trap door and hook the ladder down. I climbed up, my head just rising into the loft, when I was greeted by Mum's Book of Shadows.

"I've got it," I cheered and passed the heavy book

to Ana before climbing down.

Ana was already sitting cross-legged on the floor with the book open. "This is amazing. Is this real?"

"Mum says if you believe in magic, magic will believe in you."

"It's so beautiful and personal."

She carefully turned the ageing pages. The book had been around a lot longer than Mum's lifetime. Perhaps it had been passed down by a relative. I sat next to Ana to get a closer look. There were pressed flowers and leaves as examples of the plants required for certain spells. Some pages had little sketches to aid the instructions on ingredients or how to cast. Each spell had its own page with a delicately scripted title.

Some spells, I recognised. There were spells for healing, dreams, money, and relationships. Spells that were for special celebrations. There were pages explaining the use of different herbs, colours, crystals, and the moon. There was no mention of demons.

"How about this 'Sweet Dreams' spell?" I asked.

Ana leaned forward and read the page. "All I need is lavender?"

"It sounds pretty simple."

"Have you got a pen and paper so I can write down the incantation?"

I got up and fetched Ana a pen and paper from the bedroom. When I returned she was already on another page. The top of the page was titled 'Heal Your Scars'.

"Can we do this one now and see if it works?"

"It never works for me. I don't believe enough," I

complained but I was willing to try for Ana. I glanced at the page and saw that all we needed was an onion and a white candle. "I'll get what we need. Bring the book,"

We headed downstairs to get the required equipment and outside to the garden. One thing I'd learned from Mum was that magic is always more powerful when surrounded by nature.

We sat down in the middle of my small garden on a grassy spot. I lit the candle with a match and placed it in between us. Ana rolled up her sleeves and revealed her wrists. She began rubbing the sliced onion against her cuts and hissed as it stung.

"Why did you cut yourself?"

"It was an accident."

"Both wrists?"

"I know how it looks, but I was asleep."

"Asleep?"

I didn't need her to answer. I saw that faraway sad look in her eye, reliving a horror. Ana put the onions down.

"I have night terrors. It's why I got expelled from boarding school. Avoiding sleep makes it worse. I'm a freak - I know. Please don't tell anyone," Ana pleaded, her big eyes begging into mine

"I won't. I promise." I held out my hand for her wrists, ready for the spell.

"What now?" Ana smiled and let me take her wrists.

"We meditate. Close your eyes. Breathe in through your nose, then slowly out through your mouth. Focus

ALLY ALDRIDGE

on the sun's energy. Draw it into your body. Feel it warming and healing your scars."

Ana's eyes closed and she was doing her controlled breathing. I joined her, thinking about the warm light of the candle between us and picturing it hot and powerful, burning like the sun. My fingers sweated where they held against her scars and I tried to imagine them glowing hot and red, healing her skin as if she'd never bled.

"Burn candle, burn, burn candle, burn,
Goddess of the sun, healing light we yearn,
Hear Ana's plea, burn candle, burn,
Goddess of the sun, guide good health to thee
Burn candle, burn, burn candle, burn."

I had just finished the incantation when a strong wind raced around us and Ana squealed. Our eyes opened and the candle went out.

"Did it work?" I let go of her wrists.

Ana gasped. A smile filled her face as she announced, "Oh, Mr Griffen, I'm coming back to swimming."

She then held her hands up as if she were surrendering so I could see her perfectly healed wrists.

I grabbed one of her hands to wrists more closely. "This is the first spell that has ever worked for me. I can't believe it!"

Ana grabbed my hand and jumped up and down. "We're witches, Mariah. Full-blooded witches."

I began jumping with her and we bounced around

in a circle, around the smoking candle, and the church bells chimed six o'clock.

"Quick, Ana, we'll be dead witches if Mum catches us." I swept up the book and hurried into the house.

Saturday morning, I was laying on my bed finishing my maths homework when Jace burst in, lighting up the room. He bounced into the space next to me and lay back against my pillow. The way he casually lay there made him appear dreamed up and I almost pinched myself to check he was real. I put down my homework and lay next to him. Our faces were so close I could feel his breath on my cheek.

"I've so much to tell you! I guess you do, too!" he gushed.

"Not really."

I couldn't think of anything I wanted to tell Jace. I certainly didn't want to talk about Murray and I'd barely been to the pool as I was avoiding him. I couldn't tell him about the spell with Ana without breaking my promise to her about keeping her scars a secret, either.

"I got Kiely's ticket and Murray said he's taking you. Good work, Mariah. You keep him busy so Kiely and I can get some alone time."

I was busy fuming *'how dare Murray say that*!' but all I could muster was, "Oh!"

"I can't thank you enough. Murray's got terrible

timing. That's why it's so great you two are together."

He brushed a curl from my face. My heart jolted at his touch and I didn't want any part in helping him take his relationship to the next level with Kiely.

"I'm not going," I sulked and rolled onto my back.

"Does Murray know? He keeps winding me up that he's taking you. It's not kind to lead him on," he scolded.

"I'm not leading him on!" I sat up, offended by his judgemental tone.

"What's up, then?"

I want to go with you, idiot!

"I don't fancy it. What would I wear?" I fumbled for an excuse.

Jace sat up and put a comforting arm around my shoulder. "Kiely will lend you something. I'll speak to her. She's got tons of dresses."

Yippee! I thought sarcastically. I could wear Little Miss Perfect's clothes and look only half as good in her dress. It couldn't get much worse!

Jace carried on, "I thought you were nervous about being alone with Murray and were going to ask to practice again."

Practice? My ears perked up. I twisted to check his face, to make sure he was being serious. A crease furrowed his brow making him look genuinely concerned. It felt naughty to take advantage of his misinterpretation of the situation, but I couldn't help myself.

"I am nervous."

"You're going to kiss him?" Jace's draw dropped which was odd considering the idea had been his.

I nodded. "I've only kissed you... I just don't know..."

He mumbled, "I guess, I can't say no. You'd do the same for me... well, you did. It's just..." He wrapped his arms around his legs. "Kiely and I, we're exclusive now."

"She'll never know," I whispered naughtily.

I leaned towards him, our lips so close they tingled. I paused. I couldn't bear to be hurt again. I waited for him before I felt the burning heat as our lips touched. He kissed me.

He let go too soon. "You've nothing to worry about. Promise, you won't tell anyone about this."

I nodded, still a little lost for words and feeling like his dirty secret. For the first time, I felt cheap for kissing him. I needed him to tell me I was worth more but he got up and headed towards my bedroom door.

"Let's grab some snacks before we get too deep into revision."

"Are you serious about revising?" I whined a little. My real complaint was how brief the kiss had been and how meaningless I felt.

Jace shook his head at me. "You don't want to do resits."

"No, of course not."

I got up to follow him downstairs. I'd need a whole bowl of ice-cream with sprinkles and syrup to pick me up from this. And - maths revision on top - I couldn't help but sulk.

I had to find Murray and tell him I'd changed my mind about the ticket, and was now onboard with the ruse. I'd spent my lunch running around the school on my mission.

I'd thought about Mum's warnings. So long as I didn't kiss him, and avoided the pool, I should be fine. There was no harm in speaking to him, especially with other people around.

My feelings for Jace were getting stronger every day and the thought of him kissing Kiely killed me.

Where was he when he wasn't swimming?

Break was almost over. I gave up and headed to my favourite spot to enjoy fleeting glances of Jace running across the pitch. I spotted Kiely and her friends sitting on the benches, looking perfect while watching the boys play.

Then, I saw Murray.

It never crossed my mind he might play football, too. He was jogging across the pitch to speak to his sister when he looked up and saw me. I felt struck by lightning, caught in a flash of those silver eyes. Suddenly, he was running towards the building. My heart began to pound and my hands were clammy.

He'll think I was spying on him, I fretted.

There was nowhere to escape but up. The top floors

were reserved for sixth formers. I hoped they wouldn't notice me taking a quick detour. I raced up the last flight.

I flung open the double doors and walked briskly along the corridor, searching for another way out. I stood out like a sore thumb in my school uniform; all the sixth formers were in casual dress.

I kept my head down.

I heard the thud of the doors behind me hitting the wall.

"Goldie!" Murray yelled.

I could have died. If they hadn't noticed me before, they did now. I could hear Murray closing in on me.

"What are you doing up here?"

"Exploring."

"I saw you spying. How often have you watched me play?"

"I don't watch *you* play!" I emphasised the word 'you' to make a point.

"Does Jace know you watch *him*?" He emphasised the word 'him' in the same manner I had but there was malice to his tone.

Murray made me nervous and I needed to get this over with. I grabbed his hand and pulled him out the door, relieved to find another stairwell. I began my descent to familiar ground.

"Actually, I was looking for you."

"Me!" he choked as he followed. "I find that hard to believe while you're running away."

"Jace persuaded me to go." I nodded at one of the

posters.

"I know. Kiely's lending you a dress."

"Well...," I blushed. I couldn't believe I was going to ask. "Are you still able to take me? Jace thinks we're together and I think it's working. Perhaps, your idea isn't totally dumb." Realising I was babbling, I panicked that I may have lost him, so added some incentive: "He plans to kiss Kiely!"

"Actually, some girls have asked me." He smiled smugly.

"Oh," I was taken aback. My hands sweated. How do I explain this to Jace without looking like a total loser?

Murray lifted my chin up. "Don't worry, Goldie, I told them I already have a girl."

Overwhelmed with relief, I flung my arms around Murray. The moment I realised what I had done, it was too late. I was firmly in his embrace. I fought the urge to squirm away. It felt good in his arms, maybe going together wouldn't be so bad. He was sexy and smelled amazing – what more could a girl ask for? It wasn't like I was in any position to be fussy.

"But first, I think you should make good on your promise."

I pushed myself away from Murray but found my back pressed up against the rough, brick wall of the stairwell. He wasn't going to make me kiss him, not here where anyone could see?

The warning!

Murray placed a hand against the wall by my ear.

He had me pinned into the corner. In no time his lips were against mine, too quick for me to consider turning my face so he got my cheek. His kiss felt arrogant and confident.

Shamefully, my body pushed against his, weakly surrendering to his charm. I allowed myself to enjoy it, like a kiss of freedom; I was no longer in his debt.

He let me go, but, oddly, I wanted more. I gently opened my eyes only to be confronted by the screen of his mobile phone. Us, kissing, frozen in time in a photo.

"Why did you do that?" I reached for the device but he turned his body and held it up high out of my reach.

Mortified, I screamed: "Delete it! Now!"

He shoved it into his trouser pocket and when I tried to pull it out, he teased me, "Hey! Hey! Don't be so keen!"

"As if!"

I gave up. I was burning with humiliation. My skin prickled with heat. He grinned as the bell rang overhead.

"You can deny you want me all you like but the evidence is here. You enjoyed it. I'll pick you up at seven on Friday."

I dreaded who he might show the photo to. Was this why Mum warned me? I was so angry with myself, I had to get away. I raced out of school. A black cloud hovering over my head all the way. Rain - just my luck!

I thrust my key in the lock, and swung the door open with such force the handle dented the opposing wall. As it ricocheted off, I caught the door in my hand

and manoeuvred around it. Swiftly, I kicked it shut behind me.

"Alright!" Mum yelled.

She stormed into the hallway to greet me, her arms folded over her chest, flour on her apron, and the sweet aroma of freshly baked cakes followed. Her expression scolded me.

"What?" I spat as my temper sought someone to blow at. It was building up inside me, pressing against my chest, begging to be let out in a violent whirlwind.

"Don't 'what' me, Missy! What do you think you're doing slamming my front door like that?"

Something terrible and dark brewed inside me, my fingers tingled with rage. An uncontrollable force was taking over.

I screamed to let it out and, as I raised my hands up above my face, white lightning danced between my fingertips. The beautiful white strings of light, their brightness almost blinding, twirled and danced as I felt myself diffuse. A rush swept over my body like nothing I'd felt before.

A gust of wind whipped around me and I heard every door in the house slam shut. The bangs echoed as a final exclamation that this torrent had ended.

My hands shook with fear and my eyes were wide with shock.

What had happened?

Without saying a word, I turned to Mum for answers but she looked angry. Confused, I glanced around for what caused the phenomenon but there was nothing I could have been electrocuted by. It didn't make sense.

"You kissed him, didn't you!" It wasn't an accusation, she knew. She didn't wait for my answer. "Oh, Mariah, I warned you. Why didn't you take heed? I don't tell you these things for fun."

"What's he done to me?"

CHAPTER 11

MUM GRIMACED. It was clear she didn't know how to explain the unexplainable. Her face washed with relief when the oven timer rang. She waved her arm for me to follow. My legs were wobbly as she led me into the kitchen. She lifted buns out the oven and onto a cooling rack.

Red curls fell around my face as I looked at my shaking hands. They were paler than usual, and the tips of my fingers had a strange grey-blue colour as if pen ink was smudged over them. I touched them to my forearm. They were icy cold.

Was I dying?

Alarmed by that thought, my head shot up, and I caught Mum watching me. She gave a heavy sigh.

"Oh, Mariah, where do I start?"

How should I know? I didn't care where she started,

as long as whatever she said started to make sense.

"I know you love Jace."

My cheeks flushed red at her revelation.

"But, he's not the one. You're meant for someone else. I just hoped...," her voice trailed off and she returned to the sink to wash the baking tray. "I didn't think you'd meet him so soon."

"Who?"

"Murray."

"Murray?" I spat out. Her powers must be off. There was no way. "I don't even like him!"

"Really?" She was surprised. "What was that in the hallway?"

"What's that to do with him?" I felt my fingers tingle, the hairs on my arms lift, and I knew it could happen again. Beads of sweat prickled my brow and the sudden heat made me feel faint. I wrapped my arms tightly around my body, and lowered myself onto a stool. "I feel unstable."

Mum placed the baking tray on the drying rack by the sink and dried her hands on a tea towel. "I've been sworn to secrecy until the time is right."

"The time is right now!" I spat the words out and realised I'd been holding my breath.

"It's not my place to say." Mum's brows furrowed in sympathy.

"Mum!" I wailed. "Please, I need to know!"

Mum walked across the kitchen. She tossed the kitchen towel onto the counter-top. "You don't know what you're asking."

I stood, gripping the sideboard. "Yeah, because you won't tell me anything and you know! You know!"

For a split second, I thought she was going to hug me but instead, she gripped the top of my arms and pinned them to my sides.

"Calm down! Right now!" Her voice softened, "Mariah, I beg you."

Mum's eyes welled up. Seeing her sad frightened me more than anything that had happened.

"I'm scared."

"Oh, Mariah," she gushed and gave the hug I craved. She stroked my hair and whispered in my ear. "Please, heed my warning. Don't kiss him again. Not unless you're ready to give up everything you know."

She kissed my forehead and freed me. "I need to finish up here. Why don't you take a bath before dinner? I'll cook your favourite - admiral pie."

"Mum...," I began.

She stroked my hair. "Shh! You'll be fine. Stay calm."

"But..."

Her eyes narrowed as she rubbed her neck. "Give me a moment to think. I'll fix this. Don't worry."

She returned to her cakes, packing them into boxes ready for the charity sale tomorrow. I knew any further questions would be treated as background noise. I sighed, made my way upstairs, and ran my bath.

Mum wasn't long behind me. She entered the bathroom carrying a large jar. "You can use my homemade bath salts. It'll help you relax."

She used a wooden scoop to measure the salts to pour into the hot water. The air filled with the soft scent of lavender.

"I made it myself." Her lips brushed my cheek as she passed me with a kiss.

"What's in it?" I asked.

"Jojoba oil, lavender, frankincense, vetivert, chamomile, and a touch of magic." She winked at me. "Nothing but the best for my little girl."

"We need to talk about what's going on with me."

"We will. As soon as you've rested. Enjoy your bath." She smiled as she left the room.

My head buzzed with all the unanswered questions as I got undressed and into the bath. I lay back, allowing the warm water to surround me and melt away my worries. The sweet, gentle aroma rose with the steam and made my mind feel hazy, the questions that troubled me no longer mattered. My body became heavy and I struggled to keep my eyes open. I reached up to pull myself out, but my arm dropped back like a dead weight. I was slipping down under the water, unable to save myself. I was going to drown... but I was too tired to stop it and too tired to care. My body lay beneath the water and I shut my eyes to sleep.

I woke in my room, full of light. I yawned and stretched for my mobile to check the time. The screen was blank;

the battery was dead. I scrambled out of bed and plugged it into the charger but it still wouldn't come on - the bloody thing wasn't working. I pressed the power button and, to my surprise, heard the cheerful startup tune. As the screen came to life, I noticed the battery was full... Someone deliberately switched off my phone! And, I was already late for school.

I jumped into my slippers and threw my dressing gown around my shoulders. I raced downstairs to confront Mum. She was sitting on the sofa reading her book.

"Did you switch off my phone ?" I demanded.

"Yes, you felt unstable and must take a day off."

A wave of relief washed over me and my shoulders dropped. I wasn't aware of how tense I felt about going to school, and avoiding Murray, and controlling my powers, until the pressure was off. He had a knack of winding me up. I dreaded to think what he might do today or, worse, make me do.

Mum patted the cushion next to her on the sofa.

I didn't sit. "What was in that bath oil? Did you drug me?"

Mum laughed, "Don't be silly."

"What's going on? What's happening to me? Am I sick? Is it... magic?"

"Part of the joy of life is the gift of surprises."

I shook my head and paced the room, never taking my eyes off her. "Please, Mum, I need to know!"

She watched me carefully and in a quiet voice said, "I'm not sure how to tell you delicately."

"I don't care. Just tell me!"

"I saw you kiss Murray," Mum said.

I froze but wished to run from the situation. There was something unpleasant about the idea of her seeing me kiss a guy. It felt the wrong kind of naughty.

"Then, you took his human life."

I coughed. "What? That didn't happen!"

Sadly, Murray was alive and kicking, running around, sharing that picture. Oh, how I'd kill him if I could, but I'm no murderer! As much as he drove me crazy I didn't seriously wish harm on anyone, not even him.

"Mariah, this is serious. You mustn't kiss him again! I'm thankful you made it home before anyone got hurt."

"Am I dangerous? I kissed Jace too," I blushed. I didn't mean for it to slip out but I needed to know he was safe.

"No more kissing." She glanced at the clock. "There's too much to tell you and I can't be late. Stay home and we'll talk more when I return."

She took her empty mug to the kitchen and grabbed the cake tin on her way out. She began putting on her coat and scarf.

"Mum, you can't leave me like this!"

She leaned forward and kissed my forehead. "Everything will be okay." She moved me aside to reach the front door, and tossed the words over her shoulder. "You'll be safe here."

But her words offered no comfort. She was gone. I

was alone.

I wandered into the lounge-diner and slumped onto the couch wondering what to do with myself. Still holding my mobile, I messaged Ana.

Mariah: Not swimming. I'm off school.

I was sure she'd reply later wanting more information but that gave me time to decide what to tell her. Would she believe the truth? She'd been pretty understanding so far of the craziness I'd exposed her to. I smiled as I remembered jumping around upstairs as we celebrated our first spell together.

Then, I noticed the only thing left on the dining room table: Mum's crystal ball. It was possibly full of all the answers Mum refused to give, if only I could use it.

I'd seen Mum use it countless times and there was no harm in trying. So, I set about preparing the table as she would. I laid out the purple, silk, embroidered cloth reserved for magic and placed her pride and joy in the centre. Her crystal ball sat proudly on its gold stand, glistening at me, full of promise.

I pulled up a chair and greeted it. My fingers hovered tentatively over the forbidden glass.

I'd asked Mum straight out, more than once, and she'd refused to tell me anything – surely she'd expect I'd do this. Maybe she left the crystal ball out on purpose? Ana would say that's permission. I fought with my conscience telling me not to mess with it but the need for answers ate at me.

Greedily, I leaned forward on the small wooden chair, my fingertips pressing against the cool glass. I began to deepen my breath in the same manner I'd seen her do so many times before. I looked intently into the sphere, trying to conjure up images.

The glass began to cloud as if someone was breathing on the inside. My heart quickened with excitement. No matter how hard I believed, magic never worked. But, right now, there was no denying something was happening. Something had awoken inside me, like a magic pilot light.

The clouds blew around in circles; a trapped wind encased in glass. I sought through the smoke for an image. It thinned into stringy spirals, the magic tingling in my fingertips. The stormy image twisting and swirling like a whirlwind, spinning around and around, trapped within the glass, fighting to break free. A patch darkened and the smoke ran towards the shape as if being inhaled. The glass warmed and my fingers got hot, almost unbearably hot.

In a flash, it lit up like a light bulb but went out just as quick. The house lights flickered and the clouded image was gone. The globe darkened, almost black, except for a large, silver crack inside the glass, frozen in the shape of a lightning bolt. I bit my lip.

What have I done?

What would Mum say when she sees it? It wouldn't be good! I couldn't be here when she discovered it.

I grabbed my mobile, not sure who to call. To my

surprise, the screen was full of notifications. What had happened? Jace. Jace. Jace. He never messaged me... I unlocked my phone.

Jace: Classy pic

What pic...?
The kiss!

Ana: R U okay?
Ana: Why R U off?
Ana: OMG! Call me.
Ana: R U 2 together?
Ana: Aghhh!

I quickly opened Instagram and searched for Murray. As soon as I found him, my worst fears were confirmed. Top of his feed is the photo of us snogging and the caption: "She's official. Officially wants to get in my trunks!"

I wanted to hit reply and tell him to take it down. I felt my blood boiling. My hands were shaking, tingling... I gritted my teeth.

The rest of his feed was no better. I wasn't the first girl he had humiliated. Nearly every other picture is a photo of him with a different girl. Seeing them with their arms draped over him, fingers touching his body, breathing him in, tasting him, it made me feel sick. I tossed my phone across my bed as tears pricked my eyes and pulled the duvet over my head.

It wasn't the picture or the crude caption that bothered me. It's how cheap I feel, seeing myself on his feed like a basic bedpost notch. One of many 'nothing special' girls and what's worse was Jace had seen it. Everyone had seen it. I'm not even in school and Murray still managed to piss me off.

Curling up into a defensive ball, I glared at my destructive hands. The tips of my fingers have the same distinct blue tinge that I'd seen the day before. I let out slow steadying breaths to calm myself down and saw my normal pigmentation return.

A strange feeling prickled up my back as if I were an intruder in my own home. Instinct told me I didn't belong here. In a strange way, I never felt I belonged. I always felt out of place like this wasn't where I was meant to be. Yes, it had been my home since the day I was born, but something didn't feel right.

Now, it didn't even feel safe - because of me. I'm a trespasser in Mum's house, a malicious vandal, destroying what she values most. And capable of murder, too, she'd told me that.

I'm dangerous!

It was only a matter of time before I hurt someone I love. I had to get away.

Despite having no idea of the extent of my powers, or the mechanics behind it, I knew I had no control. It was imperative I go.

Packing light, I identified the crucial items I needed for my survival. My sleeping bag came in its own drawstring bag. Seeing it reminded me of Jace and how

I used to take it next door and stay over when Mum went to her festivals. As I mourned over the way things had turned out, the value of what I was leaving behind became apparent. My bag was light but my heart was heavy.

My hand rested on the front door latch. If Mum saw me, she would try and talk me out of this. Yet, I couldn't go without letting her know it wasn't her fault.

Carrying my bags into the lounge and dropping them by the sideboard, I pulled out a sheet of Mum's beautiful homemade paper. I took her quill pen and wrote my goodbye note.

Dear Mum,

I'm so sorry about your crystal ball. It was an accident. I know how precious it was to you and wish I could fix or replace it. I hope one day I can make it up to you and you can forgive me.

This is not an easy decision to make but I must leave. I can't be around anyone right now. It's what's best for everyone, whilst I figure things out.

Please don't worry about me. I love you and I'll be home as soon as I can.

All my love,

Mariah x

Screwed up drafts filled the paper bin. It'd taken several attempts to make sure if anyone else saw it they wouldn't think I were crazy. I gave the note a final check and contemplated whether one kiss was enough when

I might be gone forever... A tear ran down my cheek and smudged the ink. I quickly wiped them away and folded the letter, placing it in the middle of the table, next to the broken crystal ball. I lifted my bags to my shoulder and entered the hallway as the front door opened.

Mum blocked my exit. She glowed like an angel with the light streaming in from behind her. Her mouth dropped as she took in the sight before her.

I sweated like a burglar caught red-handed. The bag suddenly felt heavier and the straps dug into my shoulders. My cheeks flushed as my mind spun a dial of excuses trying to find a tale I could use.

The smile vanished from her face. "Are you going somewhere?"

A lump lodged in my throat making it impossible to speak and my mouth was dry. I croaked an ineligible sound as tears streamed down. My face crumpled and my eyes shut tight like a clam. I heard some strange gurgling noise and realised it was coming from me. As I sobbed, a floral scent mixed with flour and sugar filled my nose, warm arms held me tight. Mum stroked my hair and like magic – perhaps literally - her presence calmed me.

She took me into the lounge-diner and we sat on the couch. She opened the cake tin she'd been carrying.

"One each. I'll make us a nice cuppa tea and you can tell me what's going on."

I bit my lip as I realised she was gonna want answers. I felt awful about running away. But, more so,

I was terrified about telling her I damaged her sacred crystal ball. I wasn't even supposed to touch it.

As she passed the dining room table she saw the note.

Today couldn't get worse.

She lifted it to her face. Her eyes widened and flashed back to me. "Were you running away?"

A simple nod said it all. I bit my lip and kept my eyes on my trainers, one shoe rubbed against the other to remove a piece of caked on mud. It served well as a distraction from my guilt and shame. I felt one with the dirt, worthless, and I wanted to crumble away with it into the carpet.

The room was quiet.

I didn't dare look up until I heard the click of the kettle.

I could make out my bag in the hallway. If I was quick, I could escape now. My heart anchored me to the chair, the thought of leaving too painful. The clock on the mantelpiece ticked, each long and drawn out second and taunted my rapid breaths. It felt like an eternity before Mum returned with two mugs. She placed one on the wooden coasters at the coffee table.

Holding her cup with both hands, she sat next to me. She leaned forward, peering into her cup as if she couldn't bring herself to look at me. With an unusual calm for the situation, she said: "I deserve to know why."

She waited for me to say something. I took deep breaths to calm myself down and decide what to blurt out.

"I broke your crystal ball."

"I saw." She turned her head towards the table, the corners of her mouth dipped. Her pride and joy was tarnished with a crooked line that crisscrossed within the glass.

"I don't know how I did it. I don't know what happened yesterday or today, but I know I did it! I'm sorry." It hurt to think about the harm I could cause if I'd been touching someone I loved instead of the crystal ball.

She slumped in the dining chair. Her back to me but I could see her sadness in the way her shoulders collapsed in on herself.

"Accidents happen," she said in a manner that forgave me.

I exhaled, the worst was over.

"Why is this happening to me?"

"There's no easy way to say this," she sighed.

A sense of fear and relief gripped me as I anticipated what she might reveal. It was something big. I watched her take deep breaths, building up her courage to speak.

"You know I've always loved you? You know I always want the best for you and to protect you? Well, I have to tell you something, but you need to know that it doesn't change how much I love you."

"Uhhh, okay?"

"You're not my biological daughter."

I wasn't expecting that! My mouth fell open as I scrambled for words. I shook my head and blinked.

Did she really say that?

"It doesn't change how much I love you."

I knew she'd been pregnant when Denny was with Jace. I'd seen pictures, told stories about how Jace and I were both in their bellies at the same time. We were born only days apart and grown up side-by-side. There was no way she couldn't be my mum, was there? But, there had always been something that didn't feel right. I thought it was the absence of my dad.

"What about... How?" My mind was such a jumble I stammered out incomplete questions. "The photos..."

"I faked the pregnancy, as your real mum requested. It was for your protection. She brought you here the day you were born. It wasn't easy for her to let you go."

This wasn't easy for me, either. I leaned back and my eyes widened as I tried to take this in. My chest felt tight and my words came out shakily: "P- protection? Who am I?"

"It's best we start with who I am. I'm your guardian; it's my job to keep you safe. You weren't supposed to find out until you finished school and returned to your family." She shook her head and paused. "Your family has enemies. Dangerous enemies. I shouldn't be telling you any of this..." Her shoulders rose and dropped. "You're no ordinary girl; you're a merallo."

"What's that?"

"The original mermaid bloodline. You've certain gifts, like shape-shifting."

I ran my hand through my hair. I'd never heard of a 'merallo' and mermaids don't exist. They're mythical creatures with human torsos and fish tails and only found in fairy tales.

She's making fun of me! She can't possibly expect me to believe in mermaids?

I clenched my jaw. My hands shook as my anger ran through my veins making my body tingle. I noticed the tips of my fingers change colour, like blue ink sweating from my pores, leaking into my epidermal ridges with a silver sheen. Instead of being hot and clammy, my fingers tingle icy cold.

"But, I haven't... shape-shifted? Have I?" Every time she answered a question, I had more.

Was turning into a mermaid something I needed to worry about in the pool? Should I still call her 'Mum'?

She folded my hands into fists and held them enclosed within hers. "You have to keep your emotions under control. You're only dangerous if you can't!"

What was I capable of? Deep down, I sensed she was telling the truth. It answered my questions even if it was far fetched.

"How?"

"You have the ability to manipulate elements relating to the weather." She looked apologetic, sad even. "I guess... I ought to send you home."

I shook my head. My heart raced with panic. Everything was changing too fast. It was like that dream where you are running but your legs can't keep up.

I begged, "This is my home. I don't want to go! Please, there must be another way?"

"I don't want you to go, either," she heaved with

the strain of her words.

She allowed one hand to leave mine and lift a piece of cake from the tin. She bit into the sweet bun of sugary goodness and chewed slowly. I could tell she was struggling to swallow that one small bite. Finally, with effort, the morsel disappeared.

"I'll see what else can be done."

Her face was unusually pale and didn't fill me with confidence but was my only sliver of hope. She let go of my fists, freeing my hands. She glanced at the bag in the hallway.

"I need to figure out our options. Take that back upstairs and unpack."

I got up, willing to do whatever she wanted if it meant I could stay. I swallowed a lump in my throat as I picked up my stuff and whispered, "Can I still call you 'Mum'?"

Her eyes welled up as she whispered, "If you want to, sweetheart."

CHAPTER 12

THE STENCH OF FISH FROM MY UNTOUCHED MEAL sat on my desk but I'd no energy to take my plate down. My eyes were sore and puffy from all the crying. I felt disorientated, like I no longer knew who I was or where I belonged. My mind felt crowded, like the questions were taking up too much space and pressing down on my skull.

Mum came up. She pursed her lips together but didn't say anything. She reached over to open a window and then took my plate away. The curtains fluttered as fresh air entered the room and soothed my cheeks, but it wasn't enough. The room felt too small, like the walls were closing in and the floor had flipped with the ceiling. I had to get out. I grabbed my mobile, pushed my feet into my trainers, and hurried down the stairs.

"Mariah?" Mum called as I hurried out the front

door.

I ran before she could stop me. I hate running but I needed to be as far away from her and the house as possible. I had no idea where I was going until I arrived at the beach.

I stood on the prom, catching my breath, taking in big gulps of salty air. I spread my arms wide. The ocean looked inviting and sparkled full of promise. I felt an urge to go in, to swim away, and leave my problems behind me. The idea filled me with euphoria and I smiled for the first time since the revelation.

"Are you calling me home?" I whispered to the sea.

But there was no answer. I swallowed a lump in my throat, feeling abandoned by the ocean. Maybe, when my time is up, my family won't want me back. Or, what if I don't want to go with them? Nobody cared about what I wanted.

I still didn't know anything about being a mermaid. My body was human, everything I knew was human. The sea was endless and I wondered how different my life would be once I became a mermaid, and would I want to return to dry land? My heart felt heavy, could I ever come back?

I sat on a bench. Earlier, I'd switched my phone off to ignore all the messages about the photo. It seemed so trivial now and made me mad that people had nothing better to do than gossip. I held down the power button until I heard the familiar start up tune. I saw Ana had been texting constantly throughout the day. There were no more messages from Jace.

It felt like Ana knew me better than anyone; possibly better than Jace. After all, he'd no idea how I felt about him. For the first time in my life, I was keeping a secret from him. All the secrets were wearing me out and I just wanted to get them out. I didn't need to hide myself from Ana. I liked how I could share anything with her, but this was too much to say in a text. And she'd sent too many messages for me to read. So, I called her.

"Mariah?"

"Hi."

"Are you alright? Why haven't you been replying to my messages? Why aren't you in school?"

"Just not feeling like myself."

"And your mum lets you stay off school for that? I have one of my crazy nightmares and almost kill someone before I'm allowed off - well, expelled." Ana laughed, "I'm so relieved. I thought your mum had found out about swimming and banned you."

My heart felt heavy. I missed the pool. I wondered if it would ever be safe for me to swim again - had it ever been? Now I knew why she'd been against it.

"Mariah, are you there?"

"Yeah."

Ana's voice softened, "You're very quiet. Did something happen?"

"Can we meet?"

"Where?"

"The pier?"

"Now?"

"Please."

"On my way."

I made my way along the prom towards the pier and sat on the steps waiting for her to arrive. The repetitive tunes of the arcade machines filled my ears and I missed the peaceful whoosh of the ocean like a mother soothing her child. As soon as her driver pulled up, she got out of the car and ran towards me. We greeted each other with a hug.

Ana stepped back and held me at arm's length. "Have you been crying?"

I swallowed back tears and nodded.

"Let's find somewhere quiet to talk." Her arm draped over my shoulder as she led me off to the side, out onto the decking of the boardwalk that went around the outside of the arcade and then out to sea. Halfway along we found a bench, she let me go, and we sat down.

"What happened?"

I bit my lip to stop it from trembling. I folded over, pulling my knees up to hide my face. The more I tried to talk, the more it hurt. I shut my eyes. I felt lost. The world felt vast and I was nothing, nobody, my parents didn't want me. Jace barely noticed me. Murray had made me a mockery to everyone at school, a joke. Mum, or whoever she really is, says I'm some deadly, mermaid creature. I coughed a laugh at how ridiculous it all was and with the release came the tears.

Ana rubbed my back and whispered, "It's okay. We don't have to talk. I'm here for you if you want to, and I'm here for you if you don't."

I took some steadying breaths and sat up. When I felt ready, I uncurled and gave her a hug. Maybe if I could talk it would help me make sense. Ana handled Mum being a witch well. If anyone could handle this it was her.

"Mum thinks school is unsafe."

"Not safe?" Ana leaned in as if she was going to whisper but continued at her usual volume. "Is this one of those psychic things like when she saw you kissing Murray?"

I shook my head.

"I knew it!" she gasped.

I shook my head. *How could she know?*

"It's because you kissed Murray. Your mum warned something bad would happen. What happened? Why'd you do it?"

"I didn't. He kissed me!" I clenched my fists and could feel the electricity building. This was not a good conversation for keeping calm.

"Is he a good kisser? He's sure had enough practice."

I groaned as I recalled his Instagram feed. I hadn't done anything to encourage him but it made me feel cheap. I threw my hands up in front of my body, my fingers spread as I spat out, "That damn picture!"

Ana gasped. "Wow! Is that magic?"

My heart thundered in my chest as I realised what Ana saw. Strings of white light threaded between my fingers like an electric cat's cradle. This had to be the power Mum warned me about. I looked around. Nobody was about. Nobody had seen anything but

Ana.

"I have to go."

"Mariah…" She reached to stop me.

I shook my head. Tears were already welling in my eyes. I turned on my heels and fled.

I went back to the house I'd grown up in, but no longer felt like home. It felt temporary knowing I was to be returned, and that unsettled me. Mum was waiting when I got in. I could see a variety of herbs on the dining room table and knew she'd been casting.

"Where did you go?"

Her voice sounded weak, almost as if she were begging for an answer. She approached with care, as if any sudden movement could cause me to bolt again.

"I needed to get out." I kept my eyes down and went straight upstairs to bed. I prayed she'd leave me alone. I quickly got changed and turned the lights out.

I dream about being a mermaid swimming in the ocean. Now I knew why I was here. I was searching for my family. I kept swimming and the blue was endless with no sign of any life. No fish. No plants. I tried calling for my real mum, my real dad, but the words came out garbled and my mouth filled with salty water. Nobody was here for me.

Mum and I didn't speak until the morning. She waited for me in the kitchen with a steaming, morning brew. I sat on a stool and she slid it towards me like a peace offering.

All night, I thought about the danger I had put Ana in by meeting her. I kept replaying Mum explaining I'm with her for my protection but I needed to know more.

"You spoke of dangerous enemies. Who?"

"Mainly a werewolf named Luna with a bloodlust for shifters. She's exterminated entire family lines. The merallo are one of the few survivors."

"Werewolves, too?" I had to laugh. *Why was I even surprised?*

She gave a solemn nod.

"If my family are all powerful mermaids, why'd they need you?"

"For two reasons. The first is I use your essence for my magic and, as a result, you age. The second is to keep you hidden and safe until you come into your powers."

I rested my elbows on the counter and my head in my hands. This was too much to take in. Mum moved round to sit in the seat beside me.

She placed her hand on my shoulder. "I truly love and care for you."

My eyes peppered. I believed her, but it was a bitter truth. What would happen to us when I had to return to my family. I couldn't help but feel she'd spent years deceiving me and everybody close to us. I was well aware what a convincing liar she can be, but I never thought she'd use her trickery on me.

How much of what she said should I believe?

I was relieved to stay off school. I didn't feel up to facing anyone, especially Murray and the gossip. I was angry his kiss had opened this can of worms and now I had to make sense of truths that changed my whole identity. Mum didn't want me telling anyone, not even Jace, for fear it'd blow my cover after hiding for so long.

I didn't tell her how much Ana already knew. I'd been ignoring her. I hadn't got the energy to handle the tirade of questions that came with her insatiable curiosity. She'd want to know about my powers and what could I tell her - I'm a mermaid? I hope she'd forget and drop it.

Most of the week I'd stayed in bed, crying and feeling sorry for myself, but today I was up, washed, dressed, and sorting through some old photos. I'd spread them out across the floor. The images showed everything I'd be leaving behind; pictures of nativity plays, festivals, days out to the zoo, exploring forests, and other adventures. Every picture from chubby baby to now, I was with Jace. I snatched up the only photograph of Mum and I. I'd always assumed she didn't like her picture being taken, but was it deliberate? Had she purposefully kept out of our photos because she knew she'd not be part of my future.

My hand shook. She'd always known. My heart shot with pain. The life I loved was a lie and now it was over. Something unknown and unwelcome was taking its place.

Mum entered my room carrying a large sports bag. "You need to pack."

My worst fears rushed to the surface. I wasn't ready to say goodbye. I scrambled to my feet and shook my head.

"Please, I don't want to go."

I clasped my hands together and licked my dry lips. She'd been preparing for this - getting rid of me. I didn't care if they were my real family, I didn't know them. I wanted to stay here.

Mum frowned and then smiled. "Oh, Mariah, you're going to stay with Jace."

I sat down in the chair at my desk and let out a sigh of relief.

"I may have found a solution but need to go away to get what's needed. Denny said she's happy to have you. Remember, stay calm, stay out of trouble."

"I will," I promised, quickly gathering my things to stay overnight. "Where will you be going?"

"Far away. I won't be back until Sunday. I've transferred some money to your account so you can go Christmas shopping with Jace; take your mind off things."

"Thanks."

A sleepover with Jace usually helped me feel better. But, my heart still felt heavy.

I began sweeping up the photos from the floor back into the box. I felt a bit awkward being sent to hang out with Jace. I'd been off school for a week and he'd either not noticed or didn't care to check on me. His last message had been his response to Murray's photo.

I stepped onto the curb. The house was still unfamiliar but knowing Jace was inside made everything else seem unimportant; I was here for him, not his home. Heaving my bag onto the front step, I pressed the doorbell.

When they lived next door, I'd sneak through the gap in our fence and let myself in the backdoor. Most of the time we didn't bother to tell our mums where we were going. Our homes were an extension of each other's. Waiting reminded me, once again, of how divided we are now.

The door flew open and with a cheer of 'Freckles!' my mood was lifted.

Jace grabbed my bag off the porch and carried it easily up the stairs, putting shame to my earlier struggles. I couldn't help but giggle, infected by his positive mood.

"First sleep over since the move. Mum worried we're getting too old for this, but I told her we're more like brother and sister."

My head bowed as I realized he thought our kiss was meaningless. One of my most cherished memories was non-existent in his mind. I was heartbroken to be placed in the brother/sister category - that was worse than 'just friends'.

His hot breath tickled my ear as his words raced down my neck. "No point worrying her about our kiss... right?"

"Kisses." My eyes darted to his lips as mine tingled with the memory.

As soon as we entered Jace's room, I saw a silky red dress hanging from the wardrobe.

I laughed, "What's that?"

"A dress! Don't tell me being out of school has made you forget your social calendar. I know nothing's more important than me but remember the dance?"

Oh no!

My skin prickled as I began to sweat. Light rippled down the dress like an evil glint. I knew without asking – Kiely had leant me a dress. It wasn't safe, I couldn't go. The truth was too bizarre. I stammered for an excuse.

"I... I don't have a ticket."

Bingo! A legitimate reason not to go.

I bit my lip to prevent myself grinning from my miniature achievement.

"I'm taking you, silly!" Jace announced.

There was no way to suppress my smile. My hands flew up to cover my gaping mouth. It felt like a dream come true. Being safe and careful no longer mattered.

I'd risk everything if Jace was taking me... it was an entirely different matter.

I ran up to the dress stroking the delicate fabric with enthusiasm. "It's gorgeous. Red's my favourite colour."

"That's why I picked it." Jace's smile set my heart on fire.

"Won't Kiely mind?" The thought of Kiely made my fingers tingle. I clenched my hands into fists to stop what was happening.

"Dinner!" Denny called up the stairs.

"I'm starving." Jace vanished out the door and down the stairs.

I stood still, my heart pounding. I was going to the dance with Jace. He'd not noticed how the thought of Kiely had affected me. I took deep breaths in through my nose, out through my mouth. A small vapour cloud of condensation escaped my lips alerting me to how close I'd been to putting Jace's life in danger. I hoped Mum would be quick with the cure; I needed to get these powers under control.

Calm down!

All I have to do is keep it together until Sunday morning. If I harmed Jace, I'd never forgive myself.

"Mmm."

The scent of lasagne wafted up the stairs. My mind switched to food and I followed the smell of dinner downstairs.

The silky material fell in delicate layers and gave a swaying effect. You could tell it'd look stunning on the dance floor. The tiny spaghetti straps made me feel both secure and sexy. When I got in the car, I patted the delicate fabric out in a fan around me. The dress was distracting me from feeling like a fool.

Jace had explained over dinner that my ticket was actually Kiely's ticket and she'd use the one Murray bought me. The plan was to meet them there. My heart felt like a rock as I pretended I was fine with it. Technically, I'm still Murray's date! Somehow, he'd won.

"Are you okay? You've been quiet ever since dinner," Jace's hand rested on my leg in a way that was meant to be comforting but was anything but.

"Please don't leave me with Murray."

"I thought you liked him?"

I shook my head.

"Hang out with someone else, then. There'll be loads of people you know." He squirmed and whispered so Dave couldn't hear. "It's just... I really wanted to... you know..."

"I get it!" I spat the words. He was right though, I didn't want to be around to see them making out.

My anger was simmering through my body, making its way to my fingers. Unless I wanted this to be Stephen King's *Carrie* at the prom, I had to get myself under control. I faced the window and shut my eyes.

Calm, calm, calm…

By the time we reached the school my anger had

passed. My hand reached for my allergy bracelet to fiddle with, but it wasn't there. Jace had encouraged me to take it off as the blue beads didn't go with the red dress. Not wearing it made me feel naked. I tugged at the hem of my dress as we crossed the car park towards the hall.

Jace was like a homing pigeon; as soon as we were through the doors he beelined for Kiely. She stood with Murray who leaned against the glass doors.

Due to the winter darkness, I couldn't see through the glass but I knew on the other side of the doors were the benches I'd eaten at al fresco with Ana. Beyond that in the distance, across the field, were the tennis courts and the brick building I once frequented for swimming.

Murray straightened his stance and unfolded his arms as we approached. Kiely caught me off guard by greeting me with a brief hug. She moved on to hug Jace and point out the mistletoe in a cringe-worthy, enthusiastic manner. I stiffened as Murray's arm slipped behind my back pulling me beside him. He laughed in response to my disgust.

"Looks like I'm gonna need to keep a close eye on those two," he nodded in Kiely's and Jace's direction.

Kiely was pressing her body up against Jace, her hand trailing down his chest, with a flirty look that held his gaze. Jace needn't worry about kissing her. It made me feel sick. How could Jace be into someone so cheap? I wanted to scream at her. I wanted to slap him. I could feel myself losing and shut my eyes, trying to block it out.

I pushed Murray away from me and headed off into the maze of school corridors to cool down, or warm up. I wasn't sure which, but I needed to calm down. My bones had already begun to chill. As the music became fainter and the corridors got darker, I stopped.

Where am I going?

"Goldie, are you alright?"

"Leave me alone!" I groaned and began walking again. The unused corridors felt eerie at night, part of me didn't want to be by myself but I equally didn't want Murray trailing behind.

"Are you sure? You know this place is haunted?" His hand touched my upper arm.

I paused. Nobody had told me that before. I've never seen a ghost, but I believe in them. Mum took me to shows to see mediums at work. We'd sit at the back and I'd guess if they were 'real' or 'fake'. Afterwards, she'd reveal if I was right. Sadly, most were fake but every so often she'd whisper, '*Oh, this one is good. This one is worth the money.*' A stab of pain shot through my chest as I thought of her. She may be protecting me but she'd lied to me all my life.

Murray mistook my pause as interest in his story. "The ghost is a boy who killed himself down this very corridor. He was bullied by others for being in a wheelchair. One day, he hung himself from that strange, metal bar up there."

I looked up to where he was pointing. Oddly enough, there was a metal bar.

"He seeks vengeance and wishes to cripple

151

anyone that walks in the school. Some have heard his wheelchair creaking down the hallways. The sound that he is coming for you."

I smiled at Murray. "I don't believe that. Ghosts are peaceful spirits."

"Don't run to me when he cripples you!"

"If I'm crippled, I won't be able to run," I laughed.

Murray laughed, too.

It wasn't even that funny, but it really got us and we giggled until tears ran down our faces. We sat down in the so-called haunted corridor. Murray was so close I could feel the warmth of his skin against my arm.

"You're right. It's a stupid story. How'd anyone get up there?"

"Do you believe in ghosts?"

Murray shrugged. "Seeing is believing and I haven't seen any."

"Wouldn't it be cool if we did?" We both looked down the dark corridor expectantly. No ghost came. Still, we sat in silence for a while... waiting.

"I'm sorry for kissing you," Murray said out of the blue.

My attention snapped back from the lengthy darkness of the corridor to his face. His head was bowed as he stared at his trainers.

"I'll take it down if you want? The pic. I didn't mean to embarrass you."

"Why'd you do it?"

"Impulse. Instinct. It's so strong, I can't believe you don't feel it, too."

His feelings echoed my own for Jace; how I longed to hear him speak of me like that.

"I don't regret kissing you. I have to fight the urge not to do it again. There's something about you that draws me in."

"You can't!" I raised my hands defensively. I saw the pain flicker across his face briefly at my reaction. It felt cruel but I knew it was kindness. Not only was I not leading him on, but Murray didn't know the danger of kissing me.

I understood his pain. I imagined his heart breaking every time I speak of Jace in the same way my heart does when Jace speaks of Kiely. I decided it best not to mention Jace to Murray anymore; he knew without needing to hear it.

"I missed you at swimming. I hope you didn't stop coming to school because of me?"

I shook my head. "Nothing like that."

"Good. It's not the same without you there, Goldie." He dropped his head as if for once the cocky Murray was embarrassed by his own admission. He raised his hand as if shielding his face. "Sorry, that was too much."

"It's okay," I whispered.

"Can we at least be friends?" He met my eyes.

"Okay, but, first, I need to know why you took that picture and posted it to Instagram?

"I did it for you."

"For me?"

"Yeah, the plan. Piss Jace off. Jace realises he wants

you. Jace dumps my sister."

"The plan failed."

"I know." Holding my gaze, he licked his lips as if remembering our kiss. "I also hoped you'd get a taste of me and give up wanting Jace."

"Sorry." I fidgeted and stared at the ground, allowing my hair to hide my blushing face.

It couldn't happen. He'd just have to accept that I'm not interested. The same as I had to accept that Jace was never going to be mine, no matter how much I wanted us to be more. We'll just be friends, forever. And, maybe, that's worth more...

Sometimes, I thought it would be easier to never see Jace again, but I needed him. Like a drug. I was addicted to his presence and all the joy and pain that came with it. Without him, I was a different person, someone dark and miserable.

"Can friends dance?" Murray asked.

"Yeah, but this friend isn't any good."

"Nor's this one." He got up and pulled me to my feet.

We returned to the school hall, my hand warm and safe in his. I recalled moments with Jace when my heart raced from the lightest touch; did I have that effect on Murray? The thought I could possibly do that to someone made me feel powerful.

A slow song was playing. His hands rested on my hips and I wrapped my hands behind his neck. His eyes seared down on me and I could see that hungry look in his eyes. I blushed and rested my head on his chest.

"Tell me if I'm too much," I whispered.

I knew first-hand the difficulty of remaining friends with someone you felt so strongly about. I didn't want to make this any more difficult for him than it already was.

"Never enough," he stated fondly.

I rested against him; we had resolved the issues between us. A new beginning was here. Finally, a friend who understood exactly what I'm going through with Jace even if we can't ever speak about it.

At the thought of Jace, my eyes drifted across the dance floor to find him. He stood in a similar pose with Kiely, they were fixated on each other's lips, their heads inching closer. Everyone moved in slow motion as I saw my worst nightmare come to life.

My nails dug into Murray's shoulder as I shared my pain with him. My hands circled down his chest as I went to push him away to escape the horror but morbid fascination held me there a moment longer. I tortured myself with the sight of their lips coming together.

An icy coolness flooded my body, I was drowning in the anguish as my lungs froze and my heart died. The chill was so cold that my fingers ached as if they were burning. The only heat in my body was an acid fire that stung my eyes and I knew I was going to cry. I broke free from Murray and ran out the glass doors.

CHAPTER 13

As soon as I stepped outside, the sky opened up and it poured. The rain was hard and cold, possibly even sleet. I knew the field would be soaked before my feet even touched the muddy grass.

No longer caring for my own wellbeing, I pelted across the slippery field leaving a trail of deep, wet pools in my wake. I could feel mud sucking around my sandals and oozing up between my toes but I ran away from the hall as fast as my legs could carry me.

I arrived at the pool house. The door was locked but there was a sensor light in the porch that came on. It became my little, bright sanctuary and I sank down the brick wall. The silky, red dress stuck to my body like a second skin, soaked to my bitter bones. The shoes were ruined, caked in wet mud.

From cold and fear, I shivered, knowing I needed to

inspect my hands. I lifted them up in front of my face and slowly unfolded my fists, palms up. As I inspected them, I saw the tell-tale blue tinge. I snapped them shut as bile rose at the thought of what could have happened if I'd stayed.

That was close!

My head fell back against the wall as I embraced the stillness and exhaled. The rain fell like a curtain at the edge of the porch, thumping an urgent drum overhead. My hiding place was safe and dry as I clutched my knees to me. The storm rages around me but here I can't be touched. I shivered in the wet, flimsy dress as calm gently claimed me.

"Goldie!"

I stiffened on hearing Murray's voice. I couldn't see him in the darkness but under the porch light, he could see me. I got to my feet and glanced around for an escape.

Murray came into view, flustered and mad. He came closer, coming under my shelter, looking wild and... rather sexy. His shirt was ripped open, revealing the toned body I'd become familiar with. The rain looked good on him and my cheeks warmed.

I backed up, confused and frightened by his strange behaviour. Then, I see it. There above each pectoral muscle are four dark round circles.

I squinted. "Did you get a tattoo?"

"You did this! What did you do to me?"

Shaking, I leaned closer to inspect the marks. They were fresh, his skin red as if his flesh had been scalded.

"You're burned!"

I don't understand how this happened. Only minutes ago, we were dancing. But, I knew it was me. I looked accusingly at my hands and backed up.

"Stay away! I'm dangerous!"

I felt sick as the reality struck. I'd harmed Murray, scarred his body with my powers.

It's as if time had frozen, making the rain pause, suspended in mid-flow. But time was moving; it was moving very quickly and so much was happening my mind stretched it out deliberately, allowing me to take in as much detail as possible, causing the longest seconds of my life.

Murray growled angrily and I stepped back further. His hand thrusted forward as he attempted to grab me. I dodged out of his way and noticed as he touched the raindrops they turned a frosted white. They collected in his hand, clinking like marbles in their unnatural slowness. With his arm fully stretched, the hailstones flew from his palm. They shot forward like icy bullets, smashing into the door to the pool house and shattering the glass panel.

He was as shocked as I was. He glanced down at his right hand to see a hoarfrost building, covering his fingers in delicate little white needles. He crunched his fingers to his palm and watched the ice break and fall away. Unlike the shards of glass by the door, these icy fragments melted and joined the puddles. He opened his hand and the frost began to build again. The ice cast a strange, blue glow across his features, making them dark and twisted as if possessed.

"Stop it, Murray!" I begged. "If anyone sees you..."

I didn't know what might happen but I imagined it wouldn't be good. Scenarios of being treated as lab rats so scientist's can make sense of the phenomena ran through my mind. I wondered if my unknown family would be in danger. Authorities could use my powers to harm more people or lock me up to keep everyone else safe.

Murray clenched his jaw, the fear caught in his eye. I had to get it together and take care of him.

"Come on."

I reached through the smashed glass to unlock the door. We hurried into the foyer. Once inside, I sought somewhere private to calm Murray down.

The foyer felt too wide and open. Anyone walking past could see us. I glanced around for somewhere out of sight, but the next room off was the changing rooms. Despite breaking and entering, there was something wrong about having a guy in the girl's changing room and I didn't feel I was allowed in the boy's. That only left the corridor leading through to the pool.

I grabbed Murray's sleeve and pulled him along the corridor. Once through, I sat him down on one of the brick islands. The underwater lamps illuminated the room sufficiently for us to see. They cast eerie patterns of light that danced across the walls. It comforted me and I had an urge to dive into the pool.

His fingers were blue and he now tossed an icy cloud between his hands. It was similar to juggling, except the ball was made of vapour and moved slowly. He was shaking; his expression a mixture of fear and fascination.

"You need to calm down."

"Calm?" he scoffed, getting to his feet. He paced back and forth, alive with nerves. "What the fuck is happening to me? And, how the hell are you so calm?"

He glared at me and I knew he blamed me too. My throat felt tight.

"I'm sorry."

Murray paced the poolside. The mist snaked between his fingers, leaving trails of smoke that ran over the floor and pool.

As he paced towards me, I placed my hand on his upper arm. He paused to acknowledge me and our eyes met. He felt icy cold but there were beads of sweat on his forehead.

"Hello? Is anyone there?" an unfamiliar voice called from the foyer.

My heart pounded in my chest as Murray looked wildly around the room. This wasn't helping either of us calm down. And the person who'd found the smashed door had no idea of the danger they were walking into.

I licked my lips, my mouth going dry as I tried to think what to do. I began to panic. There was no plausible lie that'd explain the broken door and why we were here. Every second felt like a ticking bomb. I spotted the fire exit on the far side of the room. If we were quick, we could make it out before being discovered. There was still time.

I reached for Murray's hand and tried to pull him along with me. My muddy shoes slipped and my heart caught in my throat as I felt myself falling. In a desperate panic, I reached out and clutched hold of Murray. We toppled together into the pool, and as we hit the water our lips met.

The water wasn't heated but our kiss was. The coolness wrapped us in a chilly embrace. Murray's hand slid up my back, holding me against him. I felt a tingle of electricity ripple between our bodies, reaching from our kiss down to my toes. My legs wrapped around him, pulling him closer as we became a tangled octopus of lust.

His body warmth felt good against mine and dispersed the cold. I didn't want to stop kissing him but I felt the intensity of his feelings building as if they were my own. We were connected in a way I'd never felt with anyone, two heartbeats pumping in unison.

Even with my eyes shut, I sensed the light to the pool room being switched on. The glow shone through my eyelids, invading our privacy and causing me to break away. I'd forgotten about the voice. Someone was checking the room for us. It brought me back to reality like a slap to the face.

I placed a finger to my lips. Murray nodded and copied me to show he understood. We grabbed hold of the vent to keep us underwater. At least we're both good at holding our breath. We just had to stay still so not to cause any ripples.

I hoped Murray had enough air; neither of us anticipated this. I grinned as I recall the big kiss instead of a deep breath. The longer we waited, the more I worried for him but he smiled back at me, unfazed.

I notice a cut on Murray's neck, just below his jaw. My hand reached forward to inspect it and I realised it wasn't a cut but... it wasn't possible. He had a gill, an actual gill!

My hand reached for my own neck and as my hair floated back I felt a strange flap of skin in the same place. Murray saw and his head jutted forward to inspect it for himself. He slowly goes through the same motions as I. Was this physical abnormality a part of being a merallo? If it was, does that mean Murray is one, too? What about Kiely?

Our eyes met and we spoke a language that has no words. I noticed that his eyes had changed. The pupils have stretched into long, thin slits like frog eyes – I remembered how Ana had described mine the day Mr Griffen offered me a place on the team. Bright and glowing like two full moons, his silver eyes shone and I could only dream that my own looked as beautiful as his.

The main light shut off. We wee alone in our underwater world with only the pools under lighting. It felt magical and a million miles from the drama of my life. Murray took off his ruined shirt and the light, cotton material floated away. My heart raced as I saw the glistening marks upon his chest. Under the water, they didn't look like burns, and shimmered. The tips of my fingers rested upon the indents, a perfect match like a key to a lock.

His arms slipped around my waist and I let myself be pulled close. I felt him drawing me in and could tell he wanted to kiss me again. Holding my gaze, he licked his lips. My heart beat in anticipation as we drew closer and our lips met. Murray felt so right but I knew it was wrong to lead him on. Somehow, with all my strength I pushed away and kicked out at the water. He clung on to me as we rose to the top. We broke the surface and I saw his face was flushed with colour and his eyes sparkled with anticipation of another round.

"We have to get out of here!"

He shook his head but I ignored him and lifted myself up out of the water. As I climbed onto the side I felt him grab my legs and pull me back. My knee slammed down hard and scraped against the hard concrete as he dragged me back into the water. I twisted around so I could see what he was doing, my butt resting on the edge.

His behaviour scared me. I snapped my legs back from his grip and, with two quick, cycle kicks, I hit one foot into his chest and the other into his jaw. I used the momentum to project myself away from him and the pool, and safely onto the side. I wriggled to my feet and backed away from the water's edge.

Murray rubbed his jaw and sucked his lip. It seemed my kick had caused him to bite down and now blood ran from his mouth and down his chin. I didn't feel guilty. He needed to get his emotions under control otherwise who knows what might happen? Besides, my knees hurt from where he caused me to fall. I can't have him getting the wrong idea about us, either! We're just friends, after all.

"What were you thinking?" I yelled. My arms were animated with too much energy to stay still. "They could come back any minute and you smashed the door, remember!"

"Sorry!" Murray swam towards the steps and fished out his shirt along the way. I felt a twinge of guilt but knew I must keep my own feelings under control, too. This was his fault anyway. Mum warned me never to kiss him but he forced himself on me in the stairwell. Now look where we are!

"We've no time for 'sorry's! We have to get out of here... like now!" I hurried towards the fire exit doors at the back of the room. I pushed down on the bar and we were back outside in the cool breeze.

The rain had stopped. My dress was soaked. I couldn't go back to the disco and drip all over the dance floor.

Murray was trying to put his shirt back on but it was too damaged, with eight black holes scorched through the fabric, thanks to my carelessness. Without his shirt, anyone could see where I scarred his body. Instinctively, my fingers reached out and ran across them.

"Sorry," I shuddered. As much as I tried to find reasons for why this was Murray's fault, I knew this was my fault for losing control when Jace kissed Kiely.

"Does it hurt?"

"Not anymore." His tone was soft. His finger caught my chin and lifted my face up to meet his eyes. "What happened back there?"

I understood how Mum must have felt when I asked her to explain the unexplainable. I didn't have any answers for Murray but he had no one else to go.

"I don't know."

"Our kiss? You can't deny it, you felt it." He drew nearer.

I shook him off. "It was an accident."

"Under the water, you were so into it."

"I only did it to calm you down."

He laughed. "That was supposed to calm me down?"

He moved closer and I found myself, once again, pinned against a wall. My heart beat dangerously fast as I recall how things went last time I was in this position. His tongue licked across his bruised lip.

"You got me all fired up!"

His lustful intent was drawn on his face and I wasn't about to allow myself to be photographed again. I ducked down and under his arm, free from his grasp.

"Murray, if you want to talk, don't hit on me, alright?

"I'll try not to," he smirked.

Never had I seen anyone behave this way. Part of me liked it - that part of me was drawn to the danger he posed. The other part of me, the sensible part, knew I mustn't let him get that close again – he frightened me.

Murray made me feel vulnerable, with no control over the way he made me feel.

"You can't tell anyone what happened today. Please, pretend it never happened."

"That's going to be hard," he indicated his damaged shirt.

"We're just friends!" I reminded him.

"I wish I had more friends like you," he joked. His laugh sounded strangled and I knew he wasn't trying to be funny but trying to shake off the pain of my words. A laugh to repress the unwelcome truth.

I understood that feeling too well, but I couldn't be the one to comfort him; affections are easily misread. I cringed at the number of times, Jace's gentle, unintentional touch or look had caused my heart to race.

"I don't know what caused this, Murray, but I do know it's dangerous. You must stay calm, no matter what."

Murray nodded as if he understood. We began to move away from the pool house and return to the party. The storm had cleared as if blown away with my mood and the silence was chilling. The hairs on my arm stood to attention. I felt I needed to say something, anything.

"How are we going to explain this?" I asked as I held out the corners of my wet dress as if curtsying.

"I think you've never looked better," he grinned.

"Seriously, Murray!" I blushed. I knew where his eyes had settled. I shivered. The flimsy fabric clung to every part of me, revealing it all. I tried to conceal myself by wrapping my arms across my chest.

"The rain?" Murray said with a shrug.

"That will work for me. What about you?"

I eyed his torn shirt, flapping loosely around him. He only had the lower three buttons left and four burnt holes on either side of his exposed chest. As my gaze lifted, I caught him watching me.

"Hope my parents don't notice, and if they do, I'll say you ripped it off me in a moment of passion and I fought you to defend my virtue."

I punched his arm. "You wish!"

The music in the distance came to an end and we heard a chorus of people flooding out into the car park. Our time to construct a convincing cover-up had passed. I hoped Murray's parents were as oblivious as he thought.

"Mariah, I can pretend this never happened if that's really what you want, but you'll need to explain this, all of it. Otherwise, I'm going to have to start talking to find answers."

"Are you threatening me?" I swallowed a lump in my throat.

"I'd never threaten you," he laughed at the idea. "But, this is the craziest night of my life. What happened did happen, no matter what we pretend. And you're a terrible actress."

"What do you mean?"

"You're too calm for someone who knows nothing."

"I swear this is new to me, too. All I know is I'm a merallo and I think you are, too."

"A merallo?"

Wasn't that my first question? I sighed knowing how ridiculous this sounds but hoped in light of the evening's events he'd understand.

"We can manipulate weather elements and can shift into a mermaid-type creature."

"You've turned into a mermaid?"

"N... No....," I stammered. "I... I... just had an accident with some lightning and... Look, I know none of this makes sense and I can't explain 'cause I honestly don't know myself."

As I held my hands in front of me I saw lightning ripple between my fingers.

"Cool," Murray said, impressed.

"No, it's not cool. If we don't stay calm, we're very dangerous. We could kill someone. You're lucky to be alive. Until we figure this out, you can't get worked up over anything. You've got to stay calm. Do you understand?"

Murray gave a solemn nod.

"As soon as I know more, I'll find you. I'll tell you."

Murray smiled. "I like you hunting me out."

I rolled my eyes and we made our way towards the masses in silence. I caught sight of Jace with his arm around Kiely as they waited for our lift. I halted, ready to turn and bolt; I couldn't face this.

Murray sensed my movements. His hand clasped my upper arm and drew me near. His hand tickled down my arm like a current, finally locking with my fingers.

He leaned close and whispered in my ear, "Calm."

CHAPTER 14

MURRAY MADE SURE HE WAS SITTING behind the driver's seat, out of sight of his dad. Kiely reluctantly got in the front. Being the smallest, I took the middle seat between Jace and Murray. I could see the displeasure on Jace's face as my dampness began to soak through his trousers, chilling his leg.

"Why are you wet?" he complained. He tried to wriggle himself away from me, but the cramped conditions proved no relief.

"Rain," Murray answered for me.

Jace wasn't convinced but he didn't ask again. I sat awkwardly in the middle, my knees folded inward to avoid touching either of them and my feet spread to either side to avoid the raised bump the drive shaft

made in the middle of the floor.

I shivered, not so much from the cold but from fear, sick with anxiety that being so close was dangerous. I folded myself in, trying to make myself small and avoid touching either of them. I didn't want to cause anymore harm. I could feel Murray trying to catch my eye, but I couldn't take my gaze away from my hands and my silent prayer that they'd stay the same peachy tone as the rest of my body.

Murray's hand rested on my knee. I considered moving it away but the warmth was soothing and reassuring, and, when I saw Jace scowl, I got a wicked pleasure. I hoped his disgust was jealousy.

Murray's dad dropped us off first. The car pulled up out the front of Jace's house. Jace took off his seatbelt and leaned forward to place a kiss on the top of Kiely's head.

"I want to see you over Christmas," she gushed behind batted eyelashes. Her bashful 'Ms Innocence' act in front of her dad wasn't fooling me. "Text me," she asked, wide-eyed and pleading.

"I'd like to walk you to your door," Murray murmured in my ear.

"Don't be silly. That'd be weird." I said flippantly. I gave Jace a shove to hurry him up and out of the car, so I could escape Murray's advances.

Jace threw me a look communicating that he didn't want to be rushed. Thankfully, Kiely's dad threw Jace an equally annoyed look, warning him to behave in his presence. Jace took the hint and got out of the car. I quickly shuffled along the seat to join him.

Murray caught my arm and said, suggestively, "Feel free to calm me down any time. Happy Christmas and new year."

My cheeks flushed as I knew the hidden meaning. I shook him off.

"You, too. See you next year, *friend*." I added that last word as a reminder. I didn't want him getting the wrong idea about us and if he did, I was going to make damn certain that it wasn't my fault. I'd enough on my conscience without being accused of being a tease.

Jace stood on the pavement waving Kiely off. I didn't bother to see if Murray was waving. I knew he would be sitting smugly in the back of the car. I guessed I was lucky he didn't hate me for marking him – I would have to ask Mum about that.... not that I had the courage to tell her I'd ignored her warning.

I waited for Jace on the front porch. When he joined my side, he opened the front door and I noticed his face seemed twisted and out of place with an expression I'd never seen before; dark and unpleasant.

"Are you alright?"

"You and Murray looked pretty cosy," he said bitterly.

"It's what you wanted! Isn't it?" I snapped. How could Jace be cross with me for having a good time, when I'd done exactly what he'd asked of me? I'd certainly kept Murray busy. Jace had his way with Kiely under the mistletoe and should be thanking me.

He was quiet whilst he slipped off his shoes. "...It

doesn't matter."

"Why don't you talk to me?"

"There's nothing to say." He shrugged and gave a false smile. "I'm just… the dance was exhausting. Can't we play some console games or something?"

Clearly, he didn't want to discuss whatever was eating at him and I was happy to take my mind off the evening's events. I held out the fabric of the wet dress.

"First, I'm going to put my PJs on."

We stayed up playing until I began resting my head on Jace's shoulders and he decided I needed to sleep. He turned the sofa into a bed with a duvet and pillow from the large airing cupboard in the hall. The bed smelled good, with the same light, fresh, clean scent I recognised from Jace's clothes.

I settled down into the fluffy softness, sinking into its depth and wondered if it could possibly be comfier than my own bed at home. I leaned on my elbow facing Jace and cooed, "I could stay here forever."

Set in the corner of the room, the head of our beds almost touched. He mirrored my pose.

"I wish you could."

The way he looked at me, combined with those words, moved me in a way I couldn't imagine anyone else ever being able to. It was simple, yet so powerful.

"This bed is unbelievably comfy," I bragged, trying

to cover my heart.

The next thing I knew Jace was out of his bed and lifting up the cover. "Let's see, then! Move over."

"Whatcha doing?" I asked, wriggling over to allow him in. The clean scent suddenly didn't smell so pure. We were breaking unspoken rules and boundaries our mums trusted us never to break.

"Testing it out," he grinned.

I giggled. "I've got a feeling this is the stuff our mums worried might happen now we're older."

"What stuff?" he asked as he started tickling me.

I laughed out loud and kicked at him.

He placed a hand over my mouth. "Shh! You don't want to wake the house up!"

I licked his hand so he would let me go.

"You'll pay for that!" He wiped his wet hand down my face.

Still giggling, I pressed my back against the wall and gave him a sharp kick and he rolled out onto the floor.

"Oomph!" He made a funny noise as he hit the floor.

"Serves you right!" I said triumphantly.

Jace rubbed his head and got up. "You're mean." He chuckled, so I knew he didn't mean it.

"You're not getting back in." I quickly wrapped the duvet around my legs.

I hoped to continue our play fight but was disappointed when he returned to his own bed.

"Don't want to. My bed is comfier."

My head was buzzing from the excitement and playfulness. Jace had been in my bed! I grinned at him from my quilted cocoon.

"Sweet dreams, Jace."

"Sleep tight, Freckles."

The night had ended perfectly, and everything was peaceful and calm outside. Through a gap in the curtain I could see the moon, round and full of promise peeking through. Tonight, I'd dwell on the fact that Jace had been in my bed and I wouldn't worry about the tiny fact that we're just friends.

I waited until I was sure he was sleeping and I couldn't keep my eyes open any longer before I whispered into the darkness:

"Love you."

My eyes drifted shut and I dreamed that I heard him reply, "Love you, too, Freckles."

The bus stop had a view over the cliff tops, a line of beach huts indicating its edge. They were equally spaced all the way except in the middle where a large gap divided them. I saw the handrail winking in the winter sun, reminding me of the first time Jace had introduced me to Kiely. They could have kissed that day on the beach if Murray hadn't saved me from the heartache with his silly antics. I hadn't seen what he was doing back then, my heart blinded by my feelings for Jace.

A double-decker pulled up. We paid our fare, boarded and hurried up the stairs to sit at the top with the front view. Looking down on the road gave us the impression that we were very high up. Jace pulled out two small, white earphones from his pocket and passed me one. We placed them in our ears and snuggled close so the wire would not tug them out.

I knew the music was a distraction to avoid talking. He'd been in the same, strange mood this morning as last night. He put on a good act, though, smiling when required, speaking politely, and even joking around when the right opportunity presented itself. Being his best friend meant I was adept at knowing when things weren't as rosy as he'd like me to think.

"You've not said much about last night?"

He shrugged. "Not much to say."

"I saw you kiss Kiely!" I probed.

"Oh, that...," he sighed and looked out the window. Something wasn't right. What could've happened after I left the hall? Was he aware of what happened between Murray and I? He couldn't have been the intruder; surely, I would have known his voice?

"I thought you wanted to kiss her?"

"I did...," he mumbled and talked at his trainers. "And, now I have."

"You don't seem pleased."

His face twisted. "I want to break up with her."

"What!?" I gasped. Surely she couldn't be that bad a kisser. "Why?"

He shrugged. "It's just not gonna work out."

There was more to it than that but he changed the subject. He placed the earphone into my ear, pushing the conversation to a close.

"Here, check out this song. Tell me what you think"

I didn't need to listen to know what I thought. I thought he was trying to throw me off the scent by changing the subject, but I knew for certain that something was up.

I couldn't comprehend why he would suddenly want to dump the girl he'd taken months to kiss. Now he had, he wasn't interested?

"It's '*Anywhere But Here*' by an American group called SafetySuit," he said as the song came to an end. "What do you think?"

"I think you should tell me why you're going to dump Kiely." I ought to be pleased by this outcome but it just seemed so out of character that it didn't sit easily. "What happened?"

"Why'd you run off?"

"I didn't. I went for fresh air!" I lied.

"I heard Murray yell and you bolted out the doors. Did he hurt you?"

"No." I shook my head and realised how that would have been a good cover story but I couldn't hang the blame on Murray.

"So, why run off?"

"You're changing the subject!"

"If you're not telling me why you ran off crying, I'm not telling you what you missed." His eyes were sad. He snapped his head to look out the window. His sharp turn tugged the earpiece from my ear which he snatched up and added to his own ear. "If you don't want to listen, don't!"

I did want to listen, just not to some old song. I wanted him to tell me what he was hiding, but instead I was forced to sit awkwardly next to him in silence. I hoped he'd cheer up by the time we got to Ipswich; I didn't want to spend all day with him in this mood. I felt trapped. Mum wouldn't be back until Sunday and Denny wouldn't let me go home by myself. My only option was to sit this one out, literally.

I decided to drop Ana a text. I'd call her but didn't fancy Jace listening in.

Mariah: OMG. I went to the disco. Got so much to tell you. Later x

I imagined her reading my message and her flipping out. I was sure to get a ton of messages and missed calls. I couldn't wait to see her when Mum let me return to school.

I sat back and tried to appreciate the silence, but all I could think about was how I could explain what had happened at the disco. In particular, how could I tell Jace why I'd been crying? Was now the time to tell him how I truly felt? His back was turned to me and the tune he had played rattled mechanically in my head taunting me - *of a love that will never be.*

The song wasn't the sort of music Jace would

usually listen to and, for a moment, I thought he was trying to tell me something. Why else would he choose such an old song?

Stepping off the bus, I was welcomed by the fresh air and the return of a regular Jace. He was enthralled with the pre-Christmas shopping panic and embraced it with enthusiasm. We got hustled and bustled in the sea of people from shop to shop, Jace holding my gloved hand so we wouldn't get separated.

I picked Mum some cosy, thermal slippers and Jace suggested a console game I could get him. Finally, we stopped at the hot dog stand to get something to eat.

"My treat!" Jace smiled as he ordered a small and large hot dog with cheese.

Our purchase was wrapped in a paper napkin and Jace squeezed a generous helping of ketchup onto each of our sausages. It was impossible to eat in the crowds as every time I tried to bite into my hot dog I found myself bumped from a different direction. Jace grabbed hold of my arm and forged a way through the tide of people until we found ourselves sitting on the steps of the town hall. From our higher vantage point, we were safe from the bedlam taking place only yards away.

I wasn't enjoying the commotion. Unlike Jace, the noise and busyness stressed me out and I knew I needed to stay calm. I longed for peace and quiet and the weekend to be over. The images of shoppers wrestling their giant rolls of wrapping paper and hauling around bags weighted with gifts was too much for me. Nobody looked as if they were honestly enjoying themselves either. I wanted to be submerged underwater, drowning the noise out.

I hadn't realised how hungry I was until the taste of food touched my tongue. I relished the salty pork with delight and Jace laughed as I made appreciative noises.

Ketchup oozed from the bun and I felt it seeping down over my smile. Jace's finger reached out to wipe it from my lip. His fingers tickled the delicate skin and I blushed. My heart fluttered in response to his touch, and I leaned forward, my lips closing around his finger as I licked it clean. It tasted even better on his finger than in the bun.

Jace coughed and rubbed the back of his neck. His cheeks blushed red and his attention was lost watching the shoppers. He continued eating his hot dog and asked between bites:

"Anything else you need to get?"

"Nah, I'm done." I gobbled up the last of my roll to fill that strange feeling in my stomach although I knew it was pointless; I was hungry for something else but Jace wouldn't let me cover him in ketchup. Savouring the small taste I had indulged in, I asked, "You?"

Jace stood and stared out across the crowd. "I've still got to get something for Dave. What do you buy for your almost stepdad?"

"I don't know. Ask your mum?"

"Good idea."

CHAPTER 15

WE STEPPED ONTO THE LATE BUS and showed our return tickets to the driver. It was possibly the same bus from this morning, but this time it was packed with no free seats on the lower deck. I followed Jace up the stairs, clutching bags full of bought gifts.

The driver didn't wait for us to find our seats, I guess he was trying to make up time. We clung to the hand rail so we didn't get thrown over by the motion. Jace reached the top of the stairs and froze. Suddenly, he began backing down the steps into me.

"Oi!" I yelped as he stood on my foot.

"Kiely's up there!" he hissed.

"Well, there's no space down here and other people are behind us," I gave him a shove in the ribs with a roll of wrapping paper. It worked; he started moving forward.

The upper deck was almost as packed but Jace made a point of finding a vacant seat as far down the bus from Kiely. The pretty girl sitting next to Kiely looked at me as if I were an offensive smell.

Looking for an available place, I saw a creepy-looking guy that had crossed his arms and legs more than should have been naturally comfortable. It was quite obvious why the seat next to him was free. The next available seat was next to a woman who kept leaning forward to avoid the swinging arms of the screaming kids behind her.

The third free seat was... next to Murray. I gasped and felt a prickly sensation over my body. I knew we'd agreed to be friends but it still felt complicated. I knew he wanted more and deep down I wondered if he'd ever really be okay with just being friends.

For a moment, I considered the other options. I glanced back at the creepy guy, he grinned, showing a gummy mouth with only two teeth in unpleasant shades; one yellow and the other black. As my gaze cast to the harassed woman, I saw one of the kids toss a sticky lollipop into the free seat and began howling.

"What did you do that for?" the mother scolded her kid, then tapped the woman on the shoulder, "I'm so sorry."

Murray smiled expectantly. It would be cruel to sit anywhere else but next to him. I dragged my way along the aisle, grabbing the backs of seats to prevent myself from falling over. The bus turned a corner and I fell into the seat next to Murray.

Re-adjusting, I placed my carrier bags on my lap. I stared ahead at the back of the creepy man's balding head and decided 'better the devil you know, when the one you don't has fewer teeth than fingers'.

"I'm glad I saw you," Murray said.

"Me, too," I said out of politeness.

"I've got you a Christmas gift... it's not wrapped... Do you want it now?"

"What is it?" I twisted in my seat. I wasn't excited, more confused. Why would he buy me a gift? I hoped he wasn't expecting anything in return. I shook my head, red curls flew around my face. "I've not bought you anything!"

"Don't worry, it's nothing."

A pink tinge touched his cheek as he lifted a small, green box out of one of the carrier bags. It was the sort that promised to reveal jewellery of some kind. He passed it to me.

I opened the lid and peeked inside. It was a crystal snowflake necklace. The snowflake attached to the chain by a row of crystals on each side.

"Wow, it's gorgeous."

"You like it?" he beamed.

I nodded.

"When I saw it, I thought of us. The snowflake for the ice and frost from the other night. And, the four crystals on either side are like how you marked me."

"Oh, Murray. I'm so sorry about that!" I felt sick at the thought of what I'd done and I'd no reason or explanation why.

"It's fine, Goldie. It didn't hurt much." His arm slipped around my shoulder and he pulled me close. His hand rubbed against my arm .

"I'm still sorry."

He reached for the little green box and took it from me. "Would you like me to put it on you?"

His fingers gingerly tickled my neck and sent a current down my spine as he took care to place the necklace and do up the clasp. He lifted the charm and placed it at the nape of my neck.

"Beautiful."

The low, winter sun flashed through the window, it's blinding light searing into my eyes. I blinked them shut yet it burned through my eyelids and I saw a golden-red race across my vision. My hands were sweaty against the plastic carrier bags. I felt myself burning up. Only when the sun disappeared behind a cloud was I able to open my eyes again.

Murray was looking over my shoulder. "You know, Kiely is very jealous of you."

"Of me?" I choked with surprise.

"She's seen how close you and Jace are."

"We're friends, nothing more," I said with a defeated heart.

"I'd like to be friends like that," he winked.

I found myself blushing. I knew what he meant even if I wasn't willing to admit it. Following his line of sight, I caught Jace watching us. He flinched and turned to face the window, past the old lady he was sharing the seat with. His bags were on the floor and his arms crossed over his chest.

"We really are only friends," I sat back in my seat.

"Do you still want more?" he asked and I could hear the hope in his voice and I didn't want to answer his question.

"What sort of a question is that?"

"The sort friends ask each other. We're friends right?" he smirked.

"Yeah, but there are some questions you don't ask. It's like me asking, would you screw your sister?"

"No way! That's completely different. That's sick! I said nothing about incest!" he exclaimed.

"Sorry." I was burning up with embarrassment and sliding down my seat in shame as people shifted in their seats to look at us. "Can you keep your voice down?"

He laughed, "Alright."

I adjusted myself in my seat to be more comfortable. "I just meant Jace and I are like brother and sister."

"If you say so," he said.

It pained me to repeat Jace's interpretation of our relationship and I didn't have the energy to argue with Murray about it. It was the way it was, and it didn't matter if I wanted more or not. My chest felt tight and I stared down at the floor trying not to let it get to me.

"Look at that."

Out the window, it wasn't a huge show, but each lamp-post was adorned with Christmas images and lights strung overhead. It was a subtle touch, as if the locals were wishing everyone passing through a happy Christmas and I couldn't help but smile.

The view from the bus became more familiar as we got closer to our hometown. Murray pointed out the houses decorated like grottos; fake icicles hung from the windows and pretend snow on the ledges, Santa's that hung half out of chimneys, and reindeer's that stood in their front lawns. There were decorated trees, stars, and wreaths above doors and some houses even made nativity scenes. We'd always had a quiet celebration at home; just the two of us, although Jace and Denny would often join us. They liked the way Mum celebrated with Yule cake and gift giving.

"I love Christmas. We've got family visiting. What about you?"

"I don't know the rest of my family. It's only Mum and I." I felt an urge to share part of myself with Murray; a part of me that I hadn't shared with anyone except Jace and his mum. "We don't celebrate Christmas."

"I thought…," he trailed off and glanced at my bags.

"My mum's a Pagan. She tries to be a good one in this busy day and age, but she doesn't have time to do it all. We celebrate Yule."

"Is that like Christmas?" he asked.

"It's meant to be celebrated on the Winter Solstice but Mum changed it to Christmas day 'cause kids were mean to me in primary school," I blushed. "It's traditional to give gifts. We have a Yule log instead of a fruit cake, which I prefer; it signifies the Oak King. Everything is symbolic of something," my fingers reached for the necklace he gave me, "a little like your gift."

"Wow, that's not so different...," he said as he processed it. "It sounds lovely."

"We give gifts to show thanks to each other, the holly wreath is for the Holly King and the mistletoe is for fertility..."

He laughed. "Woah! That'll explain why things got so heated last night; that stuff was hanging everywhere."

I blushed. For a moment there, I'd forgotten about last night. It'd been a long day.

"Do you know any more about the, 'you know', thing?"

I frowned. "The what?"

"The marks, the ice, the kiss, the lightning, the mer-thing?"

I placed a finger to my lip to hush him. I hadn't told Jace about the kiss or any of the rest of it and wasn't sure if I could.

"Can we maybe not discuss this on the bus where anybody could hear us? Mum'll be back tomorrow, and when I get answers I'll let you know."

Murray nodded in agreement.

The bus made a few more stops and people got out. I heard Jace press the bell for his stop. I stuffed the empty, green box into my shoulder bag so I wouldn't lose it.

"Happy Yule. See you next year, friend." He gave me the smug smile that he'd used for my goodbye from the previous night.

"You, too. Thanks again." I touched my chest and could feel the cool metal beneath my palm.

Murray made sure I had all my bags as I got up. Jace was right behind me. Kiely smiled and gave Jace a giggly greeting as we passed. He gave the worst fake smile ever followed by a half-hearted wave. As we passed, he tried to be as far away from her seat as possible in the tiny gangway, and I cringed on her behalf.

We wound our way down the spiral staircase. The doors hissed behind us as the pistons closed them and the bus moved away. I started walking towards Jace's house, my arms heavy with my bags.

"Are you sure you don't like Murray?" Jace snapped from behind me.

I turned to face him.

His nostrils were flared and his face was red, with a sheen of sweat. "You seemed to be all over each other. Again!"

"What?"

"You say you don't like him, but then you sit next to him! I don't get you, Mariah!"

"What's your problem?"

He was the one that kept pushing me towards Murray, pushing me to spend time with him. My eyes bulged, and my hands prickled as I felt a warm flush run though my body.

He dropped his bags to the pavement and grabbed hold of my face. His fingers slid behind my ears as his lips pressed against mine. He kissed me roughly and I felt the tension pouring out of him as he began to relax. When his kiss ended, his hands remained clasped around my head in a way that was almost uncomfortable. The heat of his passion burned in his breath.

"What have you done to me?"

"Jace?"

He went and picked up his bags. "Sorry."

I stood motionless. What had happened? My bags tugged on my arms, yet I stood like a statue watching him storm off in the direction of his home.

Without turning around, he yelled, "We need to talk! Just, give me some time to cool down... alright?"

The bus was turning the corner ahead and I hoped none of the passengers had seen what had happened. Oddly enough, I found myself hoping Kiely of all people hadn't seen us. I knew if she had, her heart would shatter like the pool door window.

Jace was disappearing around the corner. I had to keep up; I still wasn't familiar with his neighbourhood. The roads and houses all looked the same to me with their perfect, long lawns and double garages.

I was also eager to find out what was going on. When did Jace get the idea in his head that it was okay to kiss me like that? It wasn't that I was complaining but I didn't want to become his bit of fun! Although... it no longer felt fun. Too much had happened since that first kiss in the park and everything was a mess.

Thankfully, by the time we reached his house, Jace

had chilled out. He held the door open for me with a nervous smile and eyes wide with the hope that he may not need to apologise. I scowled to let him know this wasn't over.

We headed up to his room. I sat on the sofa bed which was now folded up. Jace grabbed the remote, before falling into place next to me. He was channel hopping, searching for something to watch. It made it easier for me to say something because he wasn't looking at me.

"What was that?" I asked.

He frowned and his thumb turned white as he increased the pressure on the controller. His jawline twitched as he tensed.

"Dunno."

"Jace, we can talk about anything, right? We're best friends?"

"Stupid, fucking thing!" he snapped and tossed the controller across the room. It bashed into the mirrored wardrobe creating a large crack in the glass.

"That's seven years bad luck," I laughed even though it wasn't funny. Mum always said that if a mirror broke, the only way to undo it was to bury it in the garden - but we couldn't bury a whole wardrobe!

"Perfect!"

He got up and crouched by the mark of impact and ran his finger along the crack. A shiver ran through me as I remembered what happened to Mum's crystal ball and what I'm capable of.

"What'll you do?"

"Sticky tape." Jace crawled over to his desk and began rummaging through the bottom drawer. He found a roll and began running his finger along seeking the end. Biting a piece off, he carefully applied it to the crack. "There."

I looked at his handiwork; DIY is not Jace's forte. Now, the crack was framed by the edging of clear sticky tape.

Jace leaned against the wardrobe. He faced me and chewed his cheek. Neither of us knew what to say and there's nothing left to distract us. He spun the sticky tape roll around his index finger.

Feeling uncomfortable in Jace's presence was a new experience. I ignored the plea from my feet to run and press them into the ground to stay rooted.

Jace put down the roll and sighed. "I guess we ought to talk?"

I nodded but I was no longer sure I wanted to. Perhaps I was better off not knowing?

Jace took a deep breath. "We promised we'd stay friends but since the move we don't talk anymore. You're slipping away, becoming a stranger, and I know you're keeping secrets... and... I'm keeping secrets, too."

I frowned. It was him who'd shut me out, busy with new friends, a girlfriend, and being Mr Popular. His posture was crumpled and I knew there was more he needed to say but couldn't get out.

"Tell me, then? What's your secret?"

"I can't." He frowned and turned away.

I got up and crouched next to him, placing my

arm around his shoulders. He shrugged me off. So, I sat beside him, my arms wrapped around my legs. His rejection created an invisible wall between us, built brick by brick of unspoken words.

He shifted so he sat cross-legged, his elbows resting on his knees and his head dipped towards his lap. His voice was quiet but I heard his words, chilling and clear:

"We're not friends anymore."

Chapter 16

Y LIP QUIVERED. I was frozen, except my eyes blinking back tears. My hand pressed against my chest trying to push the pain away. I'd struggled with him dating Kiely, but this? Not even friends?

I swallowed around a lump in my throat and tried to speak.

"Jace, please…," I started but it all hurts too much. "Isn't there something…"

He lifted his head from his lap. In all the ways he has touched my heart before, I've never felt as moved as right now. My face cracked as my heart shattered. I can't live without Jace in my life. I can't even picture it. My mind grasped every detail, trying to savour this painful moment, in case it is our last. Every memory now more precious than I ever realised; the colour of his eyes, the shape of his lips, the way his hair moves...

"Tell me your secrets?" he begged.

But I couldn't speak. Every time, I opened my mouth to say something, I had to suck in a breath to stop myself from crying. It's all too much. I pushed off the floor onto my feet, racing out of his room and into the family bathroom. I locked the door behind me.

I stood at the sink, leaning on it as I watched my horrible face in the mirror twisting in anguish. Taking short sharp breaths, my lip began to quiver and fat, salty tears descended down my cheeks. I shut my eyes, crushed my eyelashes in defeat as I let it all out. Sobbing, I rubbed at my puffy eyes roughly, bashing away the burning drops.

There was a gentle knock at the door disturbing my personal torture. I bit my lip whilst my red-rimmed eyes sought the source of the sound. Somebody was at the door and it's the one person I wanted to run to my rescue and the one person I won't let see me like this.

"I'm sorry." Jace waited for my response and when he didn't get one he asked, "Will you open the door?"

Numbly, I shook my head, then realised he can't see me.

"No!" My voice croaked as it broke out, torn by my broken heart.

"You wanna talk?"

"Do you?" I snapped. Why should I talk to him when he doesn't even want to be friends anymore? If we're not friends, then what the hell are we?

The temperature dropped as fast as my mood. I

shivered and glared down at the sink. The bowl had developed a sheen as if covered with frozen water and was even cold to the touch.

I growled at my reflection.

As I exhaled, an icy vapour escaped my mouth and I noticed my eyes shimmer an unnatural shade of silver, and my pupils have elongated. I checked my hands and noticed my fingertips have the deathly blue tint. There was also a white frost encrusting the tips, looking like blue snow or crushed ice.

At least I wasn't shooting lightning! And, I hadn't hurt Jace, had I?

My eerie eyes flicked up in horror to meet my reflection, my attention drawn down to my collar bone. Eight icy, clear crystals reflected back at me; Murray's necklace, as if thanking me for what I did to him. But I won't lose my calm again, I can't!

I moved away from the mirror, angry at myself for allowing my emotions to take over. My throat felt tight and my fingers reached for the clasp of the necklace, taking it off, and shoving it deep into my pocket.

I slid my back down the door until my bum reached the floor and pressed my ear against the wood to hear if Jace was still there, but I couldn't hear anything. I look at my dangerous hands and feel sick. Another white cloud of condensation escaped my mouth.

"Are you there?"

I felt a gentle thud as if he had collapsed against the door on the other side.

"I'm here, Freckles."

My heart came to life at the sound of his voice. "Are you okay?"

I held my breath in anticipation. I won't be able to live with myself if I've hurt Jace, scarring him like Murray.

He's quiet and with the silence caused dread. My heart began to thump, getting faster with each second. The temperature dropped and the hairs on my arm stood on end.

Fresh tears brewed, but these were different. These were tears of sorrow for someone else, for someone I would rather die for than ever see harmed; these were not tears for my own self-pity. I took a deep breath and gritted my teeth to hold them back. The temperature dropped further and an icy mist emitted from me, filling the bathroom in a chilling fog.

"I'm fine," Jace said.

I sighed with relief.

"Sorry, Mariah, that didn't come out how I meant. I've so many regrets; I don't know where to start."

Jace sounded more confident with a door between us. Knowing he's okay eased the prickly sensation that had swept my body. As I relaxed, I noticed the mist thin out and disperse.

"I never should have asked you to kiss me."

My heart sank. I never regretted our kiss. "Don't, it was perfect."

"There's a line friends should never cross and we crossed it!" he snapped like he was telling me off. "We'll never be the same again. It's ruined us and it's all my fault."

I shook my head. That kiss was one of the best moments of my life and I'd never see it otherwise. Taking a deep breath I allowed his words to sink in and it physically hurt to accept that he regretted kissing me. I dropped my head into my arms, folded in my lap. The icy cold sensation was building again.

I must stop, I must be calm... for Jace.

"I'm sorry I used you. I'm sorry for every occasion I disregarded your feelings and didn't put you first."

He knew? Where was this coming from?

"I shouldn't have forced you to hang out with Murray. Everything I did to get with Kiely without thinking of you - it was selfish. I don't deserve to be your friend."

"Isn't that my choice?" I asked, frightened of losing him.

"It doesn't matter. The damage is done. I can't...," he paused and I was scared of what he might say next. "I can't be your friend."

"No!" I got up, my hand reaching for the lock.

"Jace," I heard his mother's voice in the hall.

My hand paused over the bolt as I listened, a wintry cold emitted from my fingertips. It chilled the metal, a sparkling frost claimed the bolt like a wave running up the beach.

"What are you doing sitting outside the bathroom?"

"Waiting for Mariah."

"Are you sure you need to wait there?" Denny asked but didn't wait for an answer. I could almost visualise her shrugging. "I thought you might be excited to know it's snowing outside. Pretty heavily, too. We're in for a white Christmas."

Running over to the far side of the bathroom, I opened the window. Outside I saw big fluffy, white flakes, like fairies dancing in circles, gently descending to the ground. I reached my hand out to catch one. It looked like a piece of candy floss, but melted the moment it landed in my palm.

Was I responsible for the snow?

I returned to the sink, running the hot tap to warm my hands and clear the ice in the bowl.

"You still there, Mariah?" he asked.

Where else would I be?

"I'll be out in a bit."

My fingers were a normal flesh colour again. I dried my hands and shut the window before joining Jace in the hall. He stood with his hands tucked in his jeans and his chin resting on his chest. He looks sad and sorry. Instinctively, I reached for him, wrapping my arms around his neck, drawing him in for a hug. His hands slipped out of his pockets and around my waist.

"I really am sorry," he mumbled into my hair.

"I know." My fingers stroked the hair at the nape of his neck; something I knew he found comforting.

He pushed me back by my hips and held me at arm's length. My hands slide down to rest on his shoulders.

"I meant everything I said," he said painfully. "I hate seeing you with Murray; I can't ignore it any more. I'm sorry, my head, my heart - it's all a mess. I don't even know anymore. I thought… the way I feel about you, felt about you, was what you feel for a best friend. You're the person I need and that's always there for me, but… kissing you has changed everything. I don't want to be your friend, Mariah. Not anymore. It's not enough. I want... more. I'm sorry, I've fucked it all up and gone about this all wrong. But… there, I've said it. The truth."

My heart thundered in response. I didn't know how long I had dreamed of hearing him say those words. Now, he was saying it and I was scared I would lose control of my powers. I screwed my hands into fists to protect him.

"I feel the same," I whispered back.

The electricity was pulsing in my palms. I moved my hands away from his body and held them behind my back. The air between us thickened and I knew he wanted to kiss me but I was unsure if it's safe.

My neck craned towards him; my body craved him. I shut my eyes in anticipation but the image of Murray's burnt flesh flashed in my mind.

My eyes opened in alarm, remembering the danger my lust would place Jace in. He was pulling me closer, guiding me towards him. I turned my face at the last moment and he got my cheek.

"What about Kiely?"

He let me go and stepped back, unable to face me.

My heart pounded in my chest. I wanted to grab him and kiss him until I saw that goofy grin of his that I loved so much, but I had to stay in control. I gave a weak smile.

"You need to sort things out with Kiely first. No more regrets!"

He nodded.

"Let's check out that snow your mum was talking about!"

I didn't wait for an answer. I was already walking towards the stairs and I knew he was following me. We hadn't kissed but I still had that warm, afterglow feeling. We weren't breaking up as friends, we were on the border of starting something new, and I was excited.

Jace's mum made us mugs of hot chocolate whilst we watched the snow settle from the conservatory. The drink was warm and sweet and complemented my feelings.

The unexpected snowstorm was pretty thick and although it was coming to an abrupt end, it was obvious it was going to lay. Once wrapped up in our coats with the addition of hats, scarves, and gloves, Jace and I stepped out the patio door into the garden.

The snow was fresh, pure, and a brilliant white. Jace took my hand and we crunched along making big, deep footprints. He tilted his head back and stuck his tongue out to catch one of the last snowflakes in his mouth. I followed suit.

We laid in the snow so our fingers were almost touching and then spread out our arms, moving them up and down as far as they'd go while swinging our feet out. We got up with care so as not to ruin our imprints, and giggled at our attempt at hand-holding snow angels.

Every time I caught his eye, I knew he was thinking about us being more. I blushed and prayed my heart would settle, and that my gloves could keep my deadly secret safe.

I hoped Mum had found a solution. It was exhausting using all my strength to stay calm and fight his charm. With every glance, it became increasingly difficult. I ached for him and I had no idea how much longer I could keep control. I could tell he sensed it, too. We were buzzing on the same high, an anticipation of what was to come, an acceptance of a mutual need to be together. This pull, this draw, was physical. It was no longer an emotion. It tugged us together like a cord.

"Hungry?" Denny called from the backdoor.

We both nodded in unison. Trying to do the right thing had left us famished. Jace was still with Kiely and I had to stay in control.

We nipped up to Jace's room to get changed out of our wet, snow clothes. He loaned me a pair of his joggers and a t-shirt. The clothes were clean but his scent clung to them, making me feel warm and fuzzy.

We helped ourselves to pizza and chips in the kitchen, although I don't eat much. I couldn't - my tummy was unsettled and I found myself grinning at him the whole time. We dipped our chips in each other's ketchup, taking ages, and hardly eating anything.

"You two okay? You've barely touched your food!" Denny placed her hand on Jace's forehead. "You do feel a little hot. Maybe you shouldn't have played out in the snow so long?"

I had to bite the inside of my cheek to stop myself from giggling.

"Have you finished?" she directed her question at me and I nodded.

Jace nodded, too, excusing us from the table.

As soon as we were out of sight, Jace took my hand and led me to his room. His eyes sparkled with merriment and we both giggled.

Morning came too soon. Hearing the distant sound of Mum's voice in the hall got me out of Jace's bed faster than any alarm clock.

Although there was nothing wrong with Jace being in his own bed, he jumped out, too, and raced across the room to throw on his dressing gown.

"What's your mum doing here?"

I shrugged my shoulders and rummaged in my bag for my mobile phone to check the time. The display read 10:20 am. I held it up to Jace's face so he could see. We were lucky his mum hadn't checked in on us.

"I'm gonna get dressed!" I grabbed my bag and ran to the bathroom.

There, in the peace and quiet of the white tiled room, I collected my thoughts. A lot had happened since Mum sent me off in the taxi. I washed and brushed my teeth, and threw on my clothes, now dry from the snow.

I opened the window to see if the snow was still there. The grass was muddy but there were sporadic patches of ice, reassuring me that it wasn't all a perfect dream.

Once satisfied I was reasonable looking enough to leave a pleasant image in Jace's mind, I unlocked the door and headed downstairs. I could hear Jace in the kitchen, making polite conversation.

"Can I get you a drink, Gwyn?" he asked.

"No, we must rush. Thanks so much for having Mariah this weekend."

I knew the last comment was aimed at Denny, who replied, "Not a problem. She's always welcome."

I wondered if she'd remain as friendly if she knew I'd slept in her son's bed. She trusted that Jace and I were just friends and I wasn't sure how our mums would react when they discovered our feelings weren't so innocent.

Joining them, I stood by Mum's side. She ran her hand playfully through my hair messing up my curls.

"You've got your new makeup on." she cheered. All eyes turned on me. "Oh, Denny, you should have seen her first attempt at makeup!"

Aghhh! My mind screamed for her to shut up. I couldn't take another one of her embarrassing stories about my adolescent screw ups. She didn't even know half of it!

"Didn't you say we gotta rush?" I hooked my arm through hers and dragged her off the kitchen stool she's perched on.

"Alright, alright!" she giggled and I let her go.

Denny came over and gave us a hug goodbye and showed us out. Dave was driving us back. He got his car keys and picked up all of my bags.

Jace and I were left alone in the kitchen to say goodbye. It felt awkward. So much has happened, yet nothing has changed. Do we kiss? Do we hug? How do friends on the verge of dating say goodbye?

Then, Jace winked.

It felt right. I smiled and bit my lip as I turned to walk out the door. Jace and I shared a flirting glance that communicated our expectations of everything that is to come. I knew the next time we meet will be the beginning of something else.

Chapter 17

Arriving home, I noticed Mum had already begun decorating our home: sprigs of holly with red berries hung along the banister, and a bowl of the shiniest red apples were in a gold bowl in the hallway. Glass lanterns hung from hooks with cinnamon scented candles.

"Mum, do you want to see the gifts I bought?"

"Not right now, Mariah." She hurried into the house, passing me.

I followed Mum into the kitchen, keen to know how her search for a cure had gone. So far, being a merallo has been nothing but drama. The shape-shifting hadn't been too extreme with only subtle changes like my pupils changing shape and developing gills underwater. The storm summoning powers have been frightening, and there was the crazy incident involving

Murray.

"Did you get a cure?"

"Yes. I'm preparing the potion now. This *could be* the solution," Mum grinned, as she placed a mug next to the kettle.

My blossoming romance with Jace had distracted me from my 'little' problem. With no control, without Mum's help, I knew that I'd never be safe, and neither would anyone I loved.

"What do you mean by 'could be'?" I asked.

She made a hissing noise as she sucked air through her teeth. "It's mostly theory based."

"What?"

"Well... it's never been used on a human."

My eyes widened and I tilted my head. "Is it safe?"

Mum dismissed my worries with a swipe of her hand. "You're not human, anyway."

It sounded bizarre hearing it out loud. I was still coming to terms with what I am. I'd not considered what I'm not.

"I spoke with your parents," she continued.

"And?"

"If this doesn't work," she tapped her handbag, "then they'll step in."

"Why not now?" I wailed. First, these people give me up. Now, I have some genetic problems, and they'll only help me as a last resort!

"You'd have to go live with them. You'd be stuck at fifteen forever. Plus, it's in your best interests to finish school first!"

"Stuff school!"

Gwyn chuckled at my outburst. "How was the disco? Did you see that boy - Murray?"

"Hang on. What do you mean I'd be stuck at fifteen?"

"You're practically immortal..."

"I'm immortal?"

"You age differently to humans. You create an essence that keeps you young but when you're with me, I use your essence for my magic and you age like a human."

The more I learned about being a merallo the more incredible I realised I am. It was the first time I liked being different. I felt empowered about being a merallo and I began to doubt if I wanted the cure at all.

"So, did you have fun with Jace?"

I blushed and let my hair fall over my face as I recalled how we'd left things. "Yeah. Same, old Jace."

"Good. No more kissing."

I was going to tell her about Jace, when I noticed what she'd pulled out of her handbag. It was a jar containing the most beautiful flower I'd ever seen. It was glowing and had translucent blue petals and small purple leaves. She put on yellow rubber gloves from the sink and opened the jar. She plucked a petal from the unusual flower. It made me think of a rose with frostbite. The petals crumbled in her fingers and a light powder fell into one of the mugs by the kettle. I peered closer and saw that the petals sparkled as if coated in glitter.

I reached forward to see what they felt like...

Mum slapped my hand away. "Don't touch!"

She screwed the lid back on. The kettle clicked and she poured the boiling water over the powder. She passed me the mug.

"Sit down to drink this."

I placed the mug on the counter and got comfortable on one of the stools. Mum shook her head.

"Erm... best sit on the sofa."

I carried the mug into the lounge. Sitting on the sofa, I raised the white, porcelain mug to my lips. The drink smelled strange, like chlorine from the swimming pool mixed with the scent of washing powder, and there was a hint of a sea breeze. It was a strange concoction; I can't imagine any flower having such a peculiar scent. The heady scent filled me with an uplifting feeling like I was floating. I can sense the magic is strong and I hadn't yet taken a sip. The aroma was making my head spin.

"W- why do I need to sit?"

"The loss of your trigger could cause you to faint. Now, drink up."

I placed the hot liquid to my lips, and took a long sip. It was hot and spicy but when it ran down my throat it tingled with a minty coolness. Oddly enough, I thought I tasted something sweet and tangy like tomatoes. I drank it down like medicine, forcing each gulp as my nose wrinkled.

My stomach turned and my hand covered my mouth. I gripped my tummy in pain and shut my eyes.

My mind saw flashes of intimate moments, stolen and secret kisses, gentle caresses, and holding hands. My heart raced and my mind spun.

Am I dying, is this what I can feel coming?

The darkness was sudden; an empty black.

I heard a voice, but I was submerged under water. The words were mumbled and didn't make sense. Dim lights stirred my senses. I heard the sounds again, distant, but the word is familiar, getting clearer each time. Someone was calling my name. Is this the afterlife? It didn't feel peaceful and serene. Perhaps, for my sins, I'd been sent somewhere more sinister?

The voice still called my name but I was lost and confused. It got fainter and fainter until I couldn't hear it anymore... and then all that was left is blackness and silence.

The pain!

My throat was on fire. I gasped for air as if I'd been holding my breath too long. The oxygen scratched its way down my throat and filled my lungs.

Crumpled on the floor, next to the brown, glass coffee table, Mum kneeled beside me, her hand on my shoulder rocking me, waking me up.

"Mariah, Mariah?" she whispered.

Blinking my eyes as they adjusted to the light, I sat up. My chest was tight and my throat burned dry.

Embracing me in a hug, she asked, "Are you alright?"

I nodded. "What happened?"

"You fainted." She sat back on her heels, as I struggled to get upright.

"I fainted?" I croaked.

I've never fainted before in my life! I'd always imagined it being a peaceful experience, like falling asleep, but my body feels stripped and starved. My hands raised to hide my face as my head spun.

Mum started helping me to my feet. She pulled my hands away from my face to look me in the eyes.

"What is the last thing you remember?"

My heart was heavy with a loss I didn't understand. Perhaps I was still groggy from fainting. There was darkness like a shadow, disguising a hole, an empty unseen space that can't be seen in my heart. How can I explain what I'm going through when I have a strange sensation that I'm not being honest with myself? I searched for my last memory and frowned.

"Jace moved away."

"Excellent!" Mum smiled and rubbed my arm. "It worked."

"What worked?"

Mum shook her head. "Oh, nothing, I just meant you're fine. Everything will be alright now."

I nodded even though I didn't agree with her. How can everything be alright without Jace next door?

There in the corner of the room, I see a tree standing tall and proud, it's branches decorated in tinsel and baubles. Why was the pine tree here in September?

Yesterday had felt like the summer holidays ending and Jace moving away but it didn't take me long to figure it out: today is Christmas Eve.

What didn't make sense was why I couldn't remember the days in between. I remembered the loneliness but not the lost time without Jace. It was literally blank.

Mum said I'd hit my head hard on the coffee table and got a mild concussion. She believed my memories would come back soon and wasn't worried. But, I couldn't shake this nagging feeling that something wasn't right. I guessed that must be the disorientating sensation of not knowing my own mind.

Sitting in the lounge in my pyjamas, I was sticking a bow onto the final wrapped gift. Another gift I didn't recall buying. But, this last gift had been a mystery. It was a personalised notebook and mug with 'Ana' written on it and an image of a retro camera.

I'd searched my friends list to discover who Ana was. She had a Facebook album full of gorgeous pictures of me wearing outfits I didn't own. There was a picture on her Instagram of us sitting together by the pool in swimming costumes, which was odd because I'm not allowed to go swimming. I'd read the messages between us. The messages had raised more questions than answers.

Mariah: OMG! I went to the disco. Got so much to tell you. Later x

Ana: Why are you not picking up? You can't leave me hanging like that!
Ana: How come you were there? You said it wasn't safe.
Ana: I'm dying here. Text me!
Ana: Did you kiss hottie again?

I wanted to call her and demand she enlighten me on who 'hottie' is. But, I felt awkward not being able to remember her, or the hottie. What disco had I gone to and why did Ana believe I thought it'd be dangerous to go?

I placed the gift under the Christmas tree and sat back admiring the ivy and holly decorations with little red berries. I tried getting in the festive spirit but I felt restless. A niggling thought told me I should be somewhere or know something but I couldn't place it. Like trying to sing a carol when you know the tune but suddenly you've forgotten the words.

"Try one of these Yule Moon Cookies." Mum's oven-gloved hand held a baking tray out towards me. "They're fresh out the oven."

With care, I took one from the hot tray. "Mum, there's something wrong with me."

"Nothing a cup of wassail can't fix. I've been brewing a pot in the kitchen," she said as she hurried out the lounge to get me a cup. I could smell the sweet scent of apples and oranges stewing in cider and wine. Mum returned and handed me a metal goblet filled with a warm, brown, mulled juice. "To good health!" she cheered and clinked her own goblet against mine.

"To good health," I echoed back and took a swig. It felt good running down my throat but I couldn't let it go. "Mum, I can't remember the last few months."

"Clearly uneventful," she replied, dismissing me

"No, I mean my memories are blank."

She coaxed me to raise my cup, "Drink up."

"Mum, this is serious. I'm worried."

She had another swig from her goblet. "You know your problem? You worry too much. It's the culture of your generation. Hypochondriacs, the lot of you."

"Mum!" I snapped.

"It's true. If you'd relax, you'd be fine. It's stress! Stress has brought this upon you. If you were in better control of your emotions…" She waved her arms in the air as if dismissing me and then stormed off to the kitchen.

I took my drink and cookie up to my room. Mum's lack of concern was concerning. There are other strange things, too, like this necklace. I sat at my desk and lifted the snowflake charm from my makeup bag.

So beautiful, but where did it come from?

It was one of many things that didn't make sense. My thoughts were disturbed by a knock at the front door. My interest peaked. Only one person ever visited on Christmas Eve – I was almost too scared to allow my heart to hope.

I shoved the necklace back in my makeup bag for safe keeping. Checking out my bedroom window, there's no sign of a car or taxi, no nothing. The visitor has arrived on foot. There's an exchange of words, low enough that I couldn't make them out. Then footsteps on the stairs. I knew before the door opened it's Jace. He stood in the door frame; perfect. I wanted to cry.

"I've missed you so much."

"I never stop missing you," Jace replied.

I sat on my bed and he came over and dropped to one knee as if about to propose.

"What are you doing?" I laughed.

"Mariah." He never calls me that, always Freckles. Mariah sounded foreign from his lips. "Will you go out with me?"

Me!?

He was confused by my surprise. He searched my eyes for something, but I responded by frowning. Ironically, he acted as if *my* behaviour was strange.

"I dumped Kiely for you."

Kiely! Who's that?

His mouth twisted as if he had tasted something horrible. He got to his feet. Towering over my seated position, he snapped, "Why are you acting like this? I thought you'd be pleased... more than pleased! This is what you wanted!"

"Jace...?" I mumbled but I don't know what to say. I don't even understand what is happening.

"When we kissed!" he snapped.

We kissed!

My eyebrows shot up at this revelation. I searched desperately through my mind, through my heart, looking for that fact. Why can't I remember it?

Is he hottie?

"I don't remember…," I confessed.

"You don't remember?" he laughed bitterly, then pulled me roughly to my feet. His lips pressed against mine. He kissed me fiercely and there was something familiar in his kiss.

My mind flashed a bright light and, for a moment, I glimpsed a memory.

Jace is kissing me roughly in the street, my arms weighed down by bags. The bags are full of gifts; those I'd wrapped today but couldn't remember buying.

This memory must have taken place a few days ago.

"Deny that!" With a gentle shove of my upper arms, he pushed me back and, in my stunned state, I toppled back onto the bed. Dumbfounded, I watched him storm out of my bedroom.

The kiss had been brief and the memory gone before I'd made sense of it. I tried to recollect the events that built up to this moment but nothing. My lack of memory had hurt Jace's feelings.

All I had of the past three months was the one memory brought back by Jace's kiss. Perhaps, if I kissed him again, everything would make sense. The way Jace left, I was unsure I'd get a second chance though.

Jace liked me... more than just friends.

As his best friend, was it ethical to use him to get my memories back? But, I had no choice. I couldn't stand to see Jace upset. Jace asked me out and seemed pretty sure it was what I wanted, too. If only I could remember...

His kiss felt nice.

I ran downstairs, grabbing my coat off the hook as I passed. I wrapped my scarf around my neck and pushed my feet into my trainers. I didn't care that under the hem of my coat, visible to everyone, were my bright, yellow pajama bottoms with blue stars printed on them.

I raced into the street and smiled with relief as I saw he hadn't gotten far. I could still catch him. Running down the road to catch up with him, I started yelling his name over and over:

"Jace! Jace!"

No matter what, I'll get him back!

He stopped with his back towards me and shoved his hands deep into his pockets. I slowed down. I didn't need to run anymore; he was waiting for me, even if he won't turn and face me. The way he stood pulled his jeans taut around his backside and I noticed for the first time – I think – what a nice arse he has.

"Jace," I called one last time as I levelled up with him. I ran in front of him, to meet his eyes. "I'm sorry."

He eyed me as if I might rip him open and gorge his

entrails. He made me feel dangerous. His jaw twitched in response as he clenched his teeth, something he only ever did when he was upset.

"Please, Jace, I do want to go out with you," I pleaded hoping he'll believe me.

I needed him to kiss me again. I needed to know what happened to make sense of this. His kiss was a tiny speck of paint on a giant, blank canvas and I craved more.

One thing I'm certain of was that I'd do anything to save our friendship. Jace's kiss had taken my breath away, I'd happily kiss him again and again until my memories were restored. I just hoped there wasn't a good reason why I forgot in the first place.

His expression softened and his blue eyes sparkled. His hand reached up to lightly brush my cheek.

"No regrets?"

I nodded intuitively. It felt like something I knew. I shut my eyes, full of expectation, waiting for his kiss. Waiting for the response and recall of fond memories lost. The heat seared through my soul, melting away at the dark spot that shadows my heart. My heart thudded in anticipation at what I might discover. A curiosity for my own personal discovery had been awoken. There was something so right in the way we connected. I didn't need to remember what led to this point to understand here, with Jace, is where I belonged.

CHAPTER 18

FOR YULE, Mum had bought me a midnight blue dress with diamante detailing around the neckline. It was perfect for this New Year Eve party, and went beautifully with the snowflake necklace. I'd asked Mum to help me put it on and as her fingers tickled my neck it brought back a familiar sensation. I didn't get a full on memory but there was something good about the way wearing it made me feel.

"Did you get that for Christmas?" Mum asked.

"Yeah. I think it's from Ana." It felt like a lie but it was the only person I thought might have got me a gift that I'd not seen.

Mum carried our drinks to a table near the dance floor. We were still waiting for Jace, Denny, and Dave

to arrive. I was anxious to see Jace again as this would be the first time since he'd asked me out.

I stirred my straw around as I waited. My face lit with a smile when I saw him arrive, my former friend, now boyfriend. I couldn't help but be dazzled by his ocean blue eyes and part of me was lost at sea, wondering how I'd never noticed them all those years before.

"You look beautiful," Jace said into my ear as he placed a kiss on my cheek. Usually, he'd have said 'good' or 'great', something placid.

"You, too," I blushed back and was grateful for my drink to distract me. It was strange having Jace seeing me as beautiful. My hands sweated against the cool glass of cola. Every time I stole a glance at Jace a rush of red coursed through my body. My heart raced but I tried to act cool. It was like I'd taken something and now sitting still was difficult – I needed to get up and do something.

"It's hot in here," I said.

"What?" Jace screwed up his face.

He had shouted it but I could barely hear him over the music.

"Don't you think it's hot in here?" I said again but this time I leant towards his ear so he could hear me.

Jace leaned into my ear. "I can't hear you. Let's go outside. It's hot, too."

I giggled to myself and nodded. I followed Jace around the tables and past the dance floor. As we met with the crowd of drinkers near the bar, Jace reached back and took my hand. He pulled me through the crowd but, once outside, he didn't let go. We headed past the outdoor seating area, populated by smokers, and crossed the car park.

The winter wind chilled my hand when Jace let go so he could jump up onto the flood wall. He patted the space next to him and I hopped up beside him. We sat quietly watching the people milling around the front of the building. He gave me a side glance.

"So, what were you saying?"

"Just that I was hot."

"Still are."

Jace's flirting made me fidget with my necklace in the same way I used to play with my allergy bracelet.

"Fancy a walk along the beach?"

I nodded.

We swung our legs over the wall, and landed on the other side. A shingle pathway led towards the beach. This part of the beach wasn't visited much by anyone. There wasn't a promenade to make it accessible and the group of houses that backed onto the beach had a wall designed to protect them should there be a flood. It did its job well, as those houses stood untouched, but the obstruction was large and ugly. We wandered along, holding hands, and following the wall.

"It feels different, doesn't it?" he asked.

"Yeah."

Jace sat down on the shingle and laid back, his knees bent. I joined him but placed my legs flat. The wind kept rushing up my dress and blowing it up. I folded my hands into my lap so I didn't do a Marilyn Monroe. We stared up at the sky. The night was cool and the clouds shifted in the sky above, obscuring the stars as they raced overhead. Every so often a star would shine through.

"Ever wonder, what if this doesn't work out?"

"No," I answered honestly.

Jace rolled onto his side and brushed a curl from my face. "I don't think I could ever go back to being just friends."

Feeling him that close caused me to catch my breath. My body tingled with anticipation and I bit my lip. My dress flapped in the wind and I moved my hand to hold the material down more securely.

"Oh, Mariah..." His finger ran along my jawline gently turning my face towards his.

Be calm...

I had no idea where that thought came from - like a distant whisper in my mind. It was ridiculous, how could I 'be calm' with Jace behaving like this. He touched me as my boyfriend and I wondered if my best friend was still in there. I wondered whether I could have both my Jaces or if this was it and there was no going back.

His lips lowered towards mine and I waited for the memories to come crashing back like the waves thundering against the shore. There was a noise behind us. Higher up the bank, I could see someone in a heavy, fisherman's winter coat, the hood up and casting a shadow that hid their features. Jace helped me to my feet, which was tricky to do in heels on shingle, and pulled me into a protective embrace. There was something intimidating and menacing about the man's presence.

"Come on, Mariah," Jace said.

He kept me pulled close as we headed back the way we'd come. The man began walking, too. He appeared to be following us. Jace stopped suddenly. The man stopped, too.

Jace turned to face him. "What's your problem?"

I wasn't ready to see Jace get into a fight. I gripped his hand and heard a strange noise like a growl from the man. I pulled Jace towards the car park, the music getting louder as we got closer. We climbed over the wall and I saw Mum.

Mum stood there in a long, black and white maxi dress that wasn't very flattering for her short and dumpy figure. Her hair blew around her wildly, like a warrior woman gazing towards the battlefield. I've never been so relieved to have her checking up on me.

"What're you two doing out here?" Mum asked as she glanced at our interlocked hands.

We've held hands before but now I felt caught and Jace obviously felt the same as he let go of my hand as if I'd burned him.

"It was too hot inside," I complained.

"The smokers were by the door," Jace added.

"You'll have to put up with the heat for the countdown, you're not missing that," Mum said and smiled at Jace. "Which lovely man is going to kiss me if you're not there?"

Jace laughed. "With pleasure, Gwyn."

Mum started to lead the way back and I looked behind for our menacing stranger but they'd gone; a shadow of a threat.

Jace leaned into me. "I want you to be my first kiss this year, so we'll have to sneak off before your mum beats you to it."

Everything with Jace now felt naughty and the more we explored these new feelings the more I felt I was losing my best friend. It was bittersweet. I feared if we didn't work out, I couldn't be just friends, either.

I stacked some beer mats into a pyramid whilst Jace tapped his phone. He had been clock watching ever since we got back inside. His eagerness was making me nervous. The screen light went out and he pressed a button to wake it up again. This time, his eyes twinkled and he leaned across the table towards me.

"Wanna get a drink?"

Mum grabbed his arm. "It's almost the countdown."

"A drink can wait." Denny nodded at Jace in a silent order to sit back down.

Jace sank back into the hard-backed chair and Denny leaned back into Dave's arm. Mum still held onto his sleeve as if she knew his true intentions. Jace wasn't a good actor and 'gutted' read clearly on his face as he slouched in his seat.

"We'll be quick," I said, and got up and hurried towards the bar, hoping Mum wouldn't hold him back seeing I'd gone. I wondered where he planned to kiss me; surely he wouldn't do it at the bar in front of everyone.

His hand slipped into mine. "We can get a drink after the countdown."

I looked back over my shoulder to meet those cherished, blue eyes. A mischievous twinkle sparkled and I wanted to kiss him right then.

"10... 9... 8..."

Panic flushed my face. "Not here!"

"No," Jace agreed. His hold on my hand tightened as he quickly led me outside. As soon as we stepped out, the cool air soothed my flushed cheeks. The smokers had already headed indoors and we were alone.

"5... 4... 3..."

Jace didn't even wait for the countdown to finish. His lips pressed against mine and I stumbled back against the wall. His lips were hot and searing against my own, and I felt the rough brick rub against my skin.

My eyes closed, my vision changing from a passionate red to a burning white and a sensation like deja vu caused the hairs on my arm to stand on end.

His hunger was dangerous, like I was the prey, willingly captivated. I didn't want him to stop and then... It felt as if he had but I could still feel his lips warm against mine. His kiss didn't feel enough, as if I was pushed underwater, drowning and starved of oxygen. Gasping for more, I opened my eyes, only to be confronted by a mobile phone. There on the screen was a picture of me kissing Jace, but his hair was dark, not blonde. All I could see was the phone but slowly the rest of the room came into focus and I recognised the brick stairwell from school. Jace wasn't in focus, his arm stretched out towards me, showing me the picture but there was something not right. It didn't feel like Jace.

Trying to make sense of what I could see, I tried to pull away and pushed Jace back. This time, I really felt his lips leave mine.

"What's wrong?"

"Nothing," I shook my head unsure why my mind thought remembering the mobile phone was important. "We should probably get back inside before they notice we're gone."

Over Jace's shoulder, I saw something move at the far end of the car park. A man, similar to the one we'd seen earlier, stood in the corner. He was gone before I could say anything and I realised someone saw us kissing. I wasn't ready for anyone to know about us yet.

"Are we alright?" Jace asked.

"Never better." I gave an empty smile and hoped I was better at acting than him. I had no idea if us getting together had been a gradual process or if we'd been struck by lightning. "Jace have you ever dyed your hair?"

"You know I never have," he laughed and ran a hand through his hair. "This is all natural."

He squeezed my hand and started making his way back towards the noise and people inside. Before going in, I glanced again across the car park but no one was there. Yet, the hairs on my arms stood as if they'd been statically charged and I had that prickly sensation I was being watched.

CHAPTER 19

I WAS SWIMMING IN DARKNESS *when something grabbed my ankle. It was Mum. Her dark hair swirled around her face like octopus tentacles and the streaks of grey shone a vibrant silver. My legs were a fishtail and she had hold of my fin. She had a malicious grin on her face, dark shadows cast across her features making her appear menacing. She was pulling me down, deeper into the darkness. The further she pulled me, the harder it was to breathe. I tried to shake her off, to free myself, but the light from the surface was fading, my lungs were tightening...*

I sat up, wheezing as I sucked in a desperate breath. My navy satin dress lay crumpled on the floor from last night. Falling asleep, I'd been content from a wonderful night but now I was in a cold sweat, my heart racing. I

checked my mobile and saw the time was 3:30 am. I'd barely slept.

My room felt small like the walls were folding in on me and I was desperate to get out. I pulled back the curtain so I could open the window. The fresh air blew in and I shut my eyes whilst I inhaled. When I opened my eyes, I saw him. There, under the streetlight, a figure stood in the rain wearing a heavy coat with a black dog. The man looked like the guy from earlier at the beach and appeared to be staring up at my window.

I dived back behind my curtain and hoped he had not seen me. My heart beat so loud I worried it would wake Mum. I let out a slow steady breath and, once I felt more composed, I peeked through a gap in the curtain.

The man was gone.

I searched up and down the street but couldn't see him. A prickly sensation ran over my body as I wondered where he'd gone. I laid back in bed and struggled to fall asleep, but, at some point, I must have drifted off because the next thing I knew was being woken by my mobile phone ringing.

"Hello," I mumbled bleary-eyed. I laid back and shut my eyes. I hadn't even bothered to check who it was. Who else would be calling me other than Jace, anyway?

"Why haven't you called me? I've been going out of my mind waiting. Then, I thought, why am I waiting for *you* to call me when *I* can call you? No more waiting, I've got questions and need answers," an angry girl's voice poured into my ear.

"I think you've the wrong number," I said and went to hang up.

"Mariah!" she yelled, stopping me. "You're not getting out of this that easy."

I looked at the screen. "Ana?"

"Who else were you expecting? Murray - the guy you apparently have no interest in - but rumour has it you went to the Mistletoe Disco together? Or, Jace?" Suddenly, her voice softened, "Well, I guess he is your best friend as well as your crush."

"He's my boyfriend."

"Oh my god! It's true. I bumped into Fallon this morning and she threatened me. She said, 'Make sure your skanky friend keeps her dirty paws off Jace'."

"What's it to do with Fallon?" I asked. This Ana seemed to know me better than myself.

"She's always like that, protective of her friends. I guess she thinks she's doing Kiely some kind of justice."

Kiely! There was that name again. It was increasingly sounding like I was some relationship wrecker.

"We need to catch up."

"Duh!" she laughed. "I'm inviting myself over on Wednesday. Alright?"

"Okay."

"I want *all* the details."

I had a sinking sensation as I knew that would be a problem. I didn't want to offend her like I had Jace, and it wasn't like I could kiss her for information. I was worried about what I'd agreed to, but it had to be better to resolve this before we went back to school. Right?

Mum wriggled into her coat as she said goodbye: "If you need me for any reason, call."

"Mum, I'll be fine." I wondered why she was being so weird about leaving me at home on my own. It wasn't a big deal. She'd left me before but I guess in the past Jace and Denny had been next door - and I wasn't recovering from memory loss.

"Okay, what will you get up to whilst I'm at work."

I shrugged. "Check my homework's done, get ready for school, nothing much."

I didn't mention Ana coming over. I didn't feel Mum was being completely honest with me and it made me want to hide things from her.

She nodded. "Good. See you later."

It wasn't long before Ana arrived. We got drinks and snacks then hung out in the lounge.

"So, how'd you end up on Murray's date?"

"Wow! Straight in there with the questions."

Ana tossed her hair. "You know me."

Actually, I didn't but I could tell I should. There was no way I would be able to answer all her questions unless I started remembering.

"How was your Christmas?"

Ana wagged her finger at me. "Don't change the subject. Did you kiss him? And, how'd you end up with

Jace?"

I shrugged. I felt like a deer in headlights.

"That's not an acceptable answer."

I grimaced and clenched my fists. "I can't remember."

"What?"

I was burning up under her interrogation and rubbed the back of my neck. "I've forgotten everything. I don't even remember you."

Ana leaned forward, a gentle frown across her brow. "Are you serious? Are you okay? What happened? Did you bump your head?"

I held my hands up. "Again, with the questions."

"I'm sorry. If you could remember me, you'd know that's what I do."

"I bumped my head, right there." I pointed to the coffee table in front of us.

"Did you go to the hospital? Is that why you couldn't call me?"

Ana really did ask a lot of questions. I smiled and shook my head. "Mum wasn't concerned."

There was a gentle silence between us as she processed what I'd said. I could tell we must've been good friends. It felt familiar, like before with Jace when our relationship wasn't so complicated.

"Do you think your mum cast a spell?" Ana asked.

She knew about Mum and her spell casting. I breathed a sigh of relief and nodded. The idea had crossed my mind but it felt like a weight lifted to be able to talk to someone about it.

"Where is she?"

"Work."

"We should check her Book of Shadows and come up with a counter spell."

"We can't cast."

Ana waved her wrist at me. "What about when we healed my scars?"

"We did magic?"

Ana grinned. "We did."

She pulled me up onto my feet and led me upstairs, got the stick, and hooked the attic door down.

"What are you doing?" I asked.

Ana ignored me and climbed up, she then passed down a big, heavy book. Instantly, I recognised it as Mum's Book of Shadows.

"How'd you know it was there?"

Ana dropped her head to one side and looked very unimpressed with me. "We've done this before."

I nodded. I had to sit down to open the book as it was so heavy. I flicked to the end but there was no mention of any forgetting spell. I felt a little defeated.

"Maybe it wasn't my mum?"

"Maybe."

"Maybe it's the creepy man."

Ana grabbed my wrist in alarm. "What creepy man?"

"I keep seeing him. First, on the beach New Year's Eve, spying on Jace and I. But, since then, I've seen him in the early hours, standing in the street watching my bedroom."

Ana gasped: "Call the police."

I shook my head. "They can't arrest someone for standing in the street. Plus, he doesn't stay long."

"What does he look like?"

"He wears a yellow fisherman's jacket with the hood up so I can't see his face."

"Serial killer."

"No, he has a black Labrador with him."

"Do you think he might be walking his dog and it shits outside your house?"

I laughed. That made me feel better.

"Ana, we're friends?" I checked and she nodded. "What can you tell me that I should know."

"Let me see..." She thought about where to start. "Murray wanted to take you to the Mistletoe Disco but, you told me, you didn't want to go with him." Her eyes narrowed as she looked accusingly at me but I have no idea why I lied or changed my mind. "Fallon says you went together but is more pissed off that Jace dumped Kiely on Christmas Eve!" Ana pulled a face. "That is pretty cold."

I nodded in agreement.

"Somehow, Jace has gone from being the friend you're crushing on to your boyfriend."

"He came to my house and kissed me. He thought it was what I wanted."

"Maybe you finally told him?"

"When he kissed me, I remembered a little bit."

Ana threw her hands up. "There we go. Snog Jace. Get your memories back."

"That's my plan," I smiled.

Ana's jaw dropped in surprise and I giggled, realising this was one of those rare moments she was speechless.

I remembered reading a story, once, about how frogs remember where they were born and return to the same pond to lay their spawn. It felt a little like that as I entered the school building. It was instinct that I knew the combination to my locker and where my homeroom was. I could see in my mind where I needed to go but people's faces were hazed out.

Some of the lockers in the building were bright, fun colours, but not ours. Now I was in the upper years, the school has to be taken seriously. This message was communicated in every way the school found possible - like dull, grey lockers. I opened my locker's chrome door.

Ana appeared next to me. "I can't wait to get back in the pool. I've missed it so much. Please tell me you remembered we did that?"

Swimming?

I recalled the photo I'd seen of us at the pool. I'd thought it strange as I wasn't allowed to go swimming.

"I don't swim."

She winked. "Don't forget how lucky you are to be on the team!"

"I'm on the team?" I laughed, not sure if she was joking.

She tilted her head to one side. "Practice tomorrow?"

"Definitely," I replied with false enthusiasm but inside I allowed her words to wash over my mind. Could I really be on the swim team? Me?

Entering my homeroom was a little scary. Everyone knew who they belonged to and sat with their groups, in their normal places. They were exchanging stories about their holiday celebrations. I took a seat next to the window and watched the clouds making pictures. For January, the sky was a nice shade of blue and it could be mistaken for a summer's day.

Three months isn't long, I can't imagine much had happened in such a short time frame, but, as I listened in on people's stories, I realised a lot had happened in only a few days, and I began to doubt my theory.

Miss Michaels entered the room with a small, leather briefcase which she promptly placed on her desk and opened to reveal her laptop. After some clicking and tapping, followed by some huffing and puffing, she pulled out a pad of lined paper and a pen. Placing them on her desk next to the redundant laptop, she stood up in the centre of the room and deliberately coughed to get our attention.

"Welcome back," Mrs Michaels projected her voice so the last few people would fall silent. "Did you all have a lovely break?" She waited as if expecting us all to implode with answers but instead received mumbles trailing off into silence. "Well, the laptop doesn't seem willing to join us, so I'm going to have to do the register manually. If you could all please write your name down on this piece of paper," she tore a sheet from her pad and gave it to the student at the front of the classroom, "pass it around, then you can carry on catching up."

It was then that I realised Jace wasn't in my form group. All I could hope for was that we at least share some classes together. I got a sinking feeling that today would be a really long day and wondered how I got through it before.

I refused to spend the rest of the day feeling out of place and decided to text Jace. Mobile phones aren't allowed in lessons. We have to keep them in our lockers, 'at our own risk'.

I leaned against my locker as I sent Jace a text. It felt like ages since we kissed and I wanted to check if it was real, that I hadn't dreamed up the whole thing.

Mariah: Meet me for lunch?

I started but have no idea of where to tell him to meet me. Do we have a meeting spot already? What is our usual arrangement for lunch?

Mariah: At the library

I pressed send and made my way to the meeting point. I don't know why I chose the library for our rendezvous point but the location popped into my head. As I made my way there it felt familiar.

I hoped he had his phone on him and not left it in his locker. I wasn't sure if I should wait outside the big double doors or inside. I felt stupid standing outside the library waiting so I stepped inside and read the notice board.

There, I saw the advertisement for the swimming club; training was on a Wednesday after school. Remembering Ana talking about practising tonight and tomorrow, I realized I must enjoy swimming to be going that often. Was I practising to improve, to impress, for the team? I felt like a detective that had found a clue.

When Jace still hadn't come after ten minutes I got anxious and decided to wait outside the door so he could see me. I ignored the looks I got from people.

When Jace didn't arrive after twenty minutes I realised he wasn't coming. Like someone stood up, I slunk away in shame. I re-entered the library and sat alone in a corner.

The librarian, Mrs Hicks, approached me. She was slim, with dark, curly hair and silver streaks, and she wore deep purple-rimmed glasses that sat at the tip of her nose. She smiled with fondness as if we knew each other well and handed me some books.

"These are new in. I saw them and thought of you."

I accepted her offer with a smile and a thank you. I realised I must come here often enough for her to make recommendations. I read the back of the books and see Mrs Hicks knows I enjoy reading romance – at least some things never change.

Familiarity made me smile, as I dipped into the books, allowing them to help me escape the disappointment that I wasn't going to see Jace today. Mrs Hick's selection was so good, I didn't even realise I hadn't eaten lunch.

Mariah: Where are you Jace?

But he didn't reply to my text and when I finally went to bed that night I struggled to fall asleep as I wrestled with whether to be angry or worried about it.

At some point, I must have fallen asleep as I had the same recurring nightmare at 3:30 am, and discovered the strange man outside my window spying on me. I struggled to fall asleep again only to be woken at 5:00 am by a text.

Who texts at that time in the morning?

Jace: Sorry Mariah. Couldn't do lunch. Ring you during break X

He was the one that wanted to go out with me! Him! Now, I felt as if he was blowing me off, and for what? His text message had helped me make up my mind. Now, I was so pissed off I couldn't fall back to sleep. Maybe I didn't need to kiss Jace to get my memories back, maybe there was another way? Maybe I could kiss anyone?

My hand clutched the necklace around my neck and I wondered if this Murray person, whoever he is, could help me. The necklace brought me some kind of comfort, almost as if it were enchanted. I wished I knew where it had come from.

In a sleepy state, I made my way downstairs. My bad mood was here to stay and I started making digs at myself. To think, I believed I could actually fall for Jace if I let myself.

It was cold and dark in the kitchen as I began making myself breakfast. A nice, warm cup of tea and a bowl of porridge sounded perfect. The kettle clicked and the microwave beeped and soon I was sitting on the sofa, watching television. My feet resting on the brown, glass coffee table that I had woken up next to the day I'd fainted.

Repeats of 'Charmed' were running and I allowed my imagination to wander with the probability that some evil demon was responsible for what had happened to me, sucking my memories from my mind to feed on. However, part of me knew they were still in me. I just had to find the key to unlock them. Currently, that key was Jace. No matter how big a jerk he was being, I would have to find a way to forgive him, to use him.

"I thought I heard you awake," Mum said entering the lounge/dinner as I blew on another spoonful of porridge. "How come you're up so early?"

I eyed her suspiciously. Mum was a fortune-teller and a pretty good witch. When she found me on the floor, her initial pleasure at my last memory being 'Jace moving away' had led me to believe she knew more than she was letting on.

"I can't remember!" I searched her face for a sign of guilt.

"Well, why don't you go back to bed?" she said without flinching.

Her lack of guilt didn't clear her name. Mum had an award-winning poker face, something she developed from fortune-telling – you can't let on that you've seen something terrible in someone's future if you have no intention of warning them about it. People don't like to pay good money for bad news. Maybe that was it – maybe it was best I didn't know. Convinced that she was definitely keeping something from me, I worried why.

"I'm awake now," I shrugged.

She left me to it and I soon heard her banging around in the kitchen, loading or unloading the washing machine. I could hear the dial clicking as she turned it on.

"Mariah, come and see the sunrise!" she called from the kitchen.

I wandered through. I'd never been up early enough to see the sunrise. Mum stood at the back door with a mug of tea in her hand. It was still dark but the clouds had turned a dark burnt orange that almost completely hid the golden colour of the sky. The shade reminded me of fire. Rising up from behind the rooftop of the other terrace houses, I could see the hot white semi-circle as the sun.

Mum wrapped her arm around me and pulled me in close for a cuddle and placed a kiss on my forehead.

"Beautiful, like your hair."

I snuggled into her. She smelled sweet like freshly baked cakes. A feeling of safety and security doused the suspicions that shrouded her. If she didn't want to tell me something, I respected that. Right there and then, I decided to forgive her. We stayed close, as the sun crept up, until fully revealed in its fullness.

Chapter 20

WATCHING THAT SUNRISE had been a positive experience for me and turned my morning around. I saw it as a new day, a new start, and anything could happen. I was ready to give Jace a chance to explain; I'm sure he had a good reason why he couldn't meet me for lunch.

At break, I stood at my locker, staring down at my mobile, willing it to ring. I slumped. I'd become one of those sad girls that hung around waiting for a guy to call. I decided if Jace failed to ring me, I'd dump him.

Part of me knew thinking it was easier than actually doing it. I had begun to fall for him already. Either that or I was remembering why I loved him in the first place. Love – that was a strong word. I wasn't sure yet if I meant it.

"There you are."

I didn't need to look up to know that sing-song voice was Ana, but I did.

"What're you doing?" she asked.

"Waiting for Jace to call."

"Have you seen the broken window?"

"What broken window?"

"Someone broke into the pool house over the holidays." Ana shook her head. "I don't get it. Why would someone do that?"

I shrugged.

"Are you going to get that?" Ana nodded at my phone.

My phone was still on silent – in accordance with school policy – so I didn't realise it was ringing. Jace's name flashed on the screen, demanding my attention. I quickly answered, unsure how long he'd been waiting.

"Jace!" I cringed hearing the desperation in my voice, especially with Ana there to witness it.

"Freckles," I felt my heart thump in response to his voice. "Sorry, I couldn't meet, I play every lunch so I don't get subbed by the team."

"Oh…"

Jace had never been into football before! He was snubbing me for a game he never liked to impress lads he didn't even know that well. Where the hell did that rank me?

"Don't be like that. You can always come and watch?"

"Oh, thank you," I said sarcastically. "I'd love to come and sit in the cold whilst you kick a ball around a muddy pitch."

"Don't come then!" he snapped and hung up.

I stared at the blank screen. How dare he hang up on me?

I threw my phone into the back of my locker with all my force. There was a loud dong as it collided with the metal. Little sparks shot off it and zapped my fingers... it had looked more like sparks had zapped from my fingers, but that was ridiculous. Regardless, sparks and a phone weren't a good combination.

There was a heavy feeling in my stomach. I retrieved my phone and grimaced over the large crack along the screen, making the display unreadable. The glass reflected back at me, like a mirror of myself. Broken.

"Are you okay?"

I almost jumped. In the moment, I'd forgotten Ana was there. I swallowed around a lump in my throat.

"I'm fine. Jace is a dick."

"Do you wanna talk about it?"

I shook my head and shoved my mobile into my swim bag. I felt an overwhelming urge to find a way to fix it. As if by fixing this, it'd be proof I could fix myself.

The lunch bell rang and, despite my better judgement, I found myself standing at the edge of the playing field.

I was still pissed off with Jace. We hadn't spent any time together since New Year's Eve. Our only contact had been via text, email, and instant message, and all the time he'd made out he couldn't wait to see me. Now we're in the same bloody building and all he could manage was a phone call to tell me he's too busy playing frigging football!

Everything was forgiven when he first noticed I was here. Our eyes met and everything around us disappeared. As he jogged over, I felt like the most important girl in the world.

"Freckles. You came!" He grabbed me in an enthusiastic hug and spun me around so my feet didn't touch the ground. When he finally put me down I felt a bit dizzy.

"Shame, shame, know your name," I heard a lad jeer at us.

"Ignore them." He swiped with his arm as if he could swat them away. "I'm really glad you came."

"I almost didn't," I confessed.

"Sorry, I shouldn't have hung up on you; I just felt you weren't getting what I was saying."

"It's okay," I said and could have kicked myself. It wasn't okay but it was too late to take it back.

He pecked my forehead with a kiss and then backpedalled his return to the pitch.

As he returned, the boy from before ran up to join him.

"So, that's your girlfriend then, is it?"

"Yeah, so hands off," Jace joked back.

My heart fluttered. There it was, made official; girlfriend, not 'girl friend'; my new status in his life. It felt good and despite the cold, I couldn't help but smile.

"What are you grinning about?"

One of the pretty girls from the benches had walked over towards me. She was stunning but you could tell from the way her nose wrinkled that she was a complete bitch.

As if she had slapped me with her words, my smile dropped from my face.

"Nothing!"

"It didn't look like nothing to me. It looked like you were getting off on flaunting the fact you're a backstabbing bitch! You pretended to be Jace's friend when really you're worming your way into his pants. You're the worst sort there is!" If looks could kill, then this girl would have put me six feet under. "See that bench over there? We always sit there, always have, always will. Now, if I am sitting there and see you... well, let's just say the next time, I won't bother to give you a friendly warning."

"Is Kiely...?"

Her hand pointed to the benches. "Don't even say her name! That's my best friend! And you don't want to know what I'll do for my friends!" Her face twisted into a sarcastic smile. "Obviously not what you'd do for your so-called-friend, slut!"

I followed her finger to where Kiely sat amongst a group of girls taking selfies like it was some kind of Instagram shoot. They all sat about the benches in various poses, being beautiful, and pretending not to be watching us.

"Kiely is a real friend. Not someone I'm trying to screw. If I ever find out you and Jace were fooling around behind her back, I'll kill you. You'll see me everywhere you go and nowhere will be safe!"

I had a sinking feeling that if I didn't want to get my head kicked in by the mega bitch, then I needed to keep my mouth shut.

"Are you listening, bitch! Get the hell out of here!"

"Sorry," I mumbled.

"Sorry, Fallon!" she ordered.

I wasn't going to say that, so I nodded. With my head hanging low, I scurried back into the school building and retreated to my sanctuary, the library. I came to the conclusion that today was one of those days that is destined to go wrong, no matter what I do. I felt defeated and, for the rest of the day, I waited for the bell to ring so I could go home, go to bed, and start over.

The fluffy, white clouds and warm sky of this morning had been replaced with dark, menacing rain clouds. Despite it being January, some people had been stupid enough to come dressed for summer; typical English behaviour, to celebrate the first glimpse of the sun.

Fortunately, being a redhead caused me to shun the sun like a vampire. I was one of the smart ones, wrapped up in a protective winter coat and scarf. Admittedly, I hadn't brought my hat and gloves but I didn't want to mess my hair up and I could always shove my hands in my coat pockets if it got too cold.

As I made my way home, I could feel the rain soaking my legs, through my uniform, and the wetness seeped into my flat shoes. I had my hood pulled up and I needed one hand to keep it there as the icy, cold breeze tried to rip it away. Red curls whipped out from under my hood, licking at my chilled fingers like a vicious, damp flame. My hand was so cold that my numb fingers lost their grip and the wind was quick to grab my hood and throw it back onto my shoulders.

Nothing hindered the rain as it poured down on my head and cascaded down my neck, soaking the collar of my white school shirt. Both my hands reached up and tried to replace my hood but the wind caught it like a sail, pushing it backwards. I gave up and trudged onward.

Without warning, I had my first flash of memory without kissing Jace.

I felt submerged in water, the sounds of the world were muffled and distant. I was dropping; I could feel the depth increase as I fell, going deeper and deeper. Tiny bubbles tickling the rim of my nose but my lips were warm. I was kissing someone... probably Jace?

Then, it was dark again. My legs felt shaky and I hurried home.

I felt ecstatic that I didn't need Jace to recover my memories; I felt lighter, free – in control. I just needed the right trigger.

I hung my coat up in the hallway with my scarf and took off my blazer, leaving it in an untidy lump on the bottom step. I kicked off my soggy shoes, slipped off my wet tights, and carried the soggy lump to the washing machine.

In the kitchen, I flicked the kettle on ready to make a hot drink to warm myself up. As I waited for the water to boil, I thought back to that strange vision I had. It didn't feel finished.

The rain pelted down, banging against the window, like someone urgently tapping on my brain, hinting at the last memory's need to be fully restored, drumming into me what I must do.

I had to get back out there and embrace my trigger.

Without pause for thought, I slipped off the stool and made my way out into the garden. I let the rain claim my uniform. Mud seeped between my toes. I held my arms up to the sky above, allowing the rain to reach all of me. Rain drenched my face and I had to shut my eyes. My knee-length, pleated skirt took a little longer to soak; I spun around to allow the rain to saturate it all. My lips were numb and my shirt clung to me like a second skin.

I wasn't sure if my plan would work but… it started with a strange feeling of pressure on my mind, like a dull headache. The sense of a heavy door that didn't want to open – perhaps shouldn't be opened - but I was tugging, pulling at it, I wanted in. I saw a flash of light. I turned my head up at the sky with glee, I'd done it; I had access.

This time I was running. I could feel a sense of urgency. Clothes that weren't mine and felt out of place on my body, clinging and binding to me. On my feet, I wore strappy heels and mud seeped over the front, coating my feet in a wet, sloppy brown. I was so cold and my chest hurt with a deep, physical, inner ache. The pain was so unbearable I could feel myself pulling away. I didn't want to be here. I didn't want to remember.

But I need to remember!

The vision was turning black and the pain was easing. I knew I was coming back to the real world. I fought against it. I tried to get back to the place I'd been on the walk home.

Yes, I was back in the water - engulfed. I could see the underwater lights of a pool. My hands ran across the flesh of his body, his shirt was open. Never before had I noticed how toned and muscular his chest was. There, on his chest, above each pectoral muscle, were four dark circles, similar to a tattoo, but they glowed silver. My fingers reached forward, running over them - a perfect fit, each tip slid into the markings.

"Mariah! What are you doing?" Mum yelled, bringing me back.

I shivered as I opened my eyes. My heart pounded from the intensity of what I'd experienced and my cheeks flushed with my naughty secret and the sense of being caught.

"Are you crazy? You'll catch your death in this! Get in!"

Her warning was probably already too late! My

breathing started to stabilise and I reminded myself that I had nothing to be ashamed of. Whatever Jace and I were doing in the pool, I still had my clothes on.

Chapter 21

THE NEXT SCHOOL DAY WAS UNEVENTFUL. As I approached the pool, I felt a flutter of nerves and worried about what truths I might unravel by swimming. Relief hit me when I saw Ana smile upon entering the changing room. She was already in her swimming costume.

"You made it. You worried me when you didn't show yesterday. I tried calling but I couldn't get hold of you."

I could see why I liked this girl already. She didn't get hung up on things. "Sorry about that. My phone broke and I had one of those days."

She shrugged. "No worries. Do you want me to wait for you, or meet you in the pool?"

"Meet you in the pool," I said, relieved to be left alone for a few minutes. As Ana threw her towel over her shoulder and made her way towards the pool, I noticed how she was all skin and bones. Should I say something? No, best to leave it for now, as I wasn't certain how well we knew each other.

I changed into my costume; I had no idea where I'd got it as I knew how Mum felt about me swimming. I threw my blue towel over my shoulder in the same fashion Ana had and followed the other girls out to the pool.

Dropping my towel on one of the brick islands, I slipped down the steps, into the cool water, and bounced my way along the wall towards Ana. I searched the line-up of faces for anyone that might be familiar.

Nope. Nope. Nope. What a pointless exercise. I couldn't believe how disappointed I was. What did I expect?

Then, I saw a guy making his way towards the pool. He wore loose, black shorts with a navy waistband. His chest was well toned and he had a warm tan to his skin. He scanned the faces in much the same manner as I had but when he got to me he stopped and winked.

Against my will, my body tingled in response. My heart skipped a beat and I found myself wondering who this handsome stranger was with the dark hair and eyes that shot me like a bolt of lightning.

Then, I saw the markings. I knew this guy. I knew what he did to me. The way he had made me burn under the cool water. The heated memory I re-lived when I stood in the rain. I'd thought it was Jace but this guy had the markings on his chest. Now, they were pink like a burn.

"So, it's true," Ana gasped next to me.

I sucked in air. I hadn't realised I'd been holding my breath until Ana had brought me back with her voice. There was no need to ask what was true; she was already answering my question.

"Murray got a burn tattoo!"

So, this was Murray! This guy, whose effect on me I couldn't explain.

I turned to see him pass and the strangest sensation hit me. Bubbles burst in my tummy as he smiled and I felt as if I was drowning in the sensation. I wanted to giggle, laugh, and scream. My body wanted to grab him, to kiss him. I gasped and took a deep breath, ducking under the water to calm myself down, but the feeling wouldn't go. When I popped back up, I was relieved that he had made his way to the other side.

The rest of practice, I made a point of not acknowledging Murray. I listened as Ana set me personal time goals. Murray stayed up the other end of the pool as far away from me as possible. Ana liked to be in charge of the stopwatch and sat out on the side most of the session timing me, only getting in to do her own lap.

Finally, to my relief, pool time was up. I was loving swimming but Murray was a dangerous threat to my relationship with Jace. Somehow, this guy had a power over me and I'd have to steer clear until I can figure out how to get a grip on myself.

I grabbed my towel off the island and heard Mr

Griffen call out, "Murray, can I have a word."

It caused me to notice that Murray was right next to me, as he reached down to lift up his own towel. My eyes followed droplets of water running down his toned chest, in a way that made me feel perverse. Our eyes met and I could barely breathe in his presence. I swallowed and made a hurried exit for the changing rooms.

The showers were warm and I wished they were cool. I needed something to snap me out of the warm fuzziness my mind was experiencing from my brief interaction with Murray.

"I thought you and Murray hated each other," a girl I didn't know said as she stepped into the shower next to me.

"Yeah," I said, trying to limit my input. The mere mention of his name made my blood race in the most joyous way and I wanted to giggle at the idea that I could hate him.

"Well, he was checking you out so bad, it was embarrassing," the girl said with a hint of jealousy.

"What do you mean?" I asked inquisitively and tried to hide my treacherous heart desiring that Murray like me back. *I'm with Jace.*

"His eyes never left you. Didn't you notice?"

I shook my head.

"I did," another girl interrupted. She was scrunching shampoo in her hair. "Baby girl, if I was you, I'd steer clear of that guy." She leaned back allowing the water to wash the shampoo away before meeting my gaze.

"He's a womanizer."

The first girl nodded in agreement. "He wants one thing and once he gets it you'll be a memory on his Insta feed."

The second girl wrinkled her nose whilst patting a bottle of conditioner to try and get the last bit out. "He doesn't usually go for virgins, though."

"What makes you think I'm a virgin?" I asked blankly.

"Are you?" the older girls asked with a sneer.

I blushed.

They laughed. Clearly my response told them everything they wanted to know. But the truth of the matter was that I didn't know.

I lay on my stomach on my bed contemplating how to solve my math homework, when Mum entered the room carrying a pile of my clean clothes.

"Good day at school?" she enquired.

I nodded, even though it wasn't. It was easier to lie than talk about it and I knew if I told her the truth she would need to know more. She was entitled to her secrets and I was entitled to mine!

"Look what I've got!" she said placing the pile of clothes down on my dressing table stool and lifting up a small cardboard box she'd rested on the top.

"What is it?" I asked.

"Don't get too excited. It's basic, but I know how important it is to you." Mum flipped the box in her hands so I could see the front. It was a mobile phone.

"Thanks, Mum."

She passed it over and I marvelled at her generosity. She didn't have much money but she had gone out and got this for me, despite my reckless behaviour. I felt a bit sheepish.

"Hope you don't mind it as an early birthday present. I'll bake you a cake for your actual birthday and something small to unwrap. Is that okay?"

"That's fine," I said grinning at my present and feeling a little less guilty. Mum needed some reassuring so I gave her a hug. "Your cakes are the best."

She kissed my forehead and left the room. Pausing in the door frame, she spied me over her shoulder. Already, I was pulling the box open and removing the contents.

"The store said you can put your sim card in and keep your old number."

"Thanks, Mum." Glancing up, I gave her a nod, and then scrambled under my desk to plug the charger in and bring the handset to life.

As I crawled out from under the desk, I knocked the stool and the neatly balanced pile of folded clothes topped to the floor. The smell of clean laundry wafted up from the floor. I picked up the items, catching the scent, and realised Mum used the same powder as Denny. All my clothes smelled deliciously like Jace.

Nostalgically, I picked up a jumper and held it to

my face taking a deep breath, pretending that the soft, woolly goodness was him. Had this smell ever made him think of me?

The smell took me back in time. I could feel it coming before the flash even happened. A feeling of drifting away but still being conscious, I was flying across a plane of darkness, looking for a break in the hold, a glimmer of a memory.

My legs felt bare. I could hear the distant thud of a heartbeat that isn't my own. He felt close. Something was coming into focus; I recognised the Coca-Cola duvet before I saw his face. I was in bed with Jace.

My eyes flashed open.

My heart thudded against my ribs.

It was another memory jolt without kissing Jace! I kept sniffing my clothes trying to get back. I needed to know what I was doing in Jace's bed. How far had we gone? Had we done it? Was he my first? I kept thinking about what the older girls had said earlier about Murray only going for girls that aren't virgins. Did he know what I couldn't remember?

I felt seriously disturbed that I couldn't remember my first time, or if I'd even had a first time...

The weekend was off to a good start. Dave picked Mum and I up, and we were on our way to Jace's. To me, the trip felt new but I knew we must have been before. We drove past the Victorian and Edwardian houses that bordered the town centre, then we passed a stream of new builds that followed along the cliff tops. The houses here were big and expensive. They had balconies with sea views and driveways and garages for more than one car.

We turned off into the estate and, although the houses here didn't have the sea view, they were still large. Dave pulled up the driveway of his home and I took in the brick front wall, neat green lawn, and well-kept border of evergreen plants. At the porch, there was an empty hanging basket, waiting for spring to be filled. Everything was perfect and homely. I could only imagine how happy Jace, Denny, and Dave must be living here.

Denny must have heard us coming as she opened the front door to welcome us in. Something was different. I couldn't quite put my finger on what had changed at first, but then it hit me. Denny was bigger, not fat, but pregnant. A proud, large, round bump stuck out. I'd no idea whether I knew of her pregnancy or not. I followed Mum's lead.

Mum approached Denny and placed a hand on her belly. "Denny, you're glowing. How are you doing?"

We knew – phew! I wasn't sure how I was going to pretend I hadn't noticed. She was huge! She had to be at least six months pregnant.

"Good, how about you?" she asked as she ushered us in.

"Freckles," Jace cheered as he squeezed past his

mum and embraced me in a warm hug. I felt prickly at the thought that Jace might kiss me in front of our parents and breathed out a sigh of relief when he didn't. Our new relationship was disorientating without understanding what led to us to get together. Now that I'd had flashbacks without kissing Jace, I was starting to wonder if this was a good idea, but how could I break up with him without losing him?

"I'm good, thanks. Is that the kettle I can hear?" Mum answered.

"I hope so," Dave agreed and the adults all went into the house, leaving Jace and I alone.

"I volunteered us to paint the baby's room," Jace informed me.

"Great," I smiled.

As the last one in, I shut the door behind me. Following Jace upstairs, I felt an urge to explore the house. It seemed huge and unfamiliar. I'd no idea where anything was, even though I was sure I'd been given a tour the first time I visited.

Jace pushed open a white, painted, wooden door on the upstairs landing and we entered. The floor was covered in beige dust sheets and in the centre was a fold-out table with two tins of paint, a tray, two rollers, two brushes, and some masking tape.

Jace pointed to a lump of clothes. "Mum said we've got to wear old clothes when we start painting. Sorry about them."

"Okay."

"She also said we've got to put masking tape all

around before we even start."

Putting masking tape around the windows and skirting board wasn't as easy as it sounded. We peeled off and re-stuck the tape so much that some bits lost their stick and had to be redone. It was tricky to get it to go in a straight line.

"Have you told your mum about us?" I asked.

"God, no! She'd never let you stay over again!"

I blushed as I thought of the vision I'd had of us in bed. Was Jace hoping for a repeat performance? Nerves tied a sickening, tight knot in my stomach. It'd be like my first time but Jace wouldn't know. I thought about telling him about my memory loss but I couldn't find the words. Talking to Jace no longer felt easy. I wanted Ana.

He frowned. "Your mum doesn't know, does she?"

That was a good question. As a self-proclaimed psychic, I wouldn't be surprised if she'd known before anything had even happened.

"I don't think so."

"We should keep it that way. Don't you agree?"

I nodded even though hiding our relationship made me feel uncomfortable, like it was a dirty secret. The thought gave me a strange sense of familiarity. I wished I could remember why.

"Well, that's enough masking tape." He passed me a worn out pair of joggers and faded t-shirt. "Do you want to get changed in the bathroom or my room?"

I shrugged. "The bathroom?"

I didn't have a clue where either room was and

hoped when I got in the hallway there might be clues. To my relief the bathroom door was open and I could spy the start of a bathtub. I locked the door behind me and got changed. I checked my reflection in the mirror and, as I did, I felt something shift.

My stomach turned and my chest tightened. I felt bolts of pain shooting through my heart. My lip quivered and I saw my face crumple. Tears flowed down my cheeks without cause. My hands gripped the edge of the sink so tight my knuckles were white and an icy sheen shone up from the enamel and felt cold to the touch.

I jumped back and saw the tips of my fingers had turned blue. I wiped away the tears from my cheek and ran my hands under the hot tap to warm them up.

The vision had felt so real.

Am I going insane, imagining things that aren't there? Why'd I cry real tears? I hope Jace doesn't notice – how would I explain it?

There was a knock at the door and I froze.

"Are you ready?"

"Coming."

I picked up my pile of folded clothes and I'm about to unlock the door when there's a flash.

I see my fingers there, once upon a time, but the bolt is caked in a wintry frost.

The image was brief but it was enough to tell me I had been here before even though it didn't make sense.

I was still shivering when I stepped into the hall. Jace slipped an arm around my waist drawing me towards him.

"You look cute in my clothes."

I realised that I recognised this hall. This was where I had stood when he had tried to kiss me and I had turned my face so he got my cheek. This time, his lips met mine and the kiss fluttered through me and rested on my heart.

Why had I not wanted that before?

Jace was oblivious to my thoughts and was already in the baby's room, using a screwdriver to open a tin of paint. I drifted in behind him, trying to make sense of the jigsaw puzzle of flashes. What happened in the bathroom couldn't have been real. How legit are my memories? Am I interpreting things right or had my imagination gone haywire?

Jace poured some paint into the tray and I helped myself to a roller.

"Yellow, 'cause we don't know if it's a girl or a boy."

I couldn't help but wonder about babies – my own. It's not that I want them anytime soon, but I've always thought one day, when I am older, starting a family was definitely something I'd want to do.

"Have your mum and Dave thought of any names yet?"

"They want another 'J' name. They're thinking Jade for a girl, Jaden for a boy."

"What names do you like?"

Jace shrugged. "Never thought about it."

"Don't you want kids?"

He ran a hand through his hair and shifted on his feet. "Mariah, we just got together, aren't we a bit young for this conversation?"

"What if I were pregnant?"

"Well... I don't know. I'd want to know who the daddy is?" Jace stopped painting and walked over to the paint tray and put his roller down. "Are you trying to freak me out?"

"What's that meant to mean?"

"That we best be careful, 'cos that's not a decision I'm ready to make!"

"Would you dump me?" I shook my roller at him and a splatter of yellow spots showered him.

"Look what you've done." Jace began wiping splashes from his face and out of his hair. He lifted his roller from the tray and I saw in his face that he was thinking about getting me back. "We're young, Freckles. I wanna go to university. I wanna get a good job, a career. Then, I'll think about settling down, marriage, and kids."

I was shocked. It'd been a long time since we'd talked about our futures – last time Jace had wanted to be a fireman. We'd seen a fireman rescuing a cat from a drainpipe and Jace obsessed about wanting the big ladder for climbing. He had been six at the time, but him wanting to be a fireman had stuck with me. I couldn't imagine he'd need university for that. "What do you want to do at uni?"

"Not sure yet, but Dave says if you've got a degree you can get a better-paid job."

"So, not a fireman, then?"

"I can't believe you remember that," he smiled with

warmth. "I could volunteer, and I still want to rescue animals. I was thinking about becoming a vet?"

"Don't you need to be really smart for that?"

"What are you trying to say?" he laughed.

I laughed back. Jace was top of most classes, and I'd meant that he'd need to study for quite a few years to get qualified.

"Wish I knew what I wanted to do."

"You'll figure it out," he said as if he knew it all.

I felt an urge to take that smug grin off his face. Grabbing a brush off the table, I dipped it in the paint and flicked it his way.

"Oi! Unfair advantage!" he laughed and grabbed the other brush. He was quick to load it up with paint and I raced round to the other side of the table. He chased after me and when he realised he wasn't going to catch me, he leaned over and painted a line up my arm.

The brush ran cold and wet, licking against the hairs of my arm. I ducked under the table and painted a big dollop on his left foot. He ducked down to meet me and I giggled at his yellow-speckled face and twinkling, blue eyes.

"Ooo, you asked for it," I teased and jabbed forward with my paintbrush but he caught my hand. My other hand reached out for his wrist to stop his brush getting me but there was no resistance, he wasn't trying to attack me. He was leaning forward and I knew he was going to kiss me.

He felt sure and confident; playful and mischievous.

Still clasping his wrist, his arm pushed my hand back as his fingers ran up the outside of my thighs. I tingled all over for him and let go of his wrist, allowing him free reign to claim whatever part of my body he wanted. But he didn't. He stopped. His forehead pressed against me.

"You look beautiful in yellow. I should've told you that the first time we kissed, when you wore your summer dress."

Our first kiss, how I longed to know it.

His finger ran a careless trail of yellow paint down my nose and finished with a short but delightful kiss on my lips. "I know you want to take things slow but I've waited so long, it's hard to resist you."

"Mmm," I hummed with contentment. I wanted to say more but I was a loss for words.

Moving away, he got out from under the table. "Come on, Freckles, we've got to get this room done."

Still crouching under the table like a naughty little fairy, I felt as if I had enough happy thoughts to fly me to Neverland. The tricky part was using my wobbly legs. Somehow, I managed to move backwards and return to my painting with a silly, sunshine smile painted on my face that wasn't the result of yellow paint.

CHAPTER 22

W ARRIVED HOME and, as I closed the front door behind me, I was filled with a sudden sense of dread.

My body tingled, and I felt sick with rage. I screamed to let it out, and raised my hands, my fingers spread out. I gasped as I saw white lightning dancing between my fingertips. My hair whipped around me as a gust of wind made every door in the house slam shut.

"Mariah."

Mum's voice was soft and full of concern as her hand gently rocked my shoulder. My eyes shot open as I returned to the real world. Sweat prickled my forehead. I bit my trembling lip as I looked around the hallway. I was relieved to discover my hands were perfectly ordinary.

"Mariah, are you okay?" Mum moved her head so

she could look me in the eyes.

I shook my head.

"What happened? Why did you scream?"

I took a few slow steady breaths to calm myself down and Mum rubbed my back.

"I keep seeing things."

"What sort of things?"

I lifted my hands up to my face and rubbed my eyes. "Things that can't be real."

"You can tell me." She eyed me with concern but I knew that fake smile - it was her fortune teller's poker face.

I shook my head and shrugged her off me. "Lightning! I created lightning with my hands."

"Oh, Mariah, listen to yourself. That's crazy," Mum gasped and placed a hot hand against my forehead. "You definitely have a fever – sounds like you were hallucinating.I told you standing in the rain wouldn't be good for you. You best get to bed and rest."

She helped me up the stairs to my bed. I was happy when she left me alone with my thoughts but I didn't believe for a second that I had a fever. I didn't feel hot.

Although she was *acting* concerned, I wasn't fooled. If she believed I was hallucinating, she would treat it more seriously. Wouldn't the average concerned mother rush their child to the GP or even A&E? If this was a fever, there was nothing ordinary about it...

'Nothing ordinary', now that has Mum's name written all over it.

Once alone, I called Ana.

"Hey, Mariah," her voice sang into the phone in a complete contrast to how I was feeling.

I whispered, "Ana. I've started having bizarre visions."

"Why are you whispering? Are you alright?" Her words were quick and her tone full of concern.

"No. I'm freaking out about this amnesia. If you even call it that?" I kept my eye on the door and was trying to listen out for Mum's footsteps. I didn't want her to know I was on the phone.

"Have you spoken to your mum?"

"She's not bothered."

"You know why? She did this."

"What?" I screwed up my face.

"She's not fixing you because she broke you, on purpose. The question is why? What did she want you to forget?"

I shook my head. "She wouldn't do that. And, I remember waking up on the floor."

"Well, I've done some research into memory loss. The banged head scenario is possible, and it's good news your memories are coming back."

"What if they aren't real? Mum called them hallucinations."

"What kind of things are you seeing?"

"Ice where there isn't ice. Lightning where there isn't any. And, they're like superpowers, coming from me."

"Could it be magic?"

"I don't think so." I'd never seen magic like that.

Ana sighed. "I'll do some research into hallucinations, too."

I heard the creak of the stairs and knew Mum was on her way up.

"Gotta go," I whispered into the phone and hung up before Ana had a chance to reply and shoved my mobile under my pillow. Although hallucinations did explain the bizarre things I'd seen since bumping my head, a feeling in the pit of my gut told me it wasn't right.

Mum entered my room holding a mug of her healing lemon tea. She passed it to me to drink and sat next to me. I held it with both hands, breathing in the zesty fragrance. I felt wary. Ana's words still ring in my ears: '*She broke you.*'

Mum tucked the duvet around me and chanted the spell she always used when I am unwell.

"Wrap her in cotton and surround her with love,
Send peace for her body on wings of a dove,
Give her your blessing on this shadowy night,
The brightest of light, reap her pain and take flight."

Her words didn't comfort me like they had so many times before, as I was still haunted by my conversation with Ana: '*The question is why? What did she want you to forget?*'

Mum kissed my forehead, oblivious of my thoughts. "Now, drink up."

The lemon tea was bittersweet and burned as it ran down my throat. The drink made me feel doped, and I passed Mum my cup. I closed my eyes as my heavy head sunk into my pillow.

I fell into the most vivid of dreams. I could see flashes of intimate moments: stolen and secret kisses, gentle caresses, and holding hands. Was this real or a hallucination? Is it a dream or memories coming back to me? But, I am too tired to make sense of any of it. I give into the power of Mum's lemon tea and sleep.

It was dark when I woke from the spell. Something powerful stirred me and told me to open my eyes. Once they adjusted, I noticed my curtains were still open and reached up to close them.

As I knelt on my bed, my arms stretched to pull the curtains closed, I saw a figure standing on the other side of the road. They stood in the shadows, out of illumination from the beam cast by the lamppost.

The hairs on my arm prickled as I noticed it was the man I usually see in the dead of night. He wore a heavy fisherman's jacket, the hood pulled up over his head, hiding his face. I could see he was wearing jeans and the bright whiteness of new trainers. By his side sat an obedient labrador.

He tilted his head back and two bright eyes met mine. They shone like liquid silver towards me and washed away the fear. He was watching me, I was sure. I felt drawn in, like a current drawing me to him. My heart thudded like it had when I'd been in the pool and felt Murray watching me. I wanted it to be him but I knew it must be another stupid hallucination.

Why'd I want it to be Murray?

As I crawled back into my bed, I knew the uncomfortable shiver that ran over me would not be dispelled by my blanket. It was a haunting sensation. He saw me in a way nobody else ever had; those eyes had reached inside me. Unearthly.

I had to be losing my mind.

I stretched my arms out across the counter and let out a morning yawn whilst I contemplated asking Mum my 'why's' and 'how's'.

Mum switched the kettle on and went to the cupboard to pull out her box of oils and the black, granite pestle and mortar. She began picking out the oils she needed. She made her way out the back door and I slipped from my stool to see what she had set out: clary sage, lavender, pine, and calamus roots. The little brown bottles all were identical with the green sticker and name printed in white text. Mum returned with green leaves in her hand.

"What are you making?" I asked.

"An ointment for you," Mum answered.

"What ointment?"

"Just a little something to hopefully clear up your problem yesterday," Mum gave me a warm smile and the kettle rumbled as it boiled and clicked off.

"Can I help?"

"Sure." Mum smiled as she dropped a handful of green leaves into the mortar. "Can you fetch a white candle from the living room?"

I retrieved a long, white candle from the sideboard in the living room. It was new and the wick was a clean piece of string, taut in the wax. I returned to the kitchen where Mum was rotating the pestle in the mortar, grinding the ingredients together. I waved the candle and she nodded at a pile of leaves on the counter.

"Can you roll it in those mugwort leaves?"

I placed the candle on the counter and began rolling it back and forth in the leaves. "Like this?"

Mum nodded and smiled. She stopped mixing and got two mugs out the cupboard and placed a tea bag into each. For a moment, I had another hallucination and saw *a jar with a beautiful rose made of ice. The rose sparkled as if enchanted with fairy dust and I gasped at its beauty.*

I blinked.

Mum caught my eye and asked, "Are you okay?"

I ran a hand through my hair. "Fine."

"I'd say you're done with the candle," Mum said as she finished pouring milk into the two mugs. She passed me my mug. "You know, Mariah, you may be rundown. You could be due on again?"

"Due on?"

"Your period."

"Oh!" I blushed as I slid onto one of the stools. I

recalled seeing a new app on my phone called 'Cycle' and made a mental note to check it out later, before something embarrassing happened.

Mum placed the candle into a holder and lit it. "Have I ever told you about the Arwen symbol?"

I shook my head.

Mum nodded, smiled and sprinkled some flour on the countertop.

"It's made up of three lines like the rays of the sun, each one crowned with a dot," Mum began drawing the symbol in the flour. Mum moved her mortar in front of me and I could see the oils mixed and mashed with her leaves; different to the ones I'd rolled the candle in.

"What are those leaves?"

"Marigolds. I'm going to draw the symbol on your forehead." She dipped her finger into the liquid.

I shook my head and leaned back. "What's this spell for?"

"I'm trying to help you, Mariah. It'll shed light on your hallucinations."

I gave a tentative nod. Ana said if Mum was innocent she would want to help me with one of her spells, and here she was doing just that. I still felt unsure of her but the familiarity of her casting magic was comforting.

Her cold, wet finger began drawing the lines against my hot forehead. It felt refreshing and soothing and I closed my eyes.

She made a sound as she drew each line: "Ee, Oh, Ah."

Mum paused and I opened my eyes to see her

dipping her finger in the liquid again.

Quizzically, I met her eyes, "What does that mean?"

"Their names. Modern druids believe Arwen represents the truth." Mum reached forward to mark my forehead with a dot. "Love of truth."

Her finger moved along my head, "Understanding of trust."

And then a final dot at the top of my forehead in the middle, "Maintaining truth."

"Will this stop the hallucinations?"

"There are other meanings to the symbol," she said, ignoring my question. "For the ones who want the truth revealed, you must have an open heart for secrets to be unsealed."

My brow furrowed in confusion.

Mum stepped back and coldness ran through me. A strange sensation of my energy being sapped, like my blood drawing from my body. My limbs were heavy, my arms slipped from under my chin and in their clumsy state they knocked my tea from the counter. I couldn't afford to lose any more memories.

"I feel faint," I whispered.

The mug spun in slow motion towards the floor and smashed. With hazy eyes, I found Mum. Sweat prickled where the anointment chilled my skin.

I sought Mum's bright eyes which were now lost in a darkness that didn't seem human. She continued to speak, unfazed by my loss of control. The puddle of tea pooled around the foot of my stool.

"Some are evil, some are kind, and now you must

speak your mind."

"Mum?" I mumbled.

"Don't be scared. I'll never let any harm come to you."

I shivered. "I'm sleepy."

"Let me help you to bed."

Mum was around the counter, her arm around my waist, guiding me out the kitchen and into the hall. My legs felt as if they were giving way on me. They were moving but they didn't feel strong enough to carry me and I was thankful for Mum's support as we went up the stairs.

We reached my room and Mum tucked me up in bed.

"I wish I was normal." I felt pathetic as I looked up at her from my pillow.

"What makes you think you're not normal?"

"My hallucinations…," I yawned, unable to say anymore.

"This will help it go away. You will be fine, Mariah." She pulled the stool from my dresser and sat next to me, holding my hand.

The room was spinning. "I don't feel well."

"It's only temporary," Mum said with sympathy.

"Why didn't you warn me?" I felt tricked but didn't have the energy to jump up and yell at her.

"What difference would it have made? Now, tell me what's going on with you and Jace?" She kissed my limp hand.

"He's my boyfriend," I confessed. My cheeks

burned red, I hadn't meant to tell her. It was meant to be our secret but the words came out as if they had a life of their own.

"How serious?"

"Not serious…," I began. "But…" My head was screaming at me to shut up. "I think I might love him. No! I can't. I don't know." I babble, unable to stop myself. "I have really strong feelings and I think I have for longer than I can remember."

I let out a big yawn that made my eyes water while Mum asked, "Have you had sex with him?"

"No," I answered with honesty and felt a sense of relief to finally feel sure about that.

A crease appeared above her brow and she moved forward and hugged me. A loud sigh blew into my ear, confirmation that she knew more than she was letting on. I'd seen the guilt flash across her eyes. As she sat back on the stool, I realised she wasn't surprised by my revelation but more distressed by it.

"Can you remember the night you stayed over at Jace's before Christmas?"

"No." A shiver ran through me. Mum knew something significant had happened but she didn't know what and I couldn't remember. A wave of tiredness crashed over my body and trying to stay awake was making me feel sick. "I'm so sleepy."

She patted my head. "Yes, you should sleep." Her voice was quiet and her eyes full of sadness.

My head sank into my pillow and my eyes shut. "Why can't I remember? Do you think something bad happened to me?"

Mum kissed my brow. "I'm sorry, Mariah. Some things shouldn't be forgotten."

CHAPTER 23

I HAD A FEW MINUTES before I needed to leave for school so I made myself a cup of tea. I'd only just sat down on the stool when Mum entered the kitchen. She feigned concern.

"You don't look well, dear."

"I'm fine." I busied past her.

"Stay home and rest."

There was something familiar in her request and I could almost feel a memory returning, but I didn't feel safe in her presence. Was my paranoia a symptom of losing my memories?

"Let me take care of you. We can talk and you can tell me everything that's on your mind. How did you and Jace get together?"

My cheeks burned up. "We practised kissing and

we realised we wanted to be together."

My hands covered my mouth. I could've died of embarrassment. I hadn't meant to tell her that but the words were out of my mouth before I could stop them. Words buried so deep in my mind, I didn't even know them. I took a step back, my voice shaky.

"You cast a truth spell on me?"

She opened her mouth to say something, but instead screwed up her face. She wasn't ready with a lie and her face said everything.

My body flushed with heat and I could feel my fingers tingling. I ground my teeth together as I stormed out before I lost it with her. My nose flared, and my eyes bulged, as I roughly ripped the front door open. A gust of wind whipped my hair back and took the door from my hand, slamming it shut with a satisfying bang.

I hurried down the front path and realised I still had my mug in my hand. I didn't dare go back inside so I ditched it on our wall.

I can't lie!

The symbol, the strange words, the spell Mum had cast on me! She'd stripped me of my right to privacy. Even things my own mind didn't want to know she could now demand from me. My thoughts, my hidden memories, what right did she have to take them from me?

Now, she knew about Jace and I.

Her actions made Ana's theory that Mum was behind my wipeout seem more credible. I pulled my mobile from my pocket and realised my hands were still shaking. I opened my messages and replied to an old text from Jace.

Mariah: First break, meet me at the library.

First break came and, as I waited for Jace, I saw Murray. He came up the stairwell, his silver eyes met mine. His lips parted ready to say something.

"Goldie –," he started, but was interrupted.

"Freckles!" Jace cheered enthusiastically. He cast Murray an unpleasant glance and checked my reaction.

"Jace," I bubbled back. My fake enthusiasm was almost given away by a sigh that marked my effort. Something about Murray and the way he looked at me pulled me in a direction I didn't want to go. I headed off with Jace, fighting against Murray's invisible force.

"What do you want to talk about?" His brows furrowed, a mix of vulnerability and concern.

"Can we go somewhere private?"

"Is everything alright?"

I nodded, but that was a lie. "It's Mum."

My hand slipped into his and he gave it a squeeze. I began leading him down the corridor out of sight from Murray.

"Is she alright?" Jace asked while we walked. He checked over his shoulder and frowned.

"Yeah," I followed his gaze. Murray appeared to be

following us.

"What's his problem?"

I shrugged and pulled Jace on. "She knows."

We headed down the far stairwell. My hand felt hot and sweaty in his as I pulled him along with me.

"Knows what?"

I pushed open the door that leads outside and the cool air felt refreshing. "She knows about us."

"What!" Jace froze but I tugged him out into the open, away from the ears that might be listening.

"It doesn't matter; we both knew our mums would find out eventually."

"Was it through her crystal ball? She could be watching now...," Jace whispered and looked around as if he could catch her spying on us.

I shivered at the thought even though I knew it didn't work like that. The sensation of being watched pricked my skin but that was Murray's doing.

"No, I told her."

"What? Why?"

"She asked and I couldn't...," I trailed off.

"Lie?" Jace finished for me. "Great. Now you'll never get to stay over again."

"Is that all you're bothered about? When will I sleep with you again?" I snapped back.

"No, that's not what I meant. I've always liked it when you stay over, even before this. I'm worried our mums will be funny about us seeing each other, and we're never alone at school." Jace frowned at Murray who appeared to be watching us.

He wore a thick cream hoodie and dark, navy jeans, one pure white trainer pressed against the wall. His eyes locked with mine. Stuffing his hands deep into his pockets, he stared back without blinking. It was as if he were waiting for me to speak, anticipating something. Perhaps he, too, felt the draw between us, not that I wanted to talk about that, let alone admit it. Murray felt dangerous and scary, whereas Jace felt familiar and safe. Or, at least, he used to.

With a shake of my head, I shook off that disturbing feeling. "I don't care who sees us. We'll find a way to be together... I'll use swim practice as an excuse to see you after school and you can skip football."

"Mariah, I'm part of a team. They need me. And, you can't give up swimming for the same reason. I've heard how good you are."

"What about us?"

His thumb caressed down the side of my face, wiping away my frown. I felt as if everyone was trying to make things difficult for us. The thought of never spending time with him wore heavy on my soul. Surely Mum would understand and wouldn't do as he suggested?

"We'll think of something. It'll be hard with your mum being a psychic. If you scheme to see me instead of swimming, she'll know. Then, you won't get to do either."

"She doesn't know about my swimming."

"What?"

I shook my head. I didn't feel like explaining it to

him. My chin lowered to my chest.

"She seemed alright about us."

"I hope so." Then, he whispered, "Mariah?"

I looked up.

"If we need to, we'll find a way." His lips met mine in a soft, reassuring kiss. I could have spent the rest of the day like that but he jumped away at the sound of the bell ringing overhead.

Jace held the door open for me so we could go back in. His hand rested on the small of my back as if guiding me back into the school, away from Murray. Murray was right behind us, waiting to get inside, too, except his eyes were fixed on me; watching, waiting.

I froze like an ice sculpture caught in his cold stare.

"What's wrong?" Jace's warm breath tickled my ear, melting me back to normality.

"Goldie," Murray's fingers trailed along my arm, causing the hairs to stand up, static and charged. He paused and I blushed. "See you later."

My heart raced uncontrollably and I nodded. Murray was gone. It all happened so fast but that moment lasted long enough for Jace to register it.

"What's going on between you two? I thought we were being honest but..." Jace's eyes narrowed and his chin jutted out towards me.

"I'm drawn to him," I answered without thinking.

His eyes bulged and he took a deep inhale as if I'd punched him in the gut.

"We have a connection." I slapped my hand over my mouth to stop myself from saying anything more.

OMG! It's not just Mum, I can't lie to anyone.

He held me with wounded eyes. "Are you saying..."

Dread smacked into me as I realised I couldn't let him finish that question. I grabbed him, and kissed him to shut him up. He pushed me back.

"What are you doing?"

"Silencing you with a kiss," I admitted and shut my eyes, wishing I could blink myself away from this disaster. I could feel my tongue itching to tell the truth and my heart feared what he'd ask me next. I had to escape.

"Go run off with him, then!" Jace said harshly.

"No!" I could feel my eyes starting to sting with the threat of tears.

Jace pushed me roughly out of the way of an oncoming crowd of students heading to class. I found myself trapped between him and the lockers. Jace's face burned red and his jaw twitched.

"You never did tell me what happened between you two!"

"I have to go." Even though I couldn't remember, I knew I was hiding something. Maybe if he asked it'd rise to the surface and we'd both know the truth. But, I feared the unknown and what it could do to us.

"No, not until you tell me." He held onto my wrists.

"Tell you what?"

"The Mistletoe Disco!" He was furious, but let go of my wrists and ran a harassed hand through his hair and kicked a locker in frustration.

I flinched.

"Just ask me!" I screamed.

"I just did!"

Suddenly, Murray stepped between us, his back toward me, his body facing Jace.

"Get to class," he said sternly. He glanced over his shoulder at me. "Is everything alright?"

"No." My voice was shaky.

"It's none of your business, Murray. She doesn't even like you!" Jace spat like venom. His attention was back on me. "Next time we meet, I want to know all about what happened that night!"

He purposefully knocked my shoulder with his as he passed and headed off to his classes, leaving me behind. I couldn't even remember a Mistletoe Disco, not even a flash. Did I want him to ask? Did I want to know what happened? Hopefully, he would forget about it – as I had.

"What was that all about?" Murray asked.

"He wants to know what happened at the Mistletoe Disco," I confessed before I could stop myself and panic shot through me. I ran down the corridor to my class. I needed to get away from Murray fast, before I got asked any more personal questions.

Heading to the pool was like sleepwalking, I wasn't consciously thinking about where I was going but my feet knew where my body craved. If I'd been thinking, I may have chosen to go home and end the day, or even noticed Murray sneaking up on me. He grabbed my arm, pulling me to a halt.

"This has got to stop!" he snapped.

"W... What?" I said taken aback by his anger.

He clapped his hands with sarcastic praise. "Very good! Well played! Oscar award for you!"

"What's your problem?" I turned red with the unwanted attention of passers-by.

"Pretend it never happened!" he growled the words through his teeth, getting up in my face. "I didn't realise you literally meant it." His nose wrinkled in a snarl and he tugged at the necklace around my neck. "Then, you parade around school with the memory of our kiss around your throat, acting as if it means nothing to you."

My hand reached for the snowflake necklace. "Our kiss?"

It couldn't be true. The kiss underwater.

"Oh, have you forgotten?" he asked sarcastically. "Convincing!"

But the question caused something to click inside me. I was obliged to answer with the truth. I could feel it compelling the words inside me and I spilled everything:

"Yes, I can't remember anything, not just you, but Jace, too. I don't recall Jace with Kiely? You and I? It's all a mystery. I'm trapped in a world that no longer makes sense and it's driving me insane!"

Murray's face softened as the truth flowed from

me. Concern washed his feature as he let me go. "Are you serious?"

"Deadly. When I kiss Jace, I get glimpses of memories. I remember little things but not the whole picture. I honestly wish I could remember."

"Oh my god, you're not joking," Murray pulled my shaking body into his and held me, my head rested on his shoulder.

His arms felt good around me and I gave in to their comfort. "I know. You can't tell anyone, please."

"Mariah, I've kept all your secrets. I'd never betray your trust. Have you seen a doctor?"

I shook my head.

Murray sighed. "And I thought getting kicked off the swim team was a big deal."

"You got kicked off the team! Why?"

"You."

"Me!"

"It doesn't matter. You won't remember," he sighed. Despite the power he had over me, I believed he'd never hurt me. His shoulders relaxed. "Is there anything I can do, to help you... remember?"

I blushed as the thought of kissing him crossed my mind.

"Jace won't speak to me until I tell him what happened between us at the Mistletoe Disco. Do you know?"

"You want me to help you fix things with Jace? You really don't remember," Murray laughed.

"Please," I begged.

"So, let me get this straight. You can't remember that night at all?"

"I can't remember anything after the summer holidays."

"But, when you kiss Jace it comes back?"

"Yeah, there've been other triggers, too."

"So, if I refuse to tell you, you'll have to kiss me?" The corner of Murray's lips peaked a little in a smirk.

"I guess so." I shook my head. My skin prickled with a bizarre sensation, almost as if I was on the verge of one of my memories returning. "I feel like we've been here before?"

"We have," Murray grinned. He dug his hand in his pocket and pulled out his mobile phone. He showed me a picture on his screen. It was the picture from my flashback. The one where I am lip-locked with Jace... no, with Murray!

"You!" Fury boiled inside me and I realised the memory I'd had whilst kissing Jace on New Year's Eve was of Murray. I felt as if I'd cheated on Jace by thinking of someone else. If only I could remember how serious Murray and I had been. Could I trust anything he told me?

"Are you sure you don't remember?" he laughed and stuffed the phone back into his pocket. "You were mad then, too. But you owed me."

"What could I owe you for?"

"Together, we broke Kiely and Jace up."

"I'd never!" I choked. That didn't sound like me at all.

"Well, enjoy your happily never after, it's the worst thing I ever did. My sister is a mess and you've ruined my life!"

"Your life! That's a bit dramatic!"

"Don't act like you know anything about what you don't remember, Mariah!" he laughed but it was an empty sound and I could tell he was hurting. He walked away, seeming to disregard me but still muttering under his breath. "I'll never forget us, especially not that night."

I needed to know about that night. The only person who knew was Murray. I ran after him.

"Please, tell me what happened at the Mistletoe Disco?"

Murray weaved between parked cars and pulled keys from his pocket. He pointed them at a new, black car. The car beeped in response with a friendly, chirpy greeting. Murray looked me dead in the eye and I felt the force between us.

"Kiss me?"

I stopped chasing after him and backed up. "I... I can't."

Murray nodded and got into his car. The door shut with a thump. He drove out of the car park so fast that his tires spun and squealed over the tarmac.

"Murray's new car is nice," Ana appeared next to me. I worried how long she had stood there. She giggled. "Kiss me!"

I cringed, she'd heard it! "I'm with Jace!"

"You could use him, like how he used you to get

Jace to stop dating his sister."

"He used me?"

"Let's burn that anger off in the pool," Ana said with a wink.

I didn't think I could risk being at school any longer. "I need to get home."

Ana grabbed my arm and begged, "Don't go."

I shook her off. "I'm not feeling up to swimming."

An urge to chase after Murray and kiss him took me and I had to remind myself he'd sped off in his flashy car. I should be angry with him. He could have told me what I needed to know. Seriously, how hard would that have been?

CHAPTER 24

"M ᴜᴍ!" I slammed the front door behind me and threw my bag at the foot of the stairs.

"Mariah? How was school? Anything new to share?"

She entered the hallway, the homely smell of freshly baked cakes wafting with her. My nose wrinkled, feeling betrayed, it didn't match my mood and turned it unpleasant and too sickly.

"Your spell last night! What did you do?" I knew what she'd done but I needed her to confess.

"Why? What happened?" she asked wide eyed.

"I have to tell the truth!"

"That's a good thing, dear," she smiled and returned to the kitchen, with a chuckle. "You should have stayed home as I recommended."

"Mum!" I chased after her.

She lifted a warm bun from a cooling rack and passed it to me. "Try one."

"No, thanks, who knows what's in it?" I tossed it across the counter.

"Nothing untoward."

"Mum, admit what you did!"

"I'm sorry." Her smile vanished and she put her focus into her cake decorating.

Relieved that I wasn't going crazy, I took her apology as a sign of admittance. I recovered my cake and freed it from the paper wrapper. The warm cake was sweet and lush in my mouth. It crumbled and broke into spongy, sugary lumps of yum. I sunk onto a stool and through a mouthful of cake I demanded: "You have to undo it!"

She glanced up at the clock on the wall in the kitchen. "It can't be undone but it'll run out soon. It only lasts twenty-four hours."

"Thank goodness!" I shook my head at her. Why couldn't I have a normal mum like Denny? I got up and grabbed another cake off the cooling tray before running up to my room to forget about my day.

Switching on the computer, I chose some tunes to listen to - I needed something angry and empowering to complement my mood. A notification on my instant messenger popped up. I could see I had mail - I clicked the link to my inbox and the message opened.

It felt as if everyone was against me. Mum, robbing me of the right to choose what information I share. Jace, forcing me to find a way to discover information that I don't know. Murray trying to take advantage of my vulnerable situation.

An idea struck me and I didn't wait to read the email or see who it was from. Running down the stairs, skipping as many steps as possible, I bound into the kitchen. Mum was surprised to see me.

"Ask me what happened at the Mistletoe Disco?" I demanded.

"What happened at the Mistletoe Disco?"

"Jace kissed Kiely." For something I couldn't remember, I felt oddly pained at the thought of him with another girl.

"Why did you want me to ask you that?"

"Jace won't speak to me until he knows what happened with Murray and I, but I don't remember."

"That's a different question. What happened between you and Murray at the Mistletoe Disco?"

It felt like the one thing I didn't want to remember. My mouth was forming the words but I could feel my mind fighting to conceal the truth. An eternal battle erupted inside me.

"I... I..."

The room went black.

I woke back in my bed. Mum sat on the stool at my computer. She was reading something on the screen.

"Mum, what happened?" I sat up and scratched my head.

"Sorry, I think the power of Arwen ran out."

Her eyes remained on my laptop screen.

My heart raced. "What are you reading?"

"Murray sent you an email about the Mistletoe Disco."

"Mum!" I squealed, wriggling out of bed and peering over her shoulder. I was worried there could be something... I don't know... something you wouldn't want your mum to read. "That's private!"

I tried to shoo her out of my room but she twisted around on the swivel chair and I knew she had read it. The colour was drained from her face.

"A burn tattoo?"

"It's like a tattoo but it's done by burning the skin," I explained.

"How'd he get it?"

I shrugged. "I dunno. We're not exactly friends."

"Don't know or can't remember?" Mum tilted her head.

"How about you tell me what you know? You're casting spells on me, snooping through my stuff. Where's my free will? Where's my privacy?"

Mum's face reddened and her eyes cast at the floor. "Everything I do is to protect you. It wasn't my intention to cause upset. I promise, no more spells..."

She looked genuinely sorry.

"Thanks!" I sighed.

"Unless absolutely necessary."

"Mum!"

Mum sighed. "Only with your consent?"

This was a breakthrough in her allowing me some space. It was the start of our negotiations and I saw my opportunity.

"No more spying on me in your crystal ball."

She paused. "Mariah, I can't control what I see."

"You can guide your sight," I knew that when people paid her she was able to focus on them and their questions. She might not be able to control what she saw but she could guide the subject of her visions.

Mum groaned, and agreed. "I won't purposefully look."

"Thank you," I said more calmly with a small sense of victory.

Mum stood up to leave my room. "You should invite Murray over one day, he sounds interesting and clearly cares a lot about you. I'd like to meet him and learn more about burn tattoos."

I shook my head. "No, Mum, we don't get on."

"I'll help mend your bridges," she grinned.

"No meddling, Mum." I gave her an encouraging nudge out of my room and closed the door behind her.

I returned to my laptop to read Murray's email and find out why Mum thought he 'cares a lot'.

Mariah

Sorry for my behaviour today. I wasn't in the best of moods. The school feels my 'burn tattoo' doesn't portray the right image for the school. I'm no longer allowed to represent.

Getting kicked off the team sucked, and then discovering you don't even remember me was the icing on the cake.

I can't lie, I'm not overjoyed you're with Jace but I guess I only have myself to blame. I got you together. It was my stupid idea. The more time we spent together, the more we dated, the more I needed you.

And, the night of the Mistletoe Disco. Jace kissed Kiely and you took off. I went after you, and don't regret anything that happened after that. I want you to know what happened but if I told you, you'd never believe me.

That's why I'm writing. Please let me help you find a way to remember us. A way that doesn't disrespect your relationship with Jace.

Please give me another chance.

Murray x

The next day, I wanted to find Murray to see if he was serious about helping me remember without kissing. But, I had no clue where to find him.

I told Jace I'd ran off at the Mistletoe Disco because I'd been upset seeing him kissing Kiely. I told him Murray followed to check I was okay, and that was it. He cooled down a little, but I could sense he knew that wasn't the whole story but it was all the story I had.

After school, I headed to the pool. I checked my phone to see if Murray had messaged again telling me where to meet him but there was nothing from him just a text from Ana.

> Ana: Are you feeling better today?
> Ana: Please come swimming.... Pwetty pwease.

> Mariah: I'm on my way. X

I found Ana at her locker; her face lit up when she saw me. "Yay, you're here. I've been researching hallucinations like I promised."

"And?"

"Is there any chance your mum is drugging you?"

I thought back to yesterday and the truth spell, "I wouldn't put it past her."

"There you go."

"I dunno, are there any other causes?" I held the door open for her as we left the building. I wasn't convinced about drugs, but I was seriously suspecting she may have used magic on me.

"It can be caused by a lack of sleep. Are you having trouble sleeping?"

I felt a strange current run up my arm, "I still wake in the night and see the creepy guy out front."

"What if he's an evil warlock and coming for us because we did magic?"

"If evil warlocks existed mum would have been in trouble years ago."

As I crossed the car park towards the pool block, I saw Murray's car. I nudged Ana, and nodded towards it, "Murray emailed me and offered to help me get my memories back."

"You should definitely take him up on that. He's so hot."

"No Ana, I'm with Jace. He offered to help me find another trigger."

"That doesn't sound as much fun."

As we neared Murray's car, he came out of the school building. Upon seeing him, my body flushed with heat as if somehow he'd know what we'd been talking about.

"Goldie!" He smiled and jogged over. When he joined us he smiled and nodded to acknowledge Ana.

My heart fluttered in response to his presence. My emotions felt more conspicuous with Ana standing next to me. "Thanks for your email. It helped."

"With Jace?"

I nodded and bit my lip.

He wrinkled his nose. "Shame."

Ana snorted.

"Well, I wanted to say thanks." I shuffled my feet.

"No worries," he clicked his key fob at the car.

Ana's voice hissed into my ear, "Ask for his help!"

"Murray, will you help me remember the rest?" My heart fluttered as I met his gaze.

He raised an eyebrow. "Are you asking to kiss me?"

I heard Ana gasp beside me.

"N- No!" I stuttered.

"Didn't think so," he said ruefully. He ran a hand through his hair as he walked around the car and got in.

Dumbstruck on the other side, I watched him go.

Ana shoved me forward, "Go after him."

The car door sprung open on the passenger side, "Get in! I'll take you for a drive down memory lane."

I didn't argue. I got in and put on my seat belt. I glanced out the window back at Ana, who grinned and waved at me. The car had a strong, new smell. Murray turned the key and revved the engine, I felt like everyone was watching us as he pulled out the car park.

"Where are we going?"

"Before you'll believe what happened that night, you need to remember who you are. Does 'merallo' mean anything to you?"

I shook my head but when I realised, he was watching the road and not me, I said, "No."

I felt nervous in his presence. He felt powerful and connected to me in a way that I couldn't fathom.

"What can you remember?"

"Nothing much," I shrugged. The silence felt intense like I was being sucked into it, submerged and all that was left was just us. I felt the need to say something to break the spell. "My last memory is the day Jace moved away. He moved up this way."

We were racing along the cliff tops, and it wasn't long before we passed the estate where Jace now lived.

"My neighbourhood," Murray informed me as he pulled into the viewing point. I knew what this place was famous for and the words of the older girls in the changing room came back to me.

"Make out viewpoint? We agreed, I'm not kissing you!"

"Don't keep rubbing it in," he gave a pained laugh as he turned off the engine.

"Sorry." I felt horrible for hurting him. Something had definitely happened between us for him to feel so strongly about me. Murray was rumoured to be a player and here I am sitting next to him at 'make out' viewpoint. Where else would a guy like Murray take a girl? I started to feel tricked and the car felt tight and stripped of air. "What are we doing here?"

Murray opened his door. "Trying to get your memory back."

He got out and I walked round to meet him on his side of the car. We stood side by side staring out to sea.

"Do you remember coming here to meet Kiely?"

"No."

He started walking and I followed. We made our way down the steps to the beach. The only memories I had of this place were from when I was younger. Our mums had brought us here for a picnic. Denny held Jace's hand as they waded in the surf with their trousers rolled up. Jace screamed as the waves rolled around his shins, splashing against him and sprinkling his top in salty droplets. Denny encouraged me to come in, too, but Mum held onto me fast. She said it was dangerous, the water was dirty and it was so hot my skin would burn the moment the sea washed off my sun protection. She threatened to take me home unless they dropped it. I stayed on the shingle beach with Mum, wishing I was frolicking in the sea with Jace. The waves whispered to me a sweet swooshing of a sound with each roll, calling me in. It felt more real than the screams and laughter from the pair jumping at the waves. Mum, maintained her grip on my wrist, her voice distant but persistent. She told me that it wouldn't always be like this, that when I was older, I'd be stronger and I'd play in the sea for as long as I liked.

As we reached the bottom of the steps, Murray turned towards me.

"Anything?"

"No." I shook my head.

Murray looked up at the sky as if searching for answers. He reached down and picked up a pebble, and threw it into the sea. It bounced and plopped into the ocean.

The sensation of butterflies erupted in my tummy as if what he'd just done was the most wonderful thing I'd ever seen. Warmth wrapped around my school shirt as if someone was holding me. It wasn't comforting but more arousing and when the feeling passed, I noticed how cold it actually was.

He held a pebble out to me. "Do you want to try?"

I took the stone from him and turned so I was facing the sea, side on.

'*Skim it. Don't throw it.*'

I heard the words in my head and recognised it as Murray's voice.

I threw my stone and it bounced once before going under. I knew we'd been skimming stones but it irritated me that I couldn't quite remember it. I frowned and turned to face Murray.

"I give up." Defeated, he dropped down in a crouched sitting position on the shingle.

"Sorry," I said, wishing I could remember. "Can't you tell me what happened here?"

"For me, it was different than for you. I came to make sure Jace didn't get too close to my little sister. You... you were clearly into him and looked pained every time they looked at each other. Jace ditched you for some mate and I walked you home. He doesn't deserve you, Mariah, he doesn't know you like I do."

"Jace knows me better than anyone!" I said defensively.

"So, why don't you ask him what happened? Why drag me through this?" Murray snapped. He pressed his lips together as if stopping himself from saying anymore and began walking back towards the steps.

My body tingled with panic as I worried he might leave me here. "Don't go?"

He stopped and turned on the bottom step to face me. He looked pained.

"This is torture. I think you don't want to remember me!"

"Murray, why would I want to forget you?"

Murray unbuttoned his shirt. His eyes maintaining contact with me, the light picked up the silver colours of his eyes and they sparkled like the ocean. As the loose cotton material flapped in the winter breeze, I could see his hard, toned chest and, at the top, four round burn marks on either side of his chest. My hands reached forward, and my fingers slid into place, a perfect match. My heart thundered as I realised how close we were.

My voice was just a whisper, "I did this."

I was drowning in my emotions. I felt sick with guilt that I'd scarred his perfect body; how could he still care so much for me when I'd done something so wicked? His presence made me vulnerable and I feared that if I let him get close he could break me. At the same time, I wanted him to be closer. I bit my lip.

Murray's voice was deep and warm. "I need answers, too."

I was mesmerised by the power between us. Could he feel it too? The way he was drawing me closer and making it impossible for me to look away?

He turned to glance up the steps, and his hold over me was broken. I felt relief and disappointment to no longer be in that moment. My hands dropped away. He pulled his shirt back together and began buttoning it back up. My legs shivered as the cold whipped up my school skirt.

Murray's words were strained. "I promised never to force a kiss on you again. Next time, it'll be because you made it happen."

A breath caught in my throat at the thought of kissing Murray. My body craved it and I couldn't take my eyes off his tempting lips.

Murray noticed.

"Just kiss me if that's all it takes for you to remember!"

The chill in the air caused vapour clouds to form with each angry word. Murray wasn't asking me to kiss him, he was giving up. He began making his way back up the steps. I waited at the bottom, not sure if I should follow, until he added, "Come on, I'll take you home and think of something else to help."

The ride home was tense. I was like a blind spot. As he drove, I wondered how he knew where I lived without me saying and it dawned on me that he must have taken me home before.

I checked my phone and wasn't surprised to see a text from Ana. She must have sent it the moment I'd got Murray had left the school grounds with me in the car.

Ana: You know I'll want all the details!

Mariah: It didn't help. ☹

As we neared my house, I worried about Mum seeing us and her eagerness to meet him. I'd thought about breaking the ice by extending Mum's offer, but I was annoyed by his sulking.

"Can you drop me off here?"

Silently, Murray pulled over. He looked out the driver's window so he didn't need to look at me. I picked up my school bag and opened the door. I mumbled a thanks. I wasn't sure how to say bye to someone that's ignoring me. I slammed the car door and yelled, "See you!"

As soon as the door shut, he sped off without a word.

CHAPTER 25

"**H**APPY BIRTHDAY TO YOU, happy birthday to you, happy birthday, dear Mariah. Happy birthday to you."

I opened one eye to see Mum standing by my bed with a tray in her hands. I rubbed my sleepy eyes as it dawned on me: today was my birthday and she'd made me breakfast in bed. With all the drama in my life, it had slipped my mind.

In a tumbler, she had picked a handful of snowdrops from the garden and I could see their bright green stems through the glass and the delicate bow of the white flower spilling over the edge.

I sat up. "Thanks."

"You enjoy your breakfast and I'll be back with your present."

My fingers brushed the gentle petals of the flowers,

while I crunched jam on toast. I enjoyed the novelty of staying in bed. It was a tradition since before I could remember.

Mum returned with a present wrapped in thick, red paper. I peeled the tape off with care so we could reuse it for the next birthday.

"I hope you don't mind but Jace has asked to plan your joint party and I saw no issue in allowing this, now he's your boyfriend."

I cringed, it still felt odd hearing him called that. "What has he planned?"

She smiled. "I'll tell you in a minute. Now, hurry up with that. I want to know if you like it."

I reached into the parcel and pulled out a black dress with sequins and a ruffle hem.

"It's gorgeous, I wish I had somewhere to wear it."

"Tonight," Mum answered. "You'll have plans and this'll be perfect."

"Thanks, Mum." I gave her a hug and kiss, and we both got jam in our long hair.

"Oh, no!" we laughed, not minding at all.

Jace picked me up in a posh, vintage car.

"This will be Mum's wedding car. You'll get to ride in it again on the big day."

"It's beautiful. Your mum must be so excited." The car was too much and I still wasn't comfortable with dating Jace. It felt odd.

"Oh yeah, I meant to tell you. She's booked your dress fitting in for the first weekend in April."

The driver took us to La Passione, a small, Italian restaurant along the seafront, that had large windows with views across the choppy, winter sea. From outside, I could see they had decorated the restaurant specially for Valentine's Day.

We hurried inside so the wind didn't ruin my hair. Jace gave our name and we were taken to our table. Every table had a single, red rose and scattered across the tables were love heart confetti.

The first two courses were amazing but the last course was vanilla ice-cream and a red velvet sponge cut in the shape of a heart. It was artistically presented on trendy, square, white plates using the sauce to decorate.

"I'm not sure I can eat anymore. I'm stuffed," I complained with a satisfied grin on my face.

"Don't force yourself. There's more to come."

"More food?"

"No, the entertainment." Jace raised his mobile and took a picture of me.

"What are you doing?" I blushed and bowed my head.

"You look beautiful."

I smiled and tried to force myself to eat but there was no way I could manage another bite, instead I pushed food around with my fork. I looked up. Jace was staring at me, with a dazed expression on his face.

I'd not seen him look at me that way before, and that's when I had a flash.

I saw us eating cheese and tomato sandwiches and I had a fluttery feeling just looking at him.

The moment was brief but I was certain I'd been in love with him before. It compelled me to tell him everything I knew.

"Jace..."

Before I could say anymore, I was interrupted by a man on a microphone. He introduced the entertainment:

"Please join Savannah and Joaquin on the dance floor for this evening's entertainment, where you will learn to salsa dance."

It felt silly standing with Jace in the poised position, too grown up. I giggled and blushed as we stumbled in our attempt to follow the steps and keep up. The teachers circulated and helped us out with the basic steps and rhythm.

"One, two, three, four! One, two, three, four!" the teachers chanted.

Jace held eye contact, his hand hot against mine. He was trying to be serious, so I tried to as well. I was surprised that he was so into this, it wasn't something he'd ever shown an interest in before - like football. But his attitude made the dance feel more intense.

We were taught some flash dance steps and the girls got to tease the guys. The guys were shown how to dip the girls. Jace dipped me and brought me up slowly and, when I reached him, he pulled me close for a kiss. It was the first time he'd kissed me with an audience.

My head spun from the rush and my body flushed with heat.

The class was over and they announced they'd be bringing out the final course. We returned to our table.

I said, "I can't eat another thing. I've got a stitch."

Jace chuckled. "It's just coffee and mints."

I sighed with relief.

"Mariah?"

Jace was suddenly very serious. I nodded.

He leaned across our empty table for my hands. "I'm sorry about my behaviour. I guess I was jealous."

"It's okay."

"It's not," Jace dismissed my forgiveness. "You know me. It's not who I am. Everything's changing, us, my home, exams, and I lost it."

"You've nothing to worry about," I assured him.

"The move created a distance and I'm missing out on being with you, and I blamed Murray," Jace continued.

I squeezed Jace's hands. "I miss you, too."

A waiter arrived at our table and put down the pot of coffee and cups, together with the mints.

"Shall we just take the mints and go?" Jace asked.

I nodded.

As we got up, Jace grabbed the rose from the table, "For you, my love."

"Why, thank you, kind sir."

As soon as we left the restaurant, I regretted it. We decided to cross the road and walk along the beach but the bitter winter wind was ice cold as it blew in from the North Sea. My hair was thrown around in every direction and I could barely see where I was going. Jace held onto my arm as I stumbled on.

I heard him laughing.

"What?"

"One, two, three, four," he chuckled.

"This wind is crazy."

"You look like you're salsa dancing."

"It's killing me."

He pulled me out of the wind and into one of the shelters. "I'll call us a taxi. So much for a romantic walk home in the moonlight. Your hair - you look like a crazed woman."

"My poor rose!" I felt sad as I saw the poor thing had lost some petals.

"Winter sucks," he said, holding me in a hug.

When Jace finished on the phone, he took the battered flower and held it between his teeth, "Dance with me Savannah."

I laughed at him mucking around. "Try to stop me, Joaquin."

We messed around trying to remember the steps we had been taught and adding in some moves of our own by cat-walking along the bench and doing some jumps off. We were in a fit of giggles by the time the taxi honked its horn and we realised the night was over.

We sat in the back seat and Jace held my hand.

"I hope you had a happy birthday. You look beautiful even with crazy hair."

I smiled. "It was magical. I hope you enjoyed your

birthday, too."

Jace squeezed my hand and nodded.

Jace: Meet me on the front steps. Before school!

Jace's text on Monday morning was abrupt. No kiss. It didn't sound like the Jace I'd been with on Saturday night. I felt nervous as I made my way to the steps to meet him. Seeing his golden hair shining in the sun made my heart flutter, but his expression clipped my wings before I glided to any height with my happiness. And, he now had a very bruised, swollen eye.

"What happened?" I gaped and reached to touch it.

He flinched and pulled away. "Did you tell me the truth about Murray?"

"Well, yeah," I mumbled and took a step back.

Jace looked as if he'd smelled something bad. "Right. So, there's really nothing going on between you?"

I blushed. "Where's this coming from?"

"This!" He thrust his phone in my face and I briefly saw a video of Murray's shirt flapping in the wind and my hands pressed against his chest.

"It's not what it looks-"

"I'm done with your lies." He raised his hand as he cut me off, and started walking away.

"Jace!" I called for him to stop and grabbed his

sleeve. I knew everyone was watching, maybe even recording us like the moment I'd had with Murray.

"Don't bother, Mariah! We're over!" Jace shook his arm so I'd release him.

His words punched me in the gut and I couldn't breathe. My world stopped and there was silence as everyone stared. Whispers filled the air like a humming getting louder and more alarming, the world was spinning at a rapid pace. The sound rose, accompanied by a building mocking laughter.

My hands covered my face as I tried to make sense of the situation. A sudden wind rushed across the steps, lifting my hair and thrashing it about. Leaves and sheets of papers blew up into the air. People screamed as they scrambled to retain their belongings. Grit stung my eyes as dust and debris flew into my face.

I hurried to the toilets, escaping the chaos caused by the sudden change in English weather. Droplets of sweat clustered above my brow. I ran the tap and splashed cold water on my face to cool down.

I forced myself to breathe in and out, trying to gain control of myself, and fought the urge to cry. Feeling better, my breathing regulated, but I was still shaking. The tips of my fingers were tinged blue. I rubbed them, thinking it might be ink, but it didn't come off. I began washing with soap and vigor but stains wouldn't budge.

"Oi, fish bitch!"

I froze at the sink. I didn't have to turn around to see who it was. I knew.

"What did I say about keeping out of my way?"

I turned around to find her and some other girls blocking me in. I was trapped against the sink with no way out.

"It made my morning seeing you get dumped," she laughed. "Whoring it with Kiely's brother."

"I'm not!"

"We've seen you," one of the girls shouted.

I shook my head. "It's not true."

Fallon turned to the other girl. "What do we do with dead fishes?"

"Flush them down the loo," the girl grinned.

"Dead fish!" Fallon yelled and the girls grabbed my arms. I pulled but three against one was impossible. One girl held the cubicle door open whilst the other two dragged me forward. I pulled backwards, putting my weight into it as they tried to drag me.

Something bubbled inside me – was it adrenaline? My body tingled with electricity and I felt alive and powerful. The danger made me aware of my will to survive. I threw my head back as I felt the rush course through my body. Water shot up from the toilets and hit the ceiling. Jumping back, the girls let go of me as they screamed in disgust. I scrambled to my feet and turned to face them, I had to get out. They reached to grab me. I threw my arm up in defence, but we didn't even make contact. They shot across the room, thrown by an invisible force.

Fallon sat on the wet floor, her eyes wide with horror. "You're a freak!"

I shook my head and opened the door to escape, running straight into a teacher.

She saw the panic on my face. "Are you alright?"

I shook my head.

The teacher saw the three soaked girls behind me. She frowned. "What happened?"

Fallon spat, "She flooded the toilets!"

I shook my head. "I didn't."

The teacher was uncomfortable by the situation she now found herself in. "All of you to reception. Let's sort this out."

Fallon pulled the wet clothes away from her skin and made some noises to express how gross she felt.

The teacher tilted her head. "Come on, we'll find you girls dry uniforms."

In reception, I was given a seat to wait for the headmistress. The other girls were taken to get dry clothes. I felt uncomfortable sitting in the waiting area. It was very quiet and I felt like I was in trouble. I'd only ever seen the headmistress during year group assemblies and outdoors during fire drills.

The wait was long and the ticking of the clock made me nervous. I tried to rub the sweat from my hands onto my skirt without drawing attention to myself. The other girls still hadn't returned when the headmistress came to get me. She looked at me with disapproval.

"Come on."

I followed her into her office and took a seat opposite the desk. She leaned back in her chair and made a pyramid with her fingers.

"What happened, Mariah?"

"I don't know."

"You must have seen something? I've spoken with the other girls." She raised her eyebrows and I could tell she didn't believe me. She'd already made up her mind based on the other girl's accounts..

"The toilets exploded and the girls were hit by the impact and flew across the room."

"Are you saying the water threw them?"

"No," I shook my head.

"Did you throw them?"

"No."

"How did they 'fly' across the room?" She used air quotes. "Do you want me to believe they have superpowers?"

"No. I... I didn't see."

The headmistress sighed. "You know, the other girls are saying you did it."

"I didn't touch them!"

The headmistress sighed again. "I've three accounts that you flooded the toilets and all three accounts claim you pushed them into the water."

I shook my head. "No, they were attempting to bog wash me."

She squinted her eyes. "So, you're telling me these girls are bullies? They were trying to dunk your head in the toilet when they all combusted at the same time. And, you want me to believe that your head was the one being forced into the bowl but, somehow, you're the only one dry. How is that?"

"They didn't manage to get me into the cubicle."

The headmistress leaned her elbows on her desk. "If you were being bullied why didn't you report it sooner?"

"I thought I could stay out of her way."

"You should have reported it, no matter how small the incident. We take bullying very seriously," she sighed. "It sounds rather convenient that you only make this claim against them once you are caught for vandalism."

"I didn't!" I felt exasperated and stared out the window. Why had I run to the toilets? I should have ran out the gates and all the way home. If only I hadn't made Mum make that promise, she could have warned me not to get out of bed this morning.

"Mariah, you've never been in trouble and this is out of character. I don't know what to believe. You want to keep out of their way and I agree that would be for the best. I can grant that." The headmistress reached for her phone. "You're suspended, Mariah, for one week to think about the incident."

Why was I being punished?

I frowned. As she pulled the phone towards her face, a spark of white lightning flickered over the plastic, causing her to jump and drop the phone. The lights on the cradle's display screen went out. The headmistress looked at the phone with confusion and stood.

"Wait here. I'll get a secretary to call your mum, mine appears to be faulty."

"But, I didn't do anything wrong."

The headmistress paused at her office door. "Use the time to revise for your exams."

CHAPTER 26

As I walked home, a black car slowed down and stopped beside me. I knew it was Murray before the window slid down.

"Goldie, get in."

I sighed. "I don't think that's a great idea."

"Don't be daft."

"Leave me alone."

"That usually means you need a friend."

"You're not my friend. I lost my friend because he thinks I'm cheating on him with you!" I started walking faster to get away from him and before anyone saw us together.

Murray began driving alongside me. "Last chance, then, I'll have to go or people'll think I'm stalking a school girl."

Why won't he give it up? Can't he take the hint that

I'm not interested? The first tear rolled down my cheek and I swatted it away with the back of my hand.

"Are you crying?"

I shook my head but another tear escaped.

"Get in before anyone sees you," he demanded.

I gave up and got in. I sat in silence in the passenger seat regretting my decision as soon as I got in but Murray pulled away too quickly for me to get out. I clipped my seat belt.

"I'm taking you to mine. There's something I want to show you."

"What?" I sniffed. I welcomed the distraction, it helped calm me but I dreaded anyone finding out about this excursion.

"It's a surprise." He stole a quick glance at me to give a big smile. "By the way, that crap about me not being your friend is a dangerous thing to say. The only reason I'm not still hitting on you is that you promised me friendship at the very least."

I raised an eyebrow in response. Was he blackmailing me into being his friend? But what took me by surprise was the way I felt hearing him admit he wanted to flirt with me. It made me bite my lip to stop a grin that eased the pain I had been feeling.

Murray pulled up at a metal gate and clicked a button on his key fob. The electronic gates opened and we drove up a long drive. He parked in front of the double garage, getting out and I followed him.

We went into his house and across a large open plan lounge through to the kitchen. Built into one of the cupboards was a fish tank.

"Meet Red and Blue, I'm sure you can tell which is which."

Inside were two fish that were rich in the colour of their namesakes. They had long fins that fanned out around them.

"They're beautiful."

"Betta fishes were my granddad's favourites. He left them to me."

"Oh…," I muttered and wasn't sure if he needed consoling or not. "Were you close?"

Murray nodded. "Yeah, I'll get you a drink and tell you a bit about him. There's a story he told that you'll enjoy."

I was intrigued that Murray knew me well enough to think of stories I might like and accepted his offer. "Thanks."

Murray opened the back door but remained in the kitchen. "Did you want something cold or hot?"

"Tea?" I asked.

"I've got a machine that can make you any type of coffee you desire, even hot chocolate, and you choose tea," he laughed and pulled two mugs out the cupboard and flicked the kettle on.

"I don't drink coffee." I shook my head.

Murray walked around the island and indicated for me to follow him back towards the lounge. There, he indicated a lounger that was directed towards the tank.

"Chill out there while I get the drinks. It's the best

view."

It felt awkward to lie down on the lounger so I sat on the edge of the seat, facing the tank. It was relaxing to watch the fish and the way their fins moved around their body, wafting backwards and forwards.

I saw a large, dark shape bound in through the back door. It was a chocolate labrador, I realised. He leapt up, his tail wagging and reaching his paws up to Murray's waist.

"Get down, you daft dog." Murray patted his head and the dog dropped to the floor. "Go introduce yourself to Mariah." He waved his hand in my direction.

The dog came over and I reached out my hand for him to sniff.

"Meet Aero," Murray called from the kitchen as he made our drinks.

Aero sat down next to me and allowed me to stroke his head whilst I admired the fish.

I found myself drawn towards the red one. There was something familiar about the fish although I was certain I had not seen it before. The tingling sensation throbbed in my fingers and the flash ran through my body.

Red floated around me - was it blood? It slowly came into focus and my hand pushed it down, the skirt of a satin dress I didn't recognise but it was me wearing it. I am submerged. I am in the pool but it is dark except for the lights. I met his intense, silver eyes, hungry with a passion that frightens me. I noticed something unusual about his neck. He has gills!

The shock threw me back into reality and I was

confronted with the same, silver eyes from my vision, now holding a mug of tea out towards me.

"Did you have a memory?"

My eyes darted to his neck. "You had gills?"

"You remember," he grinned.

I shook my head. "That was real? What did you do to me?"

"Are you serious? I'm still waiting for you to explain what you did to me!"

He sounded exasperated and it made me feel uncomfortable. I got up.

"I best get home."

"No, wait. At least enjoy the drink I made you."

Good manners got the better of me and I sat back down on the lounger. He passed me my mug of tea which I took and held in both hands to create a barrier between us. We both blew on our steamy brews and took a few sips. We watched Aero sniffing around the kitchen hunting out any scraps that might have made it to the floor.

When my mobile rang, I sighed with relief that the silence was broken. I didn't care that it was Mum about to give me an ear bashing.

"Where are you, Mariah? The school rang over an hour ago and said they'd sent you home but you're not here!"

I took a gulp of tea. "I'm on my way."

"That doesn't answer my question. Don't make me break my promise."

I groaned. "I detoured to a friend's house but I'm

leaving now."

"What friend? You've got ten minutes," Mum said sternly and hung up.

I got up and placed my mug in the sink. I turned to face Murray to tell him that I couldn't stay any longer and request a lift home but he was grinning like a Cheshire cat.

"Glad to hear my friend status has been restored."

"You're incorrigible," I groaned.

He joined me at the sink and placed his mug next to mine. "I'll drive you home."

I cringed as we pulled up outside my house. "I should've got you to drop me off at the corner."

Mum sat on the front wall waiting for me and there was no way of avoiding her beady eyes. She jumped up and marched over to the car.

"Is this your friend?"

"He's leaving," I said as I got out.

"Murray, isn't it?" she caught the door and held it open.

I caught Murray grinning at me. "Your mum?"

Mum ignored him and looked at me. "The guy with a bike has a car now?"

"Like I'd know," I shook my head and headed up the steps and hoped she'd follow me in.

Mum manoeuvred around the door to lean into the

car. "I told Mariah to invite you over."

"She's told you about me," Murray smiled.

"No," I yelled. "She's a psychic."

"She never mentioned it," Murray said to Mum.

"As I've cut your truancy short, why don't you come in so I can finally meet you," Mum invited.

To my dismay, I heard the engine cut out and Murray got out the car.

"Great, I've got a free morning."

"And, I've got cake," Mum said as a gesture to encourage him towards our front door, not that Murray ever needed encouragement.

"Things keep getting better." Murray's eyes met mine and held them a little longer than necessary as if he hoped we could communicate telepathically.

We sat on stools in the kitchen with our fresh brews whilst Mum opened a cake tin and offered it to Murray. He took a carrot cake and thanked her for her generosity and, after tasting, he complimented her baking.

As Mum held the tin out to me, she whispered, "We'll discuss the incident later."

I should have guessed I wasn't going to get away with it. My shoulders sank and I cupped both hands around my tea.

"You have a familiar face…" Mum leaned towards Murray's face to get a closer look. "Tell me about your family. Who'd you live with? Have they always lived in Suffolk?"

Murray politely answered, "I live with Mum, Dad and my little sister. My dad's job means he often works away. His side of the family has lived here for years but my mum's side moved here from Ireland. In fact, before you called, I was about to tell Mariah a story about my granddad."

I sat up to pay attention. Mum tilted her head as she settled on Murray.

"We were close. When I was little, he'd take me out on his boat."

"Wow! He had a boat?"

"He was a fisherman and told some tall tales," Murray laughed. He nodded at me, "One was about a redheaded mermaid."

The colour drained from Mum's face and she looked at me as if I'd confessed to murder. Murray noticed and shifted in his seat, the twinkle in his eyes dissipated.

Mum growled, "Tell me, I want to hear this story!"

Murray shifted under her glare again but continued: "He claimed there was a terrible storm, and whilst pulling his nets in and checking all was secure, he heard a loud thud. Thud. Thud. He looked over the side of the boat and saw a woman's body and pulled her onboard. He lifted her into his arms and carried her into the warmth and safety of his cabin. That's when he noticed it wasn't a woman. With a fish tail instead of legs, he'd caught a mermaid." Murray smiled. "As a kid, I believed him. He was pretty convincing."

"What happened next?" I asked.

"Once dry, she had human legs and Granddad kept her safe until the storm was over. She was the most beautiful woman he'd ever seen. When she came to, she told him he was in grave danger for knowing about her kind. By knowing, he'd broken an ancient mer-law. They went to a harbour to see a witch who knew a spell to protect him from being seen by the soul snatchers."

"A soul snatcher?"

Hearing Murray telling this story stirred up emotions in me. Listening to him telling a tale felt familiar, the hairs on my arms stood on end. Perhaps he'd told me this very story and was waiting for me to remember it.

Murray grinned. "That's what I asked the first time he told me the story. Granddad said, if ever a human discovers a mermaid, the mermaid must make them their mate or let them be killed by the soul snatchers. The mermaid couldn't let Granddad be killed, she owed him her life. But Granddad refused to be her mate. He was already married to my grandma and couldn't love another woman, not even a beautiful mermaid. So, they broke the rules."

"That's romantic," I swooned a little.

Murray smiled at me. "Granddad advised me to marry the woman I love so fiercely that not even a mermaid can steal my heart."

"Do you still believe the story?" Mum asked.

Murray's cheeks flushed. "More now than ever."

"Why'd you think Mariah would be interested

in *this* story?" Mum's face was flushed and her lips pressed together so they looked white.

Murray looked uncomfortable under her glare. He looked to me for help but I didn't know the answer. He sighed and shrugged. Once again, I felt guilt. I knew I'd let him down but I didn't know what I'd done wrong.

"Mariah tells me you have a burn tattoo?" Mum continued her interrogative tone. "Would you mind showing me?"

"Mum!" I squealed.

But, Murray didn't hesitate. He pulled his t-shirt over his head and stood in my kitchen topless. There were the four dark dots above each pec of his toned chest and the markings made him appear stronger and more handsome. A desire pulled at me and I urged to place my fingertips upon the red marks, to own him. I blushed as I realised Murray had caught me checking him out.

"What a mess," Mum muttered.

"Don't be rude!" I scolded her.

She sucked air in through her teeth. "Damn blood magic."

"Blood magic?" Murray pushed her to elaborate.

She looked up from Murray's chest. "Your granddad's story is true. Your mum named you after him, didn't she?"

"Damn, you are a good psychic!"

Mum shook her head. "No. I know because I'm the witch that cast the spell over seventy years ago." We looked at Mum as if she was crazy but she continued,

"That mermaid, Coral, never found another mate. She's a siren, now."

"Oookay," Murray said in response to Mum but looked at me as if to say '*your mum is crazy*'.

"Blood is trying to fix this. You're Murray's grandson, Mariah is Coral's sister. This is the mark a mermaid prints on her mate when she chooses to procreate a new line," she pointed to Murray's chest.

Tea sprayed from my mouth. "Procreate?"

"Oh, man," Murray gasped and began putting his t-shirt back on. "I think you've misinterpreted the situation here."

"Why did I not see this sooner?" Mum scratched her head, oblivious to Murray and I's discomfort at the idea of starting a family of mer-heirs.

Mum grabbed our wrists and held us at the counter. "Of course, that's it! The spell protected the males. That's why Murray is alive despite you marking him and not claiming him." Mum glared at me. "Did you mark anyone else? What about the girl? The one with the blonde hair and the chocolate labrador."

I shook my head - not like I would know anyway.

"Kiely!" Murray gasped.

We stood cramped on the landing as Mum pulled the ladder down that gave access to the loft. As we made our way up, I could see dust and cobwebs but, to my relief, no spiders. Other than retrieving the book, I'd not had cause to come up here.

There were cardboard boxes everywhere with black marker pen scribbled on them to identify their contents. It reminded me of the day Jace moved away, my last memory before things got blurred out.

"Keep on the boards, I don't want any legs in my bedroom ceiling."

Mum pulled a dust sheet off a large full-length mirror with a silver filigree frame.

"That's beautiful," I gushed. "Why is it hidden up here."

"To keep it safe from the otherworld."

"The otherworld?"

"Not now," she tutted as she opened a chest that wouldn't look out of place on a pirate ship. She pulled out some dried sticks and lit them with a lighter she pulled from her pocket. "I need to show you something," she passed us a flaming sprig each. "Be careful, this is a fire hazard."

I held the twigs away from myself as the smoke they emitted gave off a strong smell that caught in my throat and made me cough.

"Mum, you promised not to cast on me again."

Murray had realised accepting Mum's tea and cake invite wasn't a great idea: "What's going on?"

Mum shut her eyes and began humming. Murray turned to me for answers but all I could do was shake my head. I didn't know either.

The surface of the mirror rippled.

"Did you see that?" Murray gasped.

I nodded.

It rippled again. It got more frequent, like a gentle wave blowing across a lake during a hot summer's day. It filled with a blur of colours and swirled with the ripples.

As the glass started to still, I could see an image reflected back but it wasn't us. Instead, it was like watching television with poor reception or a bad quality movie.

As Mum stopped humming, we saw a dark feather slowly gliding down to rest on a snowy bed where a girl lay curled up. Drops of red broke the crisp whiteness and a chocolate labrador barked at the shadows circling above. The dog was Aero.

"Is that Kiely?" Mum asked.

We could only see her feet but Murray recognised her.

"Yes, that's my sister. What is happening to her? What is this?"

The image stopped rippling. The still glass reflected us all staring at it in horror.

"It's a probable future," Mum explained. She placed a hand on Murray's chest. "I know this isn't a burn tattoo. You can tell me what happened, the whole crazy truth. I won't judge you."

Murray ran his hand through his hair and laughed. "Well, you believed my granddad's story."

He met my eyes and in that moment he looked vulnerable, as if seeking my support. Instinctively, I reached out to hold his hand and gave him a reassuring squeeze.

"We were slow dancing, Mariah and I, then it felt like fire burning through my shirt where her hands rested on my chest. She bolted out the door and I went after her. I asked what she'd done, but she didn't know."

"She marked you as her mate."

"I wouldn't! I'm with Jace." My heart broke as I remembered he dumped me. I swallowed a lump in my throat and bit my lip.

"Give her memories back. You are her true love. Kiss her," Mum instructed Murray.

"No! He's not my mate." I slammed my hand against his chest and shook my head. I threw Mum a look - Murray did not need any encouragement. With that, I descended down the ladder back to the landing and sought the sanctuary of my bedroom. "I need space."

Soon after, I heard Mum and Murray come down. My stomach tied in knots as I contemplated how Mum might bring him into my bedroom. The only boy I'd ever had in my room before was Jace.

"We need to work out if your sister is already marked and, if not, prevent it from happening. We can protect her from becoming part of this world."

"We have to warn her!" Murray insisted.

"No. Remember what your granddad told you about the soul snatchers? The three seers will see their laws are followed. She wouldn't live a day more."

"I can't do nothing."

"You won't. We'll watch her. We'll protect her."

Their voices became unclear as they headed downstairs. I waited for the sound of the front door but to my horror, the sound never comes. I realise Mum is entertaining Murray and I dread to think what he might tell her.

Slow dancing?

I think not!

CHAPTER 27

MY EYES WERE RED AND BLOTCHY. Everything had caught up with me and it was too much. I'd seen the video now that everyone was talking about. The clip of Murray and I on the steps, my hands on his chest. Someone saw us, recorded it, and posted it online.

I was so angry at myself for letting it happen. The worst part was, I couldn't deny my feelings for Murray. The look on my face, even from a distance was so blatant, and it broke my heart to know Jace had seen it. He was ignoring my calls and messages. I couldn't blame him. Although, he did that on a good day, so who knew if it meant anything?

I called Ana. It felt good to hear her voice.

"Mariah, are you okay?"

"No," I whine.

"Do you know 'bout the clips?"

"Yeah."

Since lunch, the new, trending video was Jace and I breaking up. A tear rolled down my cheek. It still hurt, and people were making fun of it.

"Are you and Murray… what's going on there?"

I shook my head and crushed my eyelashes together. More tears ran down my face. I wasn't with Murray, but I was mated to him. I could sense our connection when we're together, but without the history it felt like a trick. My life was so crazy, I didn't have any words.

"Mariah, are you still there? Should I come over?"

"I'm here. I'm fine." My voice was high pitched and my lip trembled.

"I'm coming over."

"No!" I stopped her. "I'm not ready to see anyone."

"I'm worried about you."

"Can we just talk?"

"Of course. You talk, I'll listen, for as long as you want." Her words were like a hug. I didn't know where to start but I felt stronger knowing she was there for me.

I stood in a long, purple gown whilst Denny compared the colour to a picture of the lavender anemone blooms that she planned to feature in her bridal bouquet.

"This is the one," she nodded at Mum for approval

and took a picture with her phone.

"Give us a twirl," Mum requested.

I blushed and turned on the platform. I caught glimpses of myself in every mirror. The purple was a good shade against my pale skin and red hair.

Denny held Mum's arm as she leaned into her. "I've told the photographer to take hundreds of pictures of Jace and Mariah dancing together. They're going to look gorgeous."

Mum laughed. "Remember, it's your big day, not theirs."

"Have you seen how gorgeous Jace looks in his suit?" She thrust her phone under Mum's nose. My heart ached to reach out and see the photo, and fill the Jace size hole he'd made by refusing to speak to me.

It was obvious Denny was in the dark about the breakup. I didn't want to aggravate Jace further by telling his mum when he'd chosen not to tell her. Mum and I exchanged a look but didn't say a word. I played along with the conversation where she thought there was some fairy tale romance going on.

"Is it me or has he had a growth spurt? It's like he's become a man overnight," Mum praised.

"I know," Denny gushed. "He's got higher ambitions than I ever did at his age. The other day, I caught him looking at universities and he's not even chosen his A Levels yet." Denny's attention turned to me. "Have you decided what you are doing after your exams?"

"No." My stomach twisted with anxiety. "I'm going

to get changed."

I hopped off the podium and made my exit for the changing rooms. I took my time putting my own clothes back on. Thinking about my future had always been a grey subject. But now, my future felt even more uncertain with the recent revelations about my heritage.

When I re-joined them, Denny was filling in a form with her details to purchase the dress and arrange the final fitting date. When Mum saw me, she pulled me into a quick side hug.

"You're going to look so beautiful."

"Thanks."

Denny returned the paperwork and joined us. "Thanks for agreeing to this."

"No worries," Mum smiled.

"I've got some other errands to run in town. You'll have to come over for a catch up soon?"

"Definitely, I've got to get going too. Got a beef stew slow cooking I need to check on."

When we got home, I headed upstairs. I could hear Mum hovering downstairs. When I went down, I discovered she had set the bistro table outside and in the middle, she had placed a scented tea light in a small candle holder.

"Wow, Mum, what's the occasion?"

"Oh, it's nothing," she dismissed me in that tone

I knew too well, one that revealed she was hiding something. I began snooping around to see what else she'd been up to. I checked the kitchen for scattered herbs or plants - any evidence that she had broken her promise of not casting any more spells on me. The oven had a warm glow, and the air was filled with a tantalising smell, Mum was baking something. On closer inspection, I spied one, giant Yorkshire pudding.

"Mum, did you know you're only cooking one pud?"

"Yes, that's for me."

"What about my dinner?"

"You're going out for dinner with a handsome, young man."

My heart filled with hope as I remembered my birthday and the last time Mum had arranged for me to be taken out for dinner without my knowledge. Mum loved to interfere, and a terrible realisation struck me. I rolled my eyes.

"Please, tell me it's not Murray!"

"He's your mate."

"I don't think so."

Mum chuckled which infuriated me further. She patted the stool. "Sit with me."

Reluctantly, I sat. "I'm not interested in him."

"What harm would come from spending a little time with Murray? After all, he's your future, you can't mark twice."

I recalled the scars on his firm chest. The guilt returned with a sickening wave. "I burned him."

"Branded him as yours. He's lucky to have survived - not everyone does."

"I could have killed him?"

"Only if he wasn't a match. Then, you'd have become a siren." She spoke as if this was common knowledge. She frowned. "What doesn't make sense is why the crows come for Kiely."

"What do they want?"

Mum shrugged. "Murray brought his sister to the bakery and she's a regular human. I've no idea why the crows want her or when they'll come. Someone must mark her, too."

"But, you said I can't do it again?"

"Not you. One of the others."

"More mermaids?"

Mum chuckled. "There are lots more than just mermaids."

The doorbell chimed.

"Go make yourself pretty for him. I'll entertain him until you get down. Murray and I are becoming good friends."

"But, Mum?"

"I'll tell you later."

My head was spinning as I went upstairs. Mum was finally answering my questions but it was so much to take in. The image of the crows attacking Kiely was savage and I didn't want to be responsible for that happening to Murray. The burns were bad enough. And now, she'd revealed, not only mermaids and soul snatchers, but there were more.

I headed upstairs to my room and rummaged through my wardrobe for something to wear. I was drawn to the black dress I'd worn for my birthday date with Jace.

I paused.

I wasn't sure I wanted to erase those memories with something new, something Murray. As I put the dress on, I realised that if Jace continued to shut me out, I'd have no choice but to move on. Maybe, if I could remember, I would understand why I branded Murray instead of Jace.

I walked down the side of the house to join Murray in the garden. As I turned the corner, I noticed the clematis was in bloom, decorating the wall in a subtle bloom.

Murray's cool eyes met mine as he smiled. "You look beautiful. I'd have made more of an effort if I'd known."

"It would've been nice if I'd known, too, instead of it being sprung on me."

"Your mum's just trying to help. She's not a bad person."

"You wait until she casts a spell on you," I grumbled.

"Let me rescue you from her," he said in an enchanting way.

He led me through my house and out onto the street. I could see his parked car. With the click of the fob, we parted to get in our respective sides.

Murray drove us to the harbour and parked up. As I joined him on the boardwalk, he took my hand and I let him. It was warm, gentle and felt nice.

"Tonight, Mariah, we will be dining on Star Finder, my family's boat."

"Your family has a yacht?"

"A motorboat. My dad has a number of appreciative clients," Murray corrected me and looked smug,

"What does he do?"

"Trade agreements on *big* contracts," Murray stressed the word big and I got the impression we were talking millions, or possibly billions, of pounds.

We passed a beautiful glass-fronted building and many boats. When Murray stopped, I knew we'd reached his. I don't know much about boats but it looked expensive. My jaw dropped a little as I took it in.

Murray helped me aboard. The first thing I noticed once on deck was that it was larger than when viewed from land.

Murray began removing his shoes and placed them in a rubber bucket.

"No offence, but my dad will kill me if we scuff the deck and it's really soft wood."

"No worries," I quickly removed my shoes before I caused any damage.

Murray gave me a brief tour of the boat and impressed me with what it had to offer. You could live quite comfortably here. It had a kitchen, bathroom, bedroom, sitting and eating area, and a cockpit. Murray sat down in front of the control panel and patted the cushion next to him for me to join him.

I always pictured a boat's steering wheel being outside, a large wooden wheel and a pirate at the helm, fighting the elements as he steered through the storms. This was indoors and very modern. It had comfortable seats and lots of buttons.

Murray started the engine with a key and drove us out the dock. It was liberating to watch the waves parting as the boat cut through them, taking us out to sea. All the nonsense Mum told me was starting to make sense. Even inside, I could taste the salty sea air and I knew I was where I belonged.

Murray slowed the boat down and cut the engine. "Here is where we will dine. In the middle of the ocean - fit for a mermaid?"

I gave him a gentle push as we got up. It still sounded odd hearing someone call me a mermaid, but the more I thought about it the more it rang true.

Murray led me up to an area he hadn't taken me to on the tour. It was upstairs and outside but covered by a roof. There was a little seating area. Murray signalled for me to take a seat by holding his arm out.

He ran about, setting the table. He placed a candle in the centre of the table and lit it with a lighter, and added two wine glasses and a bottle of Shloer.

"Shloer? Bringing out the hard stuff," I laughed.

"Did I mention I'm scared of your mum? Besides, you're not old enough and I've got to drive you home."

"I'm allowed one with a meal."

"I'll be back with our food." As Murray disappeared down the stairs, over his shoulder he added, "I thought you were a good girl."

I bit my lip. There was something appealing in Murray accusing me of being a bad girl. Something inside me that wanted to be bad with him. I thought about texting Ana to tell her about my impromptu date but when I checked my phone I didn't have a signal out here.

I sat back and took in the tranquillity of the open ocean. The candle was a nice touch as it was just starting to get dark. The boat rocked in a subtle way that you could only notice it when you were still. I thought it'd be quiet but there was the whispering of the waves and the wind. The ocean was as alive as I was.

Murray returned carrying two plates. He had made a salmon salad, with a fan of avocado slices. It wasn't fancy but I could tell he'd made an effort.

I tucked in immediately and realised how hungry I was. I tried to slow myself down so I didn't appear so greedy.

"Your mum keeps trying to tell me stuff about you but I want to take you out on dates and get to know you the right way. Real dates, not pretend ones that help you get with someone else."

"Oi, that was your idea."

"It wasn't my best moment."

"When is my mum trying to tell you stuff?"

Murray dipped his head. "I wanted answers. So…

I went to the bakery. We got chatting, your mum and I, and I started going everyday after school."

I felt jealous. There were so many times I'd asked questions, only to be silenced. I'd even had my memories wiped. But, he got answers, with a cup of tea, cake, and a cherry on top.

He gave a strained laugh. "I mean, haven't got swimming anymore."

I sighed and left an awkward silence. We finished our salad and Murray took our plates and returned with dessert.

When he returned he was laughing. He presented two bowls.

"Okay, I'm not a chef."

"What is it?"

"Tinned fruit and cream."

"It doesn't sound bad," I reassured him.

"Come on."

"If I was serving, it most likely would have been something burnt."

Murray smiled and sat down. "Your mum told me how to change into merform. I've not tried it yet. Have you?"

I choked. "She told you? She's only begun telling me stuff and isn't very forthcoming."

"Want to try together?"

My pulse raced and my insides buzzed with an energy that made me want to jump around. I wasn't sure it was wise, but I nodded. My body wanted to do this, I wanted to become my true self, a mermaid.

CHAPTER 28

W E WERE ON THE LOWER DECK, at the back of the boat, looking out across the expanse of blue. I smiled as we stood on a platform that met the sea, perfect for diving off and swimming. The waves sang a song that called me in and the salty air made my hair dance to its tune.

Murray took off his t-shirt and began unbuckling his jeans.

"Are you nervous?"

"I… I'm not sure about this."

"What's wrong?"

His mock concern was given away by the half smile that he was trying to suppress. Murray oozed confidence as he strutted towards me in his semi-nakedness. He licked his lips in a way that made my body burn. I cast my eyes out across rolling waves and took a deep breath to steady myself. I felt his finger trace down the far side of my face, softly turning my face towards him.

"Am I making you uncomfortable?"

I let out a nervous laugh. "Sort of. I'm not taking my clothes off in front of you." I didn't feel ready to see him in all his glory either.

Murray leaned close and I felt his warm breath on my skin. He spoke in a slow whisper that drew out my shaky breath, "I promise, no matter how tempting, I won't look."

The northern wind chilled my cheek where Murray's hand had been. He moved away, and pushed his jeans and pants down in one motion. I saw his arse before blushing and looking away. I heard a splash.

"Fuck, it's cold," he laughed. He was bobbing in the sea chuckling as he adjusted to the cold. "I mean it's lovely and warm."

I laughed. "You're not a convincing liar."

He turned around. "Hurry up, I'm not sure how long my resistance will last."

Oh no! I realised it was my turn to get naked. I hoped Mum wasn't lying about this otherwise I would feel incredibly naive for skinny dipping with Murray, especially with his reputation.

With hesitation, I slowly slipped the straps of my dress off my shoulders and allowed it to slide down to the floor, I unclipped my bra and bravely kicked off my knickers.

I dived in. As I hit the water, going under, it felt

good. I glided deeper into my element. Wishing to rise up, I kicked my legs. But they fought against me as if they were trapped. tangled and bound by something.

There was a glowing light around my waist, at a steady pace it cascaded down and as it did, I saw scales appear. My legs fused together forming a tail. Using butterfly stroke, I moved my legs together as one. With very little effort I rose up and broke the surface.

I found Murray and cheered: "I did it! It's true."

Murray lay back in the water and raised his dark blue tail above the surface. He shook his head. "I can't believe it."

I raised mine, a shimmery, silver tail that had a subtle rainbow in the moonlight. We both laughed and I flicked my tail to splash him.

"Oi!" he laughed and swam backwards. He twisted and disappeared under the water.

I lowered my tail and tried to see where he had gone. I felt hands on my waist, pulling me down under the water. I closed my eyes as I went down and felt bubbles tickle my nose. Remembering my gills, I was conscious of them opening and closing. It felt so natural, like breathing - we were breathing, just underwater. I opened my eyes and smiled as I took in the murky depths of the North Sea.

I elbowed Murray off me and swam away. I checked he was following me; I was fast but he was keeping pace.

I loved how the water rushed past me. I closed my eyes, relishing in the sensation. *I saw myself enjoying a ride home on the back of Murray's bike. The way we dipped as we raced around corners was exhilarating* and my body turned in the water to take a new direction. The way the water rushed through my hair, reminded me of the way *my hair had blown as I sat precariously on his bike.* I flicked my tail and drove myself upwards to the surface. The sea air against my wet skin felt harsh as I returned to reality.

Murray was quick to join me. "That was amazing!"

I noticed that a few dark scales had appeared on his shoulders. His eyes were a bright silver with elongated pupils. Droplets ran down his face and I felt a desire to kiss him. I found myself swimming closer, closing the gap between us.

"Why cycle when you have a car?"

"My parents wouldn't let me drive until I passed my test. They're such killjoys."

Murray was so close, I could barely breathe. I froze, aware of the fact we were both naked, on our first real date. This was moving too fast?

"I don't know if to congratulate you, or..." I splashed him, creating a distance between us.

"Oi!" he snapped. "Can't we enjoy this. It's not every day you realise you can swim to the Caribbean."

"Small steps, Murray. That's a bit ambitious for a first swim."

He closed the gap between us. "You've got beautiful markings on your face."

"On my face?" My hand reached up to my cheeks and I could feel the raised bumps of scales on my cheekbones and around my eyes. I wished for a mirror to see myself.

"We ought to head back to the boat before someone sees us," Murray said in a serious tone.

We swam back and Murray pulled himself aboard first. I held onto the ledge but remained in the water.

"Could you look away," I requested. Scales covered my breasts, but it still felt very revealing without a top.

Murray opened a chest and threw me a towel so I could cover myself and get dry. Like a gentleman, he turned his back to me.

I pulled myself up and used the towel to protect my dignity as I made my way to my clothes. I put on my bra and shimmied into my dress, taking care to conceal myself from Murray. Even though he wasn't looking, I knew he could turn around any moment.

He sat with his back towards me, I was able to admire his mer-form without him seeing. He rubbed at his tail trying to dry himself and it looked exotic, almost tribal, the way the scales decorated his body created intricate patterns. They shimmered down his arms and across his back.

"Did Mum tell you how we turn back?" I asked.

My body was scattered all over with shimmering scales. There was a patch on the back of my hand and whilst drying I'd felt them on my collarbone too.

"No. I'm sure once dry it'll be as easy as jumping in was."

We rubbed at our tails but nothing was happening. I began rubbing harder in a desperate hope that I needed to be really dry, a prickly heat creeped over my body.

"What if we're stuck like this?"

"We can't be," he said in a weak voice that didn't suit him. The seagulls squawked like they were chuckling at our predicament.

"Great idea, Murray!" I clapped my hands.

"You look like a seal. Ark, ark!" he laughed.

I growled, this wasn't a time for jokes.

He seemed to find my annoyance even more entertaining. "It's not the worst thing that could happen - you're beautiful."

"Really?" I said annoyed but softening. Despite being cross, I did find it flattering, "Now is not the time to be hitting on me."

The merriment vanished from his face and he became serious. "I'm going to call Gwyn for help."

Murray reached for his mobile phone and pressed some buttons and held it to his ear. "Damn, there's no signal. We need to get inland."

"We need to shift back," I said with urgency. I thought back to the experience in the water. The light cascading down my body. I had to make that happen again but in reverse.

I saw the bright white moon and I felt my body connect with it. It was as if it was an extension of me and I focused on the pure, bright, white light.

Closing my eyes, I pictured the moon in my mind and felt a coolness followed by a fierce burning racing up my legs. It was painful, I screamed and opened my eyes. I folded over in agony, grasping at my legs. There, at the bottom of my towel, I could see my toes where moments ago had been a fin.

"How'd you do that?"

It was tempting to let him stay stuck in mer-form but I needed him to sail the boat back. I looked up at the sky. "I focused on the moon."

He closed his eyes and looked almost peaceful as he concentrated and I caught myself admiring how handsome he is. Perhaps being mated wouldn't be so bad. He groaned as his fin glowed and revealed his toes. The light moved up towards his waist and soon he had two hairy legs. He opened his eyes and smiled at me.

"That was fun."

I nodded and wrapped the towel around myself and went to find the rest of my clothes. Murray got to his feet. He was unsteady on his legs as if he had drunk one too many and as he stumbled across the deck to get his clothes he dropped his towel and I was met by his backside.

I turned away as he made my cheeks flush for the hundredth time. Murray was sure good at making my blood race.

We were soon back inside the cabin and Murray started the engine, and began taking the boat back in. As we neared the jetty, I saw a figure standing at the end of the jetty. Mum held two willow twigs in her hands and pointed them out towards us.

Murray saw her, too, as he brought the boat into where she stood. "How'd she know where to find us?"

I frowned. I knew. She'd used magic despite promising not to.

Mum stumbled as she boarded the boat. She came into the cabin. "I'm sorry to interrupt your bonding but we must hurry. Kiely is in grave danger!"

"What are those?"

"Divining sticks - to find you. We will use them to find Kiely, too," Mum explained.

Murray secured the boat and we disembarked.

Mum held the two sticks in front of her and chanted:

"Moon, Sun, Air, Fire, Earth, and Sea,

Guide us to the one we seek.

Give us favour in this deed,

Guide us to the one we seek."

The sticks began pulling in a direction. We followed it along the jetty and across shingle walkways. It drew her onto the road and we followed behind her.

"How do you know Kiely is in trouble?" I asked.

"The bats came."

We stepped over a low-level metal fence that edged the field at the cliff tops. We could see the dark swarm of crows in the air and a sense of foreboding.

"Kiely!" Murray went to run, but Mum dropped the sticks and grabbed his arm.

"Wait!" She ordered.

She faced me. "You cannot put this off any longer.

Alone you are weak. You've no chance of defeating the crows with your fractured mind. You're blocked from reaching your full potential. It's time. Break the amnesia rose spell. Kiss Murray."

"No!" I shook my head. For all it had been tempting in the ocean, it definitely wasn't now. Not with Mum standing over me ordering me to do it.

Murray's jaw tensed and I could see the vein in his neck throb. His hands were in fists.

"I promised I'd never do this again, Mariah."

"Then don't!"

"You're making me choose between my promise to you and my sister's life." He shut his eyes. He looked torn, and vulnerable.

"Murray, I'm sorry, I…"

Murray cupped my cheek. "I love you. I wanted… you know what I wanted."

Was he begging to kiss me or threatening to? My fingers found their way to those damn marks that riddled me with guilt. I'd made him mine and I wanted to know why. Not just that, I realised as the gap closed between us, I lost all sense of the world around us. I wanted to know our past, to share our future. And, despite the present time being off…

"I want to."

Murray didn't hesitate, his lips were on mine, warm and soft. My breath was lost in his kiss, as he brought my mind alive with memories. Like a dam unblocked, running free, cutting its path with truth, I saw everything that had happened and my emotions flooded back. Everything forgotten returned.

When he let me go, tiny lights spun around us, rising up into the sky, like slow-moving, glittering fireworks. In the sky, they created a bright rose of light. The sparkles dispelled and floated down to the ground, soft as snow. The spell was broken and my body felt charged.

"I remember," I faced Gwyn with a heavy weight in my heart. She wasn't my mum. "Mu-, no, Gwyn?"

"I'm sorry, Mariah, but now is not the time. You must focus on saving Murray's sister."

I could feel the chemistry between Murray and I.

Electricity coursed through my body as Murray took my hand:

"Come on."

We raced forward into battle, Kiely was crumpled on the ground. The crows kept diving and scratching her skin. Aero at her side, barking and keeping the birds at bay. I could see they'd hurt him too.

"Stop!" Murray yelled.

He went to run towards his sister but I caught his hand. I could feel the energy in the air. I knew what we had to do. I raised our joined hands up towards the sky, a charge raced between our bodies, bubbling in my blood. The wind whipped up and my hair, blowing it furiously around me. We struggled to stand against the wind but the crows were no longer in control of their flight. They fought against the current, to stay in the sky. We were bringing them down.

I heard Aero howl and the sound was heartbreaking.

I angrily threw my arms over my head, attempting to move the wind and toss the birds but instead a bolt of lightning crackled down and struck a bird from the sky. I tried again and a cloud now lit up above us, rumbling with the lightning bolts inside. I aimed for another and shot the bird. The birds flew off, leaving Aero and Kiely in peace.

Murray ran to his sister's side. Aero was whining and nuzzling into her. As Murray checked Kiely over, Aero began licking her wounds. The storm simmered down and the lights in the dark cloud above turned out.

A crow flew towards us, a dark shadow cast down from where it flew to the ground. I felt a buzz in my veins, ready to attack. The shadow took form and became a man. There was something terrifying and stunning about him. He had dark skin and eyes that were almost black. He wore tight, leather trousers and, although he had shifted into a human body, he had large, dark, feathered wings protruding from his back.

His deep voice bellowed: "Gwynevere, you know better than to meddle in our laws."

"The girl is innocent. There's been a mistake," Gwyn argued.

"We make no mistakes. She's ours."

"How can this be?"

"She is an unclaimed wolf."

"A wolf?"

"One of Luna's line."

"Luna's been here?" Gwyn's eyes darted around searching the darkness for someone. "Does she know of Mariah?"

"I'm only interested in this girl. She's mine."

As he approached Kiely, he turned his nose up at Murray. "Move aside, small fry!"

"No!" Murray stood and Aero growled. "You can't have her!"

Murray threw his hand forward and a spear of ice shot from his hand. It hit the man in the centre of his chest but bounced off and fell to the floor.

The man laughed. "I'm an ancient. You're no match for me. Now, control your dog, I don't enjoy putting down animals."

"Murray, bring your dog to me," Gwyn ordered in a manner way too calm for the situation.

"No! I won't leave Kiely." Murray yelled.

I came over dizzy as Gwyn said, "Come, little Aero, come to me, come sit by my side, by the power in me."

Aero obediently walked to Gwyn and sat down beside her. Gwyn gave her attention to Murray.

"There are ancient laws we must follow. This is out of our hands."

"I said I won't leave her."

Gwyn waved her hand and I felt the ground sink and lock around my feet.

I heard Murray call out in anger, "What are you doing?"

"Gwyn! You promised never to cast on me again!"

"Except for your protection."

Trapped in an earth made conveyor belt, we were dragged away from Kiely. With no choice but to watch the man rip away at Kiely's shadow. Her body dragged across the field with each tug. She cried out in pain and her body squirmed in agony, as it was torn from her body. Despite the cold, I could see a fever upon her brow. She begged him to stop.

Murray's anguish felt like my own and I could feel my powers bubbling deep inside me. He dropped to a crouch as he was forced to watch his sister's torture. It was too much and he fought against Gwyn's hold on him. He dug his hands into the ground and pulled himself forward, moving like a gorilla in sinking mud. Crows swooped at him, but all it did was slow him down.

"Murray, leave it be!" Gwyn's voice had an air of panic.

"Join us," the man spoke to Kiely. He held out his hand towards her crumpled body as if offering to help her up.

The crows scratched at Murray's arms but he kept going. I saw the blood run down his bicep and knew I had to help. I summoned the storm cloud back and began striking the crows down. I would cover him while he advanced on our enemy.

Kiely threw her head back, screaming at the man. Her eyes were an unnatural, golden yellow. She bared her teeth at the swooping birds like a dog and I saw her fangs.

"To be one of us is better than to not be at all," the man smiled at Kiely as if he was just making a casual point. He didn't seem phased by Murray's advances towards him.

Murray kept on. His movements were slow as he dragged himself forward. He grunted with the strain of it and sounded more frustrated every time Kiely called out in agony and begged the crows to stop. Murray was rising as if climbing up out of the ground, until he was free.

He ran at the crows, beating them away from his sister and swung his fist at the man's face but it never connected. With a sweep of the man's hand, Murray flew up into the air and was suspended there.

I hoped to reason with Mum to help but she shook her head, her lip was shaking like she was truly scared. I noticed the man's hands were out in front of his body in a peculiar way.

"I warned you," his head dipped, casting an eerie shadow across his features, making them appear distorted and cruel. He smiled. A smile that was out of place on his twisted face. "Wave goodbye."

The man raised his own hand up and down and Murray's hand did the same, giving us a strange impression of a wave. The man threw his hands outwards as if throwing something and with the motion, Murray's body was tossed upwards and over the cliff top into the sea. His body flew as if he weighed nothing.

"No!" I screamed.

My whole body shook. The power brewing inside me was uncontainable. My body pulled towards the sea but I was trapped in the earth, so my powers reached for it, lifting the ocean up in a tsunami wave. The sea rose upwards creating a great wall of water. A great, grey mass almost black in the darkness, but where the moonlight caught the water it created beautiful patterns of light across the battlefield.

"Mariah, you need to calm down!" Gwyn called from behind me.

The fury was burning inside. She'd promised never to cast on me again, but she'd done it anyway. She'd trapped me in the ground, preventing me from fighting alongside Murray. Everytime something bad happened, Gwyn was right there messing with me, using her magic.

The wind built up, whipping my hair around me. It was so strong, I could feel it pulling my body, lifting me up. It hurt as the rough dirt rubbed against my skin as I rose out the ground.

As the power coursed through my veins, never had I felt more alive than in that moment. I directed all my anger into charging myself up, I could feel the energy vibrating inside me. The wave lifted, growing larger and larger.

I saw the fear in the eyes of the man and it thrilled me. I'll make him suffer. I will prevent him from hurting anyone else. I drew the water like a curtain. My arm stretched out, directing it. The sea and I are one and my power is as immense as the ocean.

As our connection grew, my power became greater. The wind blew my hair back as it continued to hold me in the air, my body tingled with how incredible I felt. I understood the power within me and so do my enemies as they face their destruction. I saw the crows being pulled into the mass, their flapping wings useless against the water sucking them in. I continued to control the sea, building the wall of water around me. It's a whirlpool on land, with me in the eye.

"Kiely!" I realised that she'd gotten lost in the commotion.

I let go of my hold on the sea. The water came crashing down, filling the space beneath my feet. I saw Kiely struggling against the torrent. Her body is being dragged over the clifftops, out with the returning sea.

The wind around me dissipated. I ran towards the rapidly receding water's edge. The water splashed my legs, I willed myself to stay human as the droplets harden and transform into scales. I leaped into the air, diving in a way that would make Mr Griffen proud. I gave in to my instincts and, as I flew through the air, I kicked out my legs out behind me, and shifted.

I broke into the waves, my tail beating behind me as I raced towards Kiely. The current aided me as much as it worked against me. It helped me chase after Kiely but was also pulling her away from me. She kept disappearing under the waves. I swam towards her pale, white hand like a beacon stretching up towards the sky. I was stronger than the sea and moved faster and soon reached her. I felt for her body, pulling her close up against me.

I flicked my tail, propelling us up to the surface. The cool, salty air chilled my cheek. The sea was choppy and the current strong. Kiely was heavy in my arms, a dead weight. Her body was beaten from the fight. I blinked as I battle my own exhaustion, I have to get us to land so we can rest.

"Murray!"

I called a few times with no answer, searching the darkness but can't see him anywhere. My heart longed for him, and I felt lost without him. I hesitated, hope holding me there a little longer, waiting for an answer.

I needed to get Kiely to safety, it's what Murray wanted. I swam for the beach, stopping every so often to check for Murray. As I neared the shore, I realised I need to shift back if I'm to carry Kiely out. I didn't know if it was even possible. Shifting on the boat had been challenging and we were dry on the deck. My body preferred being in merform, in the sea it was a natural transition.

The moon was the only light illuminating the sky.

 "Please, help me."

I shut my eyes and focused on it's milky glow. I replayed the change in my head, picturing what needed to happen. I focussed on my tail becoming legs. Feeling the light filled me with hope even though my body was resisting the change. I fought against my will to keep my tail.

Legs. I need legs.

A cool tingle touched the tip of my tail, below the surface I saw a glow, my legs were returning. It was hard swimming with legs when the sea water was battling to turn them back. It made Kiely feel even heavier. I held the girl that once was my enemy against my chest, as I carried her body to land and safety.

As I stepped onto the shore, my legs wobbled with the strain. My wet dress clung to my skin. I dropped Kiely onto the shingle and collapsed next to her. Rolling onto my back we stared up at the sky.

"Thank you," I whispered to the moon.

My legs still cast in a soft glow from the magic used to shift, dimming as it diffused. We had survived and escaped the crows.

"Shouldn't I be thanking you?" Kiely croaked.

I beamed. Never had I been happier to hear her voice.

Kiely and I dripped and shivered as we walked up the beach towards the promenade. It was late but the sky was clear with a full moon in the sky. We were both barefoot.

"Why were you out so late?" I asked.

"Getting some air," Kiely said.

It sounded a bit of an extreme thing to do, to leave your house in the dead of night, wearing only your nightdress, and not putting on shoes. Kiely wasn't telling me everything but, despite saving her life, I knew I couldn't make her trust me. I was sick of people lying to me, though, keeping me in the dark.

"Whatever."

Kiely snapped, "I thanked you for saving my life. What more do you want? We're not going to be friends. You stole my boyfriend. Remember?"

"Sorry I bothered?"

"Well, you can stop bothering. Have a good night!" Kiely crossed the road and began walking in the direction of her home, the opposite way to the direction I needed to go.

"What if they come back?"

Kiely stopped and shouted, "Maybe, I don't want saving."

Her eyes flashed gold before she continued away. I ran across the road to join her but stopped. I knew Murray would be upset if I let her go but where was he? The ocean whispered its song but wasn't telling me its secrets.

Murray could already be home or waiting at my house. Perhaps it was best Kiely and I split up, one of us was bound to find him sooner or later. I let Kiely go and headed for my own home.

CHAPTER 29

MUM WASN'T HOME WHEN I GOT IN. I was relieved my mobile was still working and tried to calling Murray and Mum but got no answer. I was exhausted and finally gave in to sleep. My sleep wasn't restful. Remembering everything caused me to toss and turn as I re-lived it all. I kept waking, hoping Mum was home and Murray was safe.

My mobile had no messages, no missed call, no notifications. Perhaps it was water damaged afterall. The lack of news just gave rise to the sick feeling in the pit of my stomach that something was wrong.

When my mobile read 3:30 am, I opened my curtains hoping to see my stalker. I was desperate for a familiar face, even one of a strange man that stands outside my house, but he wasn't there. Why tonight of all nights

had he abandoned me?

"Oh, Murray," I whispered into the night.

All the pieces fell into place. He wasn't my stalker. He was my lover, watching over me, drawn to me. All these nights he'd been there, wanting to be close when I couldn't even remember him.

Now, he was gone.

"Please, be safe."

My heart sang at the memory of us kissing in the pool, the way he chased me and found me interesting, even when he thought I was an ordinary girl. He made me see myself as beautiful. The way he described my mermaid form made me yearn to be in the sea with him again. He tried to protect me from getting hurt by Jace with Kiely, even at the detriment to his own feelings. He showed respect when helping me regain my memories by trying to find triggers that didn't involve kissing. I regretted all the time I'd wasted by not giving him a chance. Time, I'd wasted on Jace, a crush that had destroyed our friendship. I'd lost so much. I couldn't bear to lose Murray, too.

I needed Jace. I needed my friend. I wanted to run to his home and tell him everything and answer all his questions. He'd never believe me. I would have to shift and show him or use my weather powers. I imagine the shock on his face and the admiration. He'd think it cool... but telling him would put him in danger. I didn't want to face the crows again.

I must have fallen asleep as I woke to the sound of someone in the kitchen. I heard the click of the kettle, followed by the sound of a spoon clinking against the sides of a mug.

"Mum!" My heart sang.

Throwing on my dressing gown, I ran my fingers through my hair. Overwhelmed with relief that she was okay, I took the steps two at a time. I flung open the kitchen door, and froze as I took in the stranger. A woman with red, curly hair, grey eyes, and a face a little older than me was casually sipping a mug of tea. My heart hammered against my chest. Was she a crow? Was I in danger?

"Yay, you're awake. Shall I make you one?" She smiled as if we were friends.

"Who are you?"

"Your sister, Coral."

My heart thundered in my chest at the revelation, and knew from looking at her it was true. I maneuvered to one of the stools but didn't take my eyes off her. "What are you doing here?"

She whistled. "You caused quite a storm last night! Literally! There'll be all sorts of environmental experts trying to explain what happened, but I'm here because Gwynevere is not."

It was odd to hear her full name. I couldn't remember the last time anyone had used it except the freaky crow guy last night.

"Where is she?"

"Murray rescued her but she's recovering at the manor, being treated by our family doctor." Coral lifted the tea bag out of my cup on the back of a spoon.

As she handed me my tea, I sighed. "Is Murray okay, too?"

"Yes," Coral nodded and moved to sit on the stool next to me.

I breathed a sigh of relief.

"Murray shall be trained at the manor. We need to keep you both apart until you have better control of your powers. Together, you're too volatile."

"What about me? I need to learn my powers, too!"

"Little sister, that's why I'm here. What you did, with the sea - wow - unheard of." Coral sipped her tea. Her eyes twinkled as she watched me over the top of her cup.

"You'll teach me?"

Coral nodded.

I should be happy. I was finally getting to learn my powers but my heart ached for Murray; a guy I'd pushed away so many times, broken his heart countless times, and, now I finally remembered him, I couldn't be with him.

"How soon can we start?" I needed to learn to control my powers as quickly as possible. I had to get to the manor. I had to be with Murray.

Hi Goldie

Crazy first date - hey? I don't even know where to start. I wish I could be there with you, to help make sense of everything.

Gwyn's in a coma; she bashed her head hard. Thankfully, your family has their own doctor taking good care of her. She's in good hands.

They've insisted I stay and learn. Apparently, we're an epic power couple, and need to get the 'epic' under control before being reunited. Be a little nerd, and study hard my mer-mazing beauty.

If you can, could you keep an eye on Kiely for me? I know it's a lot to ask as you don't get on but she's been through a lot, and I worry about her.

I miss you already. I can't promise every date will end in weather phenomena but they can all end with a kiss. That's if you'll have me?

I'm thinking of you and hope you're safe.

All my love, Murray x

"What are you grinning at?"

Coral tried to lean over my shoulder to see my mobile screen, but I moved it out of the way.

"Nothing."

Murray's email stirred up a mix of emotions. I worried for Gwyn, even though I knew there was nothing I could do to help her. Knowing she was in a bad condition made me feel guilty for smiling, but, Murray's words had stirred up all the good vibes from our date and I wanted to kiss him, too. I sent a quick reply.

Oh Murray,

I'm going to be so geeky, this mermaid is going to need waterproof books. Swot up!

All my love, Mariah x

P.S. Give my love to Gwyn

"Whatever. Hurry up your breakfast or you'll be late."

"Can't I stay home and learn with you?" I grumbled.

Coral insisted I attend school and sit my exams. It seemed a rather bizarre thing to do considering everything that had happened. I felt the time would be better used learning to control my powers so I could reunite with Murray quicker.

"There's plenty of time for that after your exams."

I groaned.

"Remember, rule one, never reveal to anyone what you are. There are laws against mortals discovering our world."

"What'd you mean?"

"If a mortal knows, a drago will be sent to possess and wipe their mind." Coral clicked her fingers. "It'll be like you never existed."

The hairs on my arm stood on end as my powers surged thinking about how much Ana already knew and the thought of an impending battle. I remembered how it felt when Gwyn wiped my memories and wondered if she would sense something was missing. Would she miss our friendship even if she didn't know it was me that she'd lost? Could we meet brand new, start over, and have a friendship where she would never know my kind's secrets?

"What are you thinking?"

"I wish I could tell Jace." I didn't want to give Ana's name until I'd figured out how to keep her safe. There might be a loophole in the laws.

"Who's Jace? Murray's your mate."

"A friend." My heart ached, if only we still were.

"If you care about Jace, don't tell him. Now, get going before you're late."

"Mariah, you're early," Ana said, joining me with a water bottle in her hand.

"How come you're in so early?" I flipped the question back at her.

"The early bird catches the worm," she said with a weary sway. Her hair was wet and I could smell the chlorine on her.

Her choice of phrase made me think of the crows, and their prey. I had no idea what the drago would do if they discovered what she knew but seeing what the crows did to Kiely made me fear for her safety.

"Ana, you need to forget everything I've told you."

She frowned. "Like, what?"

"Magic and stuff. Never speak of it. Promise?"

"What sort of danger?" she leaned in and whispered.

"I daren't say more but knowing what I am puts

you in danger. Please, you're my best friend."

Ana's mouth dipped. "I know nothing. Your secrets are safe with me."

I hugged her. "Thank you. I'm sorry."

"I liked discovering magic and fins."

"Ana!" I warned.

"Does this mean no more spells?" Her bottom lip stuck out a little.

"I'm afraid so."

We were silent, as we felt an invisible wall rise around us. It was our thing, we'd bonded over it, and now it was gone. My heart ached as I felt another friend being taken from me, except this time I had to let her go. Keeping her in my world, sharing with her my secrets, put her in danger.

"So, what can we talk about now?"

"Boys?"

"Just one man for me."

"Actually, I have got something to tell you…" My cheeks burned. I needed to give Ana something to show her that we could be friends despite this.

"What?"

"I kissed Murray."

Ana's hands went to her mouth as she gasped. Her whole face lit up and I could tell she was pleased for me. "And?"

"We're seeing how things go."

Ana squealed. "You two are so hot together. Tell me more."

"There's not much to say."

"Don't you dare lockdown another convo!"

"I'll tell you more later but first I need to do something. See you at the pool later?"

Ana nodded and I took off. I wasn't sure how I was going to approach Kiely or where to find her. I remembered she liked to watch Jace play football even after they'd broken up but when I checked the field she wasn't there. I returned to the school and felt I'd let Murray down.

Someone grabbed me from behind and shoved me into a classroom.

I spun around and was face to face with Kiely. She'd changed. Her hair was pitch black, sucking the tan from her skin and making her look pale.

"Kiely, are you alright?" My feet shuffled as I backed up into the room, creating a distance between us.

Kiely's hand moved ever so slightly but I felt the grip on my wrist as if she were touching me. My skin burned and I gasped in pain. I held my arm against my chest as I tried to back away, finding myself up against the wall. My heart thumped in my chest, my fingers buzzed with my powers. I had to stay in control if I wanted to see Murray. Kiely wasn't even touching me, but I physically felt under attack. How was she doing this?

"I know what you are Mariah Turner and I won't forgive what you've done to my brother. I'm a crow now, and we're the law enforcers of the shifters. You slip up and I'm going to be right there, eager with your punishment. You understand?" As she spoke her eyes darkened, absent of the gold light that had shone the last time I'd seen her. She'd become something else.

Kiely's stood on the opposite side of the room, and raised her hand. I felt fingers as if they were around my neck. Staring into the blackness of her irises, I felt her grip tighten, and nodded. My eyes prickled with tears. How was I to protect her if she was hell bent on killing me. If I attacked Murray's sister, could he ever forgive me?

Kiely let me go and I choked on the sudden rush of air into my lungs, gulping it in like I desperate thirst.

Her expression softened and the darkness faded from her eyes, "Promise you won't tell Jace. Promise you'll keep him safe?"

I nodded.

Kiely's shoulders dropped as she exited, leaving me alone in the room. Murray didn't need to worry about her, she seemed to have figured out her powers better than us. I rubbed my neck and waited to be certain she was gone before leaving.

As I walked to the pool, I saw Jace. I clocked who he was speaking to. What was Coral doing here? And, why was she speaking to Jace. Every scenario I thought of didn't end well. I hurried over to interject.

Coral beamed upon seeing me. "There you are,

Mariah. I was asking this boy, Jace, where the pool is."

"Come on," I said as I took her arm and pulled her away.

"You should come and watch. I've been told she is really good," Coral called to Jace with a smile.

I cringed, did Coral even know who she was talking to? My shoulders tensed ready for Jace's reaction.

"No, thanks," Jace snorted.

I let go of Coral and spun round to shout at Jace: "You never came and watched me swim or took any interest in my swimming. I am good."

"Rumour has it, she's the best in the school," Coral corrected me.

"But, I watched you play, and you know what? You're mediocre at best."

"F' off, Mariah."

"With pleasure!" I screamed, hot with anger.

Coral matched my rapid pace as I hurried towards the pool house, straight into Ana. She looked past me at Coral when she spoke, "Hey Mariah, what was that about?"

"Jace being a dick."

"If he's your friend, I dread to think what your enemies are like."

Ana acknowledged Coral, with a look that asked *'Who is this?'* without her uttering a word.

"This is Coral."

"I'm Mariah's second cousin."

Ana's eyes widened and I hoped she wouldn't ask anything like *'what powers does she have?'* "Did you hear about the freak storm in Old Stowe at the weekend?"

"No," we both chimed. My cheeks flushed a guilty red whereas Coral was amused.

"All the beach huts down that end have been smashed to pieces. They called in environmental experts, and guess what? They're calling it an act of god! Sounds like a cop-out to me. Someone clearly wasn't watching their gadgets and failed to put a warning out."

As Coral tucked a red strand behind her ear, she gave me a knowing smile. Was this how humans made sense of a world hidden from them or were there more influences at play?

CHAPTER 30

THE SCHOOL BROKE UP FOR SUMMER and my days were filled with sitting in the garden, listening to Coral share the history of my family and the laws of their world. She taught me how to stay in control of my powers and the essence, a magical current that runs through us and slows our ageing.

Coral taught me more than the mermaid world. She taught me how to do my hair, my makeup, and, best of all, how to make cocktails using my powers. There was nothing better than sitting out in the sun sipping from a chilled cocktail glass. I rested back in the chair as Coral continued my teachings.

"Gwyn has stayed young for centuries living off essence sucked from our kind," Coral said as she sipped on her nojito. "She is the oldest fae in existence

on this side of the realm."

"How old?" I asked with a new kind of admiration for her. I wondered at all that she must know.

"No idea. She's been ready to retire for at least two generations."

"What holds her back?"

"No suitable replacement for her, so she stayed on," Coral explained. "Just as well, when you think of the trouble you've caused by coming into your powers early." Coral grinned at me.

"What will happen now she's out of action. Can I visit her?"

"Mum, our real mum, received a letter posted by Gwyn before your dramatics. The letter has named a successor. It's as if she knew what was going to happen to her."

"Well, she is a psychic."

Coral's drink made a loud slurping sound with her straw. She waved her empty glass at me.

"I think the next round is yours, Mariah."

I poured the water into her glass and held it with my hand. I watched as the water crystallised and gently took on the formation of crushed ice. I added the mint leaves, lime juice, and syrup. I focused on it slowly turning into an icy slush as it swirled around in Coral's glass.

Once the drink was made, I focused on my breathing to keep my emotions from bubbling over and ruining my masterpiece. I was in control.

"Virgin cocktails on me."

I met Coral's look of proud admiration. Then, she said the words I'd been waiting to hear: "I think you're almost ready to go home."

"When?"

"Soon. I'll make the arrangements."

Denny's wedding was taking place in a grand, old house. We were getting ready in one of the guest rooms, lavishly appointed with antique furniture and polished wood - by far the most elegant place I'd ever been. I wondered how it compared to the manor of my family whilst a woman did my hair and makeup and a photographer documented the process.

The photographer checked her view screen. "A few more of the bride getting ready."

The young woman posed as she applied lipstick to Denny's lips and maneuverer round to finish pinning some strands of hair.

"You're the perfect bride," the stylist gushed at her own work.

Denny smiled at her reflection, a red hue touched her cheeks. "Thank you. You've done a lovely job. I feel so beautiful."

"You are beautiful," the stylist stated. She turned to me. "Isn't she?"

"Yes," I agreed. Seeing Denny so happy filled me with a warm happiness - she'd got her happily ever after. Seeing her living it reminded me of how much I wanted it, too. I pined for Murray.

"Stunning!" added the photographer.

Denny's eyes welled up as she reached out towards me and I took her hand. "I never thought I would ever get married. I wish Gwyn could've come."

I heard the photographer's camera clicking as he captured our moment.

"Me, too," I nodded.

"Can you help?" Denny held out a rose quartz bracelet sent to her by Mum. She'd written to hand over her share of the bakery business and to excuse herself from the wedding. The gift was blessed to bring good fortune to the happy couple. I assisted by fastening the clasp for her.

It reminded me that Coral has given me a letter this morning as I'd hurried out the door. I'd folded it into my clutch bag and been so busy I'd forgotten about it. It had a postage stamp so must have arrived in the mail. I knew it was from Gwyn as it was written in her handwriting, with instructions not to open it until today's date. I excused myself to the bathroom to read it.

I sat on the toilet with the lid down and opened the envelope. It was written on her best paper and the inky, black text felt so personal, like I could feel her through the pages.

Dear Mariah,
I can't see why I'll not be at the wedding but know I

won't be. Please forgive my absence.

I promised not to meddle in your life with magic, but I also know how much you miss Jace and my meddling is somewhat responsible for that. I'm giving you the choice to allow one more meddle.

Inside this envelope you will find a candle, a pen, and two sheets of paper held by a paperclip. After the first dance, you and Jace can fix what is broken.

I admit, I may have meddled a little bit but I'm not sorry. And, I promise I've not used any magic.

All my love, Gwyn x

When I returned to the room, Denny was standing up waiting for me. Her full belly protruded out. There was no hiding her pregnancy now. She looked so stunning, she glowed, with her hair twisted up. She was more beautiful than I had ever seen her.

She took a deep breath. "Ready?"

Jace was handsome in his suit. We'd not spoken since he'd told me to f' off and I felt awkward, not knowing if I should speak to him or not. I kept thinking of Gwyn's letter and how she believed we could fix this.

During the service and photographs we were stuck together, but once that was over we went to the function room and bar. Everyone milled around listening to gentle music, waiting for the couple to newlyweds to return.

Jace was at the free bar getting a drink. We caught each other's eye across the room. Should I go over and speak to him or wait for him to speak to me? Uncertainty made me fidgety and my dress felt too fussy as I began to sweat.

The room filled with an air of excitement as Denny and Dave re-joined the guests. The DJ interrupted with his announcement:

"Let us welcome Mr and Mrs Dawson."

Everyone stopped what they were doing and surrounded the couple on the dance floor, wishing to witness their first dance.

Denny's smile was infectious. Dave looked at her, full of love as the room filled with the sound of Ed Sheeran's song 'Thinking Out Loud'. Dave held out his hand to invite her to dance with him and she took it, her eyes welling up with joy.

I saw Jace across the dance floor watching me. He wiped a tear away with the back of his hand and smiled fully. For the first time since our argument, he didn't scowl. I wanted to run over and be with him to share this happy moment.

"By special request of the happy couple, would Jace and Mariah please join them on the dance floor."

I felt sick with nerves. I didn't know how Jace would react - would he accept me? I felt a wash of relief as he started walking onto the dance floor and held his hand out towards me in the same manner Dave had to his mum. I hurried to join him. He took me in his arms and

I inhaled him so deeply that I never wanted to breathe out. I wanted to keep that rich smell of him forever inside me. All those months I'd missed him and now my heart ached with the fear of letting him go again.

"Mariah, we have to talk," he whispered in my ear.

We moved slowly around the dance floor in an embrace and I felt a lump in my throat. I was still sensitive to how he could hurt me and I didn't want to hear anything that would rip that fresh wound open.

"Why? Can't we enjoy this."

"Do you trust me?"

"Always."

He held me close as we danced to the rest of the song. As it came to an end, he led me off the dance floor and out of the manor.

"Where are we going?"

"The park," he said.

He pushed open a gate at the end of the garden that allowed us to enter the park that took its name from the manor. Jace still held my hand as we walked along the path. I could hardly breathe and knew I had to stay calm.

"I miss what we had. Do you think we can get it back?" he asked.

Was this what Gwyn meant when she said I could fix what was broken? Our friendship still felt so fragile, like any wrong word could ruin us.

"I miss you, too."

I realised where he was taking me, back to the willow tree. We went past the duck pond until we found our tree, rich in long, green, sweeping branches. We stepped under our canopy.

This time, instead of thrills my body was full of dread. We couldn't repeat the mistakes we'd made. I now knew I belonged with Murray. I was terrified of hurting Jace's feelings and losing him forever. I wanted to run from the situation, but I also need to stay calm and in control of my powers. I bit my lip. My feet rooted to the spot.

"Can we just go back?" he asked.

For a moment, I thought he meant back to the manor.

"Back to before things got complicated?" he added.

I felt terrible as I felt it was too big an ask. So much had happened that I could never share with him. Could a relationship work if it's full of secrets? My heart ached at the thought of going home after the wedding and returning to our lives without each other.

"I don't think we can." My face twisted in pain.

He revealed an envelope identical to mine.

"Your mum sent me this. We're not to open it unless it's what we both want, and we must be near a big tree."

"Our tree," I smiled. My heart fluttered with hope as I wondered if the envelope may contain some way to fix our messed up friendship. I nodded at the envelope. "Open it."

Jace ripped the envelope open. He reached in to pull out a piece of paper as a matchbox fell out. I picked up the matches as he read the piece of paper.

"It's a spell to mend a friendship. We need a candle,

pen, paper, and an envelope - where are we going to get that?"

I opened my clutch and showed him what was inside.

"Did you know?"

I shook my head. "I got a similar letter."

"When do you think she sent them?"

I shrugged.

Jace returned his attention to his piece of paper. "It says we need to each draw an arrow on the candle. Our arrows need to crossover to form a cross. We need something to cut the wax..."

I pulled the paper clip off the paper, and tested I was able to carve into the wax. As I cut in, crimped strings of wax came away. I passed the candle to Jace to add his arrow. Whilst he carved, I read the spell.

He pressed the candle into the soil to keep it upright and I struck a match to light the wick, cupping the orange flame with my hand so the breeze didn't blow it out before it took.

I passed him a sheet of paper, an envelope, and a pen.

"Now to write why we're sorry, what we'd like to happen, and how we feel about each other."

Jace took the items with a nod of understanding. We sat opposite each other with the candle flickering between us. My pen was poised on the page as I struggled with what to write.

What was I sorry for? My pen flew across the page. *I'm sorry we kissed. I never wanted to regret it but I regret how it changed us. I'm sorry for all the secrets I have to keep that creates a barrier between us. Of everyone in the world, I wish you could know what I am.*

Seeing the truth in black and white made me sad. Was there any hope for our future?

What did I want to happen?

I want my friend back. I don't want it to be awkward between us anymore. I can't stand the silence or absence of you from my life.

I was surprised by what I had written. For a long time, I'd wanted to be Jace's girlfriend but as I stared into the flame my heart filled with the notion that I'd do anything to have my friend back. It was more important to me than anything in the world.

How do I feel about my friend?

Whenever anyone asks, I answer it's complicated. As I stared into the flame, I knew the truth was actually very simple:

I love you, Jace, and I always will.

Writing my answers made me feel lighter. I exhaled and with that motion, I released all the tension trapped inside me. Everything was in a letter that would never be read.

I folded the paper up and put it in the envelope. Jace folded his up and placed it inside with mine. He lifted the candle from the ground and sealed the envelope with a blob of wax before returning it to the hole we had made.

We tried to dig at the base of the tree. Jace stood and kicked at the dirt with his posh shoes and I found a stick to try and dig a hole. We laughed at how this wasn't an easy task and couldn't Gwyn have sent us a magic, folding spade. But, finally, we managed to have a hole deep enough to bury our sealed letter.

We covered it over with the loose soil and stamped on top of the earth until it was not obvious something was buried there. Jace lifted the candle between us and I placed my hand on top of his.

"Do you remember the words?"

I nodded.

Together we recited the words from the spell:

"My friend and I have had a fight,
Please help us now to make it right,
Help us forgive and make amends.
We wish nothing more than to be friends."

Together we blew out the candle.

"Feel any different?" Jace asked as we sat down, looking out over the lake.

There was soil on our hands, on my dress, and his shoes. I knew we'd be in trouble if Denny saw us - especially if she wanted more pictures. But we didn't care, we were friends again and I couldn't be happier.

"Lighter. Does that make sense?"

"Yeah. Everything makes sense with you."

We stayed under the willow tree listening to the distant music from the wedding and watching the fireworks create beautiful patterns of light across the lake. I rested my head on his shoulder and his arm wrapped across my back and hugged me into him. My freckled leg stretched out towards the lake alongside his tailored trousers. I felt safe and loved, and, for the first time in a long time, everything made sense.

Coral: Be out front in 5 minutes for a surprise. X

I'd no idea what the surprise was but Jace walked me out. As I stepped out onto the steps, my heart caught in my throat. Like a mirage to a thirsty person in a desert, Murray stood at the bottom of the steps. He looked dreamy and too good to be real.

Jace gently pushed my back. "Go on, I'll see you later."

Murray was here. Murray was really here.

I ran down the steps and threw myself at him, my lips pressing against his in a heartbeat. I'd craved for him for so long, I was so hungry to taste him again, I could barely breathe. I leaned my forehead against his, unable to let go and needing to keep his closeness a little longer.

"That's some welcome, Goldie. But, I'm not doing this long distance thing any more. It's been torture."

Hearing his voice sounded so good, his words rumbled through me, tingling my senses. In his arms, I felt whole, and a feeling of belongings like coming home. I didn't want to let him go, for fear he'd evaporate and be nothing but some strange trick of my mind.

"It's really you. But, why are you here? I thought Coral..."

"I'm here to take you home. Your biological home."

My chest tightened with excitement and anxiety.

"Can we stay together now?"

"That's the plan."

"I really love that plan." I bit my lip as I stared up at him.

"I love you," he said grinning down at me. "And that dress. Have I mentioned you're beautiful yet?"

I'd longed for him so long, and to be with him, and hear those words, made my whole world brighter.   I laughed, still not quite believing he was actually here, and we could finally be together, "I love you too,"

He bent down to steal another kiss from my lips, and I felt complete.

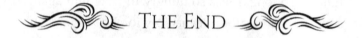 THE END

Author Note

Dear Reader,

Thank you for reading Ocean Heart. I hope you have enjoyed the story as much as I enjoyed writing it.

If you can spare a moment to write a review, I'd really appreciate it. You should be able to leave a review on GoodReads, BookBub, Amazon, or any store that sells my book. If you post a review to your social media, please tag me if you can, as I'd be interested to know your thoughts.

Visit my website allyaldridge.com to discover how you can connect with me on Social Media.

All my love

Ally

ACKNOWLEDGEMENTS

Thank you to you, the person who is reading this. I can't express how much I appreciate you taking the time to read my novel. I hope you've enjoyed it and will continue to be part of my author journey. If you are interested to know who else helped me get where I am today, keep reading...

Some people have asked if Mariah is me - she's not but there is a lot of me in her. I have red hair, was an awkward teen and fell in love with my best friend. However, in our love story, we stayed together and got married. My husband has encouraged and supported my writing and taught me to believe in myself. He gave me our children, who continue to inspire me everyday. Little children try new things, and when they fail they brush themselves off and try again. Seeing their tenacious spirits has kept me motivated, even when things have not gone to plan.

My writing started as fan fiction at the early age of 5. My first teacher is responsible for telling me what an author is and, from that moment on, I knew that was what I wanted to do. Another influential teacher was Mr Macy from my high school. He'd give me extra notebooks for story writing so I could create my novels.

I want to thank my parents for establishing a love of fiction in my siblings and I from an early age. Now I have my own kids, I know how challenging it must have been for my mum to keep three excited children under control at the library. When I look back, I still cherish those special moments when I'd snuggle up with my dad at bedtime and he'd read to me. Thank you to my cousins, who enjoyed my story telling skills and constantly demanded I make up more. I must thank my little sister, Heather, and her best friend for reading all those early attempts at novel writing and for continuing to believe in me.

I need to thank my best friends for being part of my adventures growing up. I remember sleepovers watching Stand By Me and Jo saying, "You could write about us one day, Ally. If you ever run out of ideas..." I don't think I'll ever run out of ideas, and some of our real life adventures are stranger than fiction. A big thank you to my husband's best friend Dale for reading all my drafts, offering feedback, and being my companion on trips to Book Festivals. Thank you to my friends who opened up and shared their personal experiences with me to assist in my characters development within this novel.

Thanks to Felixstowe Scribblers - my local writing group. It was good to know that I wasn't the only one with a crazy imagination. You've always made me feel welcome no matter how long I've been gone. To all the online readers whose kind and encouraging words helped me to improve and believe in myself, I thank you too.

I cannot express my gratitude enough to the online writing community across all my social media platforms. I've enjoyed being part of your journey, for your guidance in my development, and being able to call you friends. A special thanks to everyone at World Indie Warriors and founder Michelle Raab for bringing together creatives to share and support one another. Thank you J D Groom for reading my early drafts, for supporting my queries, and for inspiring me with your own self publishing journey.

Thank you to my editor, Avery McDougall, for the way you've made me laugh at my mistakes and how you've taught me to become a better writer. Thank you to Natalie Narbonne for taking my ideas and creating a beautiful cover design. Thank you to Julia Scott for making the inside as special as the outside. You guys helped turn my manuscript into the book I envisioned.

There are so many people to thank as this has been a dream I've chased for several decades. If I've not mentioned you, please know it was not intentional. I love you all.

ABOUT THE AUTHOR

Ally was born in London but grew up in Suffolk which is where most of her YA Fantasy novels are based.

She is happily married to her high school sweetheart, and together they are raising two cats, their son and daughter.

When Ally is not writing (or at her day job), she loves spending time with her family at the local beach, in the forest or watching way too much Netflix.

Ally loves a cup of tea and has been known to order one on a night out.

MORE BOOKS BY
ALLY ALDRIDGE

THE SOUL HEART SERIES

Ocean Heart (book 1)
Sky Heart (book 2) - coming soon
Forest Heart (book 3) - coming soon
Title TBC (book 4) - coming soon

I also have plans for a number of Novellas that will be spin off stories from the main Soul Heart series. Plus more books and more series...

I can't even count how many other stories are in my head but if you want to be the first to hear what I'm working on and future releases, please sign up to my newsletter and follow me on social media. All links can be found on my website.

allyaldridge.com

CPSIA information can be obtained
at www.ICGtesting.com
Printed in the USA
BVHW031448301120
594526BV00001B/72